Seven Seconds

by

Lisa Compton

The Olivia Osborne Crime Series

Seven Seconds

Cover Art by *The Wild Rose Press, Inc.*

The Wild Rose Press, Inc.
PO Box 708
Adams Basin, NY 14410-0708
Visit us at www.thewildrosepress.com

Publishing History
First Edition, 2023
Trade Paperback ISBN 978-1-5092-5160-5
Digital ISBN 978-1-5092-5161-2

The Olivia Osborne Crime Series
Published in the United States of America
Previously Published 12/2017 by Perpetuity Publishing

Olivia grasped the door handle of the victim's car. A current of energy snaked its way up her arm. Opening the door, she caught a whiff of perfume. All the dead woman had wanted was to go home and make dinner.

Olivia pushed past the residual memories and slid behind the wheel, avoiding the bloody smears, leaving those details for the forensics lab. She settled back into the seat, her feet not quite reaching the pedals. As suspected, their victim was not the last person to drive the car. The realization was the last thought Olivia had that was her own, before crashing to the other side.

Her intrusion sent ripples through the half-light. Dwellers there sensed her presence. Most only took note, but a rare few dared slither her way. Olivia wasn't safe, not like this. She was too open, too exposed.

Her innate fight-or-flight response sputtered to life as she stumbled from that place, slamming the doors to her mind as she fled. Struggling to break free, Olivia's hands flailed, seeking a return to her reality.

Outside the car, Barry heard her choking. He grabbed Olivia, and pulled her free, easing himself to the ground with her in his arms. Olivia clung to him. Barry pressed his forehead to hers, breathing deeply, willing her back to him. The soft puffs of air from her lips sent a ripple of goosebumps down his neck.

Praise for Lisa Compton

Dedication

To my Mom,
I'm so glad you passed your love of words on to me.
Without reading there is no writing.

Prologue

Seven-Second Theory: An alternative explanation for agency loss during decision making. Recent scientific findings suggest profound historical misperceptions regarding agency, moral responsibility, and consciousness. Advances in neuroscience over the last four decades tell us that unconscious process plays a bigger role in decision making than what had previously been accepted as fact; however, science offers no plausible explanation for what guides these unconscious processes.

This dissertation posits an alternative theory, based largely in theology but influenced by scientific and psychological findings, for agency loss during cognitive processing. This "Seven Second" theory has significant implications regarding brain disease and mental disorder misdiagnoses and calls into question the notion of free will.

Chapter One

Tuesday....

Monsters. She lived with them every day. Some days they came to her, other days, she went to them. Today she was going to them.

Blood was spilled. It seeped into the ground.

He had brought her to the kill spot. The lot at the end of the cul-de-sac was too small for a house as if someone had measured incorrectly when plotting the neighborhood. The untouched strip of land was nature's last stand against the growing population in this upwardly mobile subdivision. San Antonio might rank in the top ten largest cities in the country, but deer still roamed free. They weren't alone. Occasionally there were interlopers.

Olivia Osborne closed her eyes and traveled backward in search of the end. Death came at twilight, that magical time when the dark and the light swam together as equals. What did it leave behind?

Olivia stilled herself and waited for whatever was left to wash over her. She could see the residual energy suspended just above the ground, like mist. The wispy veil beckoned her; an ancient stream ran beneath it. The current below was strong enough to pull her in if she would let it. She was standing on the edge, contemplating a dive when the lieutenant interrupted her.

"So? What have you got?" San Antonio police Lieutenant Barry Bartholomew asked her, hands on his hips. They had been standing in the same spot for more than five minutes. Hours earlier a team of Crime Scene Officers had combed the area where they now stood. As the lead detective, Barry had the weight of the case resting heavily on his shoulders.

Olivia heard the fatigue that resonated in his words. Something else too. *Anger*. She opened her eyes and looked at him. Impatience rolled off of him in waves. She could almost see it. She certainly felt it. She had been trying to ignore it while sifting through death's leftovers. Olivia wondered if he was normally like this or if she was the cause.

"She wasn't afraid. At least not in the beginning," Olivia said softly. It was all she could tell the lieutenant that he would understand. He only knew one world.

"So, she was willing? She let this psychopath in her car?" Barry asked.

When would they learn? When would it end?

His thoughts swarmed inside her head, making it clear his impatience had little to do with her. It came from something older that had nested deep and twisted like a root. It made him work too hard and drink too much. He was itching for one now. She understood it all too well, but feelings stirred by a murder he couldn't make sense of interfered with what she needed to do.

"She didn't say the victim willingly let the killer into her car," Sergeant Mark Austin said.

Olivia suspected Mark felt obligated to broker peace between them since she was there at his request.

"Then what *did* she say?" Barry stopped his pacing

and stared her down. "What do you have, Ms. Osborne? I need something tangible," Barry insisted.

Olivia wanted to ignore him but couldn't. "This would work a whole lot better if you would stop interrupting me." Her voice might have been soft, but her words were steel barbs aimed directly at him. "I don't perform on command." She turned from the open stretch of land, prepared to walk away.

Barry shot a look of annoyance Mark's way.

"Excuse me, but the crime scene is back there," the lieutenant reminded her.

She heard exhaustion in his voice now more than annoyance.

"It might have ended here, but this is not where it started," Olivia said as she stalked past him. She needed distance from the lieutenant and from the dark beneath the mist that ran too deep for her liking. She couldn't wade through the jumble of both, so she had to find another way. With no destination in mind, Olivia paused at the street. She didn't look both ways. In fact, had a car been coming, she wouldn't have seen it. She moved beyond this place, tracing her way back *there*.

Instinct directed Olivia upstream from the cesspool behind her. She closed her eyes and refocused. Finding her center was easier farther away from the kill zone. There was less chaos. The two officers closely followed her as she stepped off the curb and crossed the street. She stopped not far away at the edge of the drainage ditch alongside the cul-de-sac.

"It's not an exact science," Mark said, under his breath. He sensed Barry's impatience, but they knew better than to interrupt her.

Olivia was sharing space with them, but she was

somewhere else.

"She was on her way home. She had no reason to stop." Twilight was approaching.

Barry turned his back to her, trying to talk himself out of walking back to his car and just leaving. He had already spent more time here than he wanted, and she had given him nothing useful. "This is a waste of time."

Olivia's eyes snapped open; the connection lost. "We're here because you asked *me*. You brought the dead to me because you don't know shit about him."

Her words stopped him. Barry wasn't used to the challenge but more than that, she was wrong. He hadn't asked, he hadn't even known she was about to invade the crime scene until half an hour before it happened. The only reason he hadn't sent her packing was that Mark had vouched for her. They were running out of options, and he didn't see much to lose. It didn't mean he had to like it.

"Look, lieutenant, I know you think this is all some mumbo-jumbo…." she said.

Nerves frayed, Barry wheeled around, ready to take her on.

"But that's not the real problem, is it?" Olivia asked, refusing to back down. "The real problem is time. You're running out of it."

Barry stopped and really looked at her for the first time. Intelligent. Easy on the eyes. He was trying hard not to notice her, almost as hard as she was trying not to be noticed. He guessed the minimal make-up and nondescript business attire was her attempt to blend in, but she shattered the image with the way she moved. She was confident and sleek despite the fact she had to take two steps to keep up with his one. She'd seized control of his crime scene and, he never saw it coming. Maybe because she wasn't what he had expected from a psychic or whatever she was supposed to be. The introduction had been brief, and Mark had been sketchy on the details. The contradiction was throwing him off.

Olivia didn't let up. "He hit the magic number, didn't he? Your UNSUB. Your *unknown subject*."

Her words snapped him back to attention. Barry looked over at his former partner. He'd instructed the sergeant to tell her nothing. The look Mark gave him told Barry the sergeant had followed orders.

"The kill over there in the grass is probably number three, significant from a mythological and theological perspective. Earth, wind, and fire. The Holy Trinity. Significant for another reason too. Three makes a series. You've got a serial killer on your hands. Tell me I'm wrong, Lieutenant."

Although she held his attention, Olivia sensed he was still on the fence, and he'd stay there until she pushed him off of it. She marched over and stepped in close, stopping short of a full encroachment into his personal space. She looked up to meet his eyes. His sandy hair was just starting to gray at the temples. He smelled clean and fresh like citrus.

"You're afraid." It wasn't a question. "You're about to have this case yanked out from under you. Hell, I'm surprised the Texas Rangers aren't here already, and when they come, the Feds may very well be on their heels. I give you forty-eight hours, if you're lucky," she said delivering the truth she knew he didn't want to acknowledge.

Barry stared her down. She didn't blink. How could she know his fear? He hadn't shared it with

Mark. Such a confession would have made him appear weak in his former partner's eyes. "If I'm going to lose this case to a jurisdictional pissing contest, then what's the point?"

He was pushing her buttons, his disdain for the Rangers and the FBI palpable. "That depends on you. You don't appear to be the type to let things go easily."

"And what can you do about that?" Barry challenged her.

"I can't stop them, but I can help you catch him. How close do you want to be before they get here? Get close enough and maybe they won't take it all away," Olivia whispered. She waited a beat for another argument from him. *Nothing. Thought so.* The lieutenant stepped away first and Olivia took a deep breath and retreated back into the shadows of her mind.

The silence hung heavy between them, slowly sinking in and solidifying the union. Like it or not, they were in this together. Between them, they would shoulder the horror and learn more about the unknown than either one of them ever wanted to know.

Barry gave her a moment. "Okay, tell me something I don't know," he dared her. "Anything. Something I don't already know."

"He feels comfortable here, but this is not the place he would have chosen. He didn't plan to stop here."

Again, looks were exchanged between the sergeant and lieutenant. All three of the kills had happened within a five-mile radius. Barry suspected the killer lived or worked somewhere near. If she had seen the case file, she would know this. But she hadn't.

"Then why? Why here if it's not what he wanted?"

Olivia shook her head. This part she didn't know

exactly, at least not yet. Maybe she wasn't ready to see it. "Happenstance. Something else intervened, something he wasn't even aware of."

For the first time, she sounded like a psychic. Non-committal. Barry was ready to walk away again, but she reeled him back in.

"Did you call me because it was his third or because he's made some kind of transition? Or both?"

Barry studied her again. It was another detail she couldn't have known. He had only come to the realization today. He had been on scene after the other two murders. She hadn't been as far as he knew. So, how the hell did she know this location and the method of attack was different?

Olivia considered his silence answer enough. She was correct, most likely on both counts. She didn't need him to tell her what she already knew.

"He comes across as non-threatening. In excellent shape. He has an older sense about him." Olivia unknowingly cocked her head to one side, as if listening to something only she could hear. She hesitated to assign an age. Logic dictated the killer was young enough to be agile and strong, but she sensed an older quality. Though she hadn't seen the case file she knew something about this scene was different. Something about him was different.

"As young as twenty-five, lives alone," Barry said. He was holding back until he knew more, both about the killer and about her. The details he'd just spouted off came straight from his gut, instinct being a reasonable substitute for an FBI profile at this stage. She was right though. The Feds would weigh in if he didn't get a handle on things quickly. San Antonio was the most visited city in the state. Every season was tourist season and women getting ripped up wasn't the kind of thing to boost the economy.

Olivia knew he was bluffing. "That information did not come from the FBI," she said, holding his gaze. Barry looked away first. "Maybe he lives alone, maybe he doesn't. But he doesn't do this at home, does he?"

The air cleared between them, Olivia squared her shoulders and returned fully from where she had been. Death was an unraveling. She was picking up the threads, trying to weave the events back together. She would keep on stitching despite the nonbeliever.

Besides, she had said her piece, for the time being. She hadn't meant to come on so strong, but something about this rubbed her the wrong way. She was out of practice. She had made the decision to stop, yet here she was. *Just give them something and be done.*

"This takes discipline," Olivia continued, pushing her own thoughts away. "He doesn't rush. He knows they will come. He's methodical, willing to wait as long as it takes. That's why she wasn't afraid in the beginning."

"So, he seems like a normal guy," Mark spoke up. He had been watching her and the lieutenant find their footing. He wasn't sure if they had reached common ground yet or not, but at least they had retreated to separate corners.

"Don't they always seem normal?" Olivia asked. "If they ran the streets looking like the bad men they are, you'd be out of a job, wouldn't you, Sergeant?"

Mark smiled.

"He gets them alone easily. It's one reason he seems older." Olivia would know this even if she wasn't *gifted* as some described it. She knew it because she was a single woman. Older usually meant safer, but not this time, not this one. He was different. It was the reason she was spending her evening chasing monsters. No one called her for normal.

"He blends in. He's part of the scenery," Olivia said.

"City worker," Mark suggested.

Barry immediately shook his head. "No, too easy to track. We'd have found him by now. Handy man, lawn guy. Someone with a less structured schedule."

A flash: the glint of a blade. Then it was gone. That's how it worked sometimes. Without the blood-soaked ground at her feet, Olivia's vision was beginning to clear. The streetlight buzzed to life as daylight yielded to dusk. It had only been one setting of the moon since he had been here.

"Someone helpful," Olivia said. Her gaze shifted down to the gravel at her feet. Cul-de-sacs were a place for turns.

"He earns their trust quickly," Mark confirmed.

"Everyone stay where you are," Olivia commanded.

Mark and Barry froze in place.

"That looks like blood," Olivia said.

Barry followed her line of sight. Under the light of the streetlamp, the pebbles looked purple.

Olivia watched as Barry took a look back at the greenbelt where they started. He was calculating, wanting to discount anything she had to say. They were outside the marked crime scene perimeter. "It doesn't have to be from your victim," she said.

She was for his viewing pleasure, at least until the

life force was gone. Bled out. Sacred. Satanic. Depended on what the seeker wanted and why.

The gravity of her thoughts sent a wave of vertigo through her. Olivia swayed even though both feet were securely on the ground.

Barry saw it happen. "Are you alright?" He reached for her but caught himself before he made contact.

Olivia yanked on her thoughts. Something lurked down below in the mist, she was sure of it. It called to her with a seductive whisper: *Come closer.*

Maybe she should be glad the lieutenant stopped her from treading into that unknown place. "I know I said he might be patient, but that's before the encounter. After it's begun, he becomes," she paused for a moment and waited for the veil to lift. "Frenzied," she said softly. The flash came wrapped in the scent of copper. *So much blood.* She reached for Barry, placing her hand on his arm to steady herself.

"Everything okay?" Mark asked. He had retrieved an evidence bag from the car and knelt on the other side of Olivia. He pulled a pair of gloves from his pocket and began to put them on.

"No, don't," Barry instructed him, his cell phone already out of his pocket. "I'm calling the team back. We're going to need to expand the crime scene perimeter, do another grid search, everything." Barry cast a glance Olivia's way.

She felt his blame. As he growled orders into the phone, she bent down and followed Mark's line of sight. He stuffed the bag in his pocket and pulled out a pen light. The narrow beam illuminated the immediate area.

11

"Those look like skid marks to you?" Olivia asked.

"Definitely some kind of dust-up. Too narrow for a car," Mark said.

"But not for a bike," Olivia said.

Mark directed the narrow beam of light across the cul-de-sac to the small bridge. There was an obvious white scrape on the pavement near the gravel.

Made by something metal, Olivia thought. *And there had been some velocity involved.*

"The tech guys are on their way," Barry said, rejoining them. Olivia and Mark both stood. She noticed the lieutenant's eyes had found their way back to her. His face said her time here was at an end.

****

"So, do you want to tell me what she really does?" Barry asked his former partner as they watched her drive away.

"You were here. You saw the same thing I did," Mark told him.

"She's more than a psychic," Barry insisted.

"Yeah. She's a nurse, she's a writer, she's many things," Mark said. He was dodging and he was pretty sure Barry knew it, but he didn't know how to tell Barry the truth. "Psychic was the best description I could come up with. I couldn't explain what she does," Mark admitted. "It had to be experienced."

"It was quiet the demonstration," Barry said.

Mark refused to meet Barry's stare but certainly felt the weight of it. He had seen him do the same to the suspects who found themselves in front of him in an interview room. Barry wouldn't let it go, but Mark knew how to make him stop. At least for now.

"She knew my brother. She was there. At the end."

****

At home, with the door locked securely behind her, Olivia took a long cleansing breath. Daisy came over to nuzzle her hand. She had adopted the greyhound just off the track less than two years ago. Once freed from the rigors of racing, greyhounds were totally devoted to their masters. Olivia reached for her, comforted by the feeling of something alive and warm after the jarring ugliness she had opened herself to tonight.

She dismissed thoughts of dinner, opting instead for a glass of wine, and sought solace in the warmth of a bath. It was a cleansing, a baptism not only for her body but her mind. Seeking silence, she slipped beneath the water, but something else was waiting for her there: the dark mist. In its furthest reaches, she heard the whisper of a memory. More than a memory. A summoning. *Proximare.*

No. Not this. Not tonight. Olivia gathered every bit of her strength, willed the whisper down deep and far away, at least for now.

The light in the bathroom snapped off on its own, bathing the room in blackness.

The dark called to her. It was always waiting for her there. Her constant companion.

Chapter Two

Wednesday...

She was supposed to be running errands, but she couldn't get the crime scene out of her head. That was the problem with monsters. Sometimes they stayed with you.

Olivia was familiar with San Antonio's northeast corridor, the city's fastest-growing sector before her visit to the crime scene. She took her time maneuvering through the neighborhood that boasted well-kept lawns with lots of trees, manicured flower beds, shiny cars, and yards outfitted for children of various ages. Olivia spotted the two-story treehouse long before she had any reason to explore further. The backyard where it stood overlooked the busy street that led her there. Had her own childhood included a collective of kids, they undoubtedly would have spent most of their time in a treehouse like that. From up there, she imagined she would be able to see the entire neighborhood.

Her original destination on hold, Olivia rounded the block and found herself right back at the crime scene. If she hadn't been there yesterday, she would have mistaken the trampled lot behind her for a place the neighborhood kids liked to ride their bikes. If that had been the case they wouldn't be doing it anymore, at least not for a long time.

Olivia took the turn by the drainage ditch, stopping

short of where they found the bloody gravel last night. She knew Barry had brought the techs back and they had undoubtedly been there, but she still avoided the area. She got out and walked along the sidewalk instead, stopping to lean against the metal railing and inspect the drainage ditch below. It was the spot Mark's light had illuminated last night. The city had cleared out the ditch recently. San Antonio's history of flooding meant the drainage system had been expanded and maintained regularly, especially this time of the year. Springtime was wet and messy in South Texas. '*Turn around, don't drown*' was the city's latest public plea. She scoured the bottom and saw no hiding spots.

Opting for a different vantage point, Olivia climbed onto the hood of her SUV and tried to reconcile her location. Shading her eyes against the morning sun she did a three-sixty of her surroundings. A bike leaned against a row of hedges in between two houses. She spotted the thatched roof of the treehouse. If someone had been up there two days ago at precisely the right time, they would have seen everything.

Olivia felt an overwhelming urge to call Mark or even Barry. If her phone was in her hand and not in her purse, inside the car. A clicking noise caught her attention. Her first thought was it sounded like tap shoes. And then it stopped.

"What are you looking at?"

Olivia looked down and was immediately dizzy from the sudden change in perspective. Her skin prickled with a new, latent energy and she shivered despite the warm sun.

"Are you alright?" It was a man walking a dog. It must have been the dog's tags she heard clicking.

Olivia considered both questions. She didn't have an answer for either. For a moment time stood still, frozen in place. There was a brief lag in her instincts, but once they kicked in, she had the presence of mind to study the man below. She noticed the baseball cap first. She went for the eyes next, but sunglasses hid them, and her assessment stalled. Eyes were a gateway, and she knew how to slip inside, but she was barred. Sunglasses were shutters; they blocked access to the eyes. The reflective ones he wore were a one-way mirror and Olivia knew she was on the wrong side. *A deliberate choice,* she thought. *What's he hiding?*

He wore cargo shorts cinched tight at the waist and a long-sleeve t-shirt despite the heat. There was a logo on the shirt, but Olivia couldn't concentrate under the weight of his intense scrutiny. Whether she could see his eyes or not, she could feel his stare. She pressed past it and used the temporary height advantage. If she had been on the ground with him, she never would have noticed because she rarely looked down. It was always best to maintain eye contact. That way everyone knew where they stood.

The shoes caught her eye. They were similar to cleats, but with a Velcro strap across the top of his foot, like something a child would wear. The shoes were also muddy. They must be what he wore when he worked in the yard because it hadn't rained in a week. He remained motionless as she turned her attention to the ball of fur between them. The dog appeared to be as wary as she felt. Its nub of a tail did not wag, and Olivia knew the walk had not been the dog's idea.

Ignoring her instinct to stay put, she carefully sat down and slid off the hood of her car, silently chiding herself for wearing a skirt. Once on the ground, she noted she and the dog walker were close to the same height. He wasn't more than five foot two or three, short and with a slight build. She wondered how that affected his psyche, sensing he was someone who wanted very much to belong.

He made no move to help her. The suggestion that he did not want to touch her crept across her mind. Maybe he was too distracted by the little white schnauzer with the gray Fu Manchu mustache. The dog repeatedly tugged against his tether.

"He doesn't seem to like the leash," Olivia observed.

"Not so much." There was an awkward pause, but he never once looked down at the dog. She remained the sole focus of his attention. "So, do you live around here?" he finally asked.

"I was thinking of relocating." The lie rolled off her lips with ease. "I just thought I would take a look at the neighborhood from all angles," she said as if to explain why she was standing on the hood of her car in the middle of the street. Olivia tried to force a smile but found she couldn't. She caught herself trying harder than she should to placate this stranger.

As he studied her, Olivia momentarily questioned her decision to get down and meet him on his level. Unconsciously, she reached for the small silver cross resting at the base of her throat. It was a gift from Gran on her fifth birthday and although it needed a longer chain now, she left it as it had been given to her. Touching it steadied her. She instinctively took a slow step back and connected with the bumper of her car. She had no place to go.

"I thought you were here about the murder."

Olivia opened her mouth, but nothing came out. She was uncharacteristically out of words. Over her shoulder, she heard a city truck rumbling toward them, and the tense moment evaporated. Relief washed over her. An old instinct stirred in the pit of her stomach – a holdover from her ancient ancestors, that fully engaged, would result in either fight or flight. The sensation never reached fruition.

The dog walker craned his neck to see over her head. "You might want to reconsider," he warned as the truck approached. "Relocating, I mean."

Olivia wondered briefly how he felt about the interruption, but not for long. She took the opportunity to slide past her bumper and retreat. She backed all the way to her car, keeping the stranger in her line of sight, and once tucked safely inside, she locked the doors with the push of a button. She started the engine and pulled away slowly, watching the dog walker watch her from the safety of her rearview mirror. She sensed she needed to talk to Barry, not Mark. She wasn't sure exactly why, but she knew to trust it. The buzz of an incoming call interrupted her. As she reached for her phone, Olivia noticed her hands were shaking.

****

She waited for half an hour, chiding herself for not putting the Kindle in her purse. Then again, she was supposed to be running errands. And the San Antonio Police Headquarters had not been on her list. She hadn't left her house with the intention of ending up in the lieutenant's office, yet here she was. As a result, her reading selection consisted of a six-month-old issue of *Field and Stream* and an even older copy of *Golf*

Digest. The magazines could only have been a donation. Lieutenant Barry Bartholomew didn't spend his time fishing or golfing. Too trivial for him. She knew that without even knowing him. He was all work. Not an uncommon storyline in her life.

Olivia pushed the worn copies aside when she saw him coming and guessed she should count herself lucky. According to the harried woman sitting behind the desk across from her, his projected arrival time had been forty-five minutes. He had rescued her from the boring magazines and saved her fifteen minutes. Passing her desk, Olivia saw the nameplate identifying the woman as Norma Simpson. It had been hidden by the papers on her desk. Olivia hoped they weren't important because poor Norma had done nothing but answer the phone. It never stopped ringing. The lieutenant didn't strike her as much of a phone guy.

Norma waved some pink message slips at him as he walked by, but he didn't even break his stride. Maybe because his eyes were on Olivia. The predominant theme of his thoughts was her unannounced, unexpected presence in his workplace. *Why isn't she here to see Mark?* The question was quickly replaced by the realization he wasn't entirely unhappy to see her again and was glad she had chosen him over his sergeant. At least the scenery was better than their last meeting. She had traded her business attire for casual and her blonde locks were loose giving her a more relaxed look than yesterday. She wore at least a dust of makeup and even some jewelry. No wedding band. He had noticed the detail yesterday as well.

"Any progress?" she asked, following Barry into

his space without an invitation.

"Nothing yet." Barry tried to focus on his victim's missing car, but she wasn't making it easy. He loosened his tie and stripped it from his neck. Sharing space with her warmed the room considerably.

Olivia surveyed his office. It was cramped and overflowing with papers and files that had metastasized onto Norma's desk as well. If there was a system in place only he knew it. The space was devoid of anything personal. Either he was drawing a distinct line between personal and professional or there was no line. Olivia struggled not to linger on the surroundings. It sparked the urge to tidy up and bring order to his chaos.

A dead plant occupied one corner of the window sill with a deflated balloon still attached. The first word she saw was *Happy*, the antithesis of this place. The other word was *Anniversary*. Either Norma or Mark must have given it to him. She suspected he kept it out of consideration to the giver, not for sentimental reasons, and wondered what milestone it signified.

With Olivia in his office, Barry realized the dead plant was an eyesore. He should have thrown it out already. He had not watered it once since Norma had given it to him two months ago, a thoughtful gesture to mark the one-year anniversary of his advancement to lieutenant. He had been in homicide for over five years, a union that had lasted longer than either of his two marriages. As the pitiful plant demonstrated, nurturing had never been his strong suit.

"Did you canvas the neighborhood?" Olivia asked as Barry lifted a pile of files from the lone chair across from his desk. For a moment he didn't seem to know where to put them but finally found a spot. Maybe he did have a method to his madness.

"Of course."

Olivia noticed that the impatience he exuded yesterday was gone. *What's there now?* She wondered. *Defensiveness. He's worried.* Maybe it was a transference of feelings. She suspected he was under pressure to placate the brass upstairs. Did he lump her into that same category or was his guard up because he was still trying to decide what she made him feel? She definitely had him on edge. She just wasn't entirely sure why.

"Did you see everyone?" she asked carefully.

"All but a couple."

Olivia nodded. The missing ones had the information. She was sure of it. They were missing for a reason. "Did you find the bike?"

The question stopped him short. "What bike am I supposed to be looking for?"

"The bike that left the skid marks. I'm sure you saw them. The tread was too narrow for a car. The bike you're looking for is going to have some damage."

"Those marks couldn't have been made by anything," Barry cautioned. The lab forensic technicians had been noncommittal, though admittedly, the marks on the ground looked to have been made by metal scraping on pavement. Easy to do when riding in the gravel. Take the turn too fast and you could lose control.

"I found a bike," she told him. "A straight shot across from the drainage ditch. I think you should come back with me to check it out."

"Ms. Osborne." Barry resisted.

"You can call me Olivia. Or Livie."

Barry considered the options. In his opinion, Livie didn't do her justice. Olivia had a classic ring to it and suited her much better. He had just come to the decision when Olivia challenged him again.

"Think about it," she urged. "Have you figured out how he got to the crime scene? If he had a car, why did he take your victim's?"

Damnit, how did she do that? He had wondered the same thing.

"Have you found an abandoned car in the neighborhood? If he came in on a bike, he couldn't ride out the same way after killing your victim, could he?"

Barry held up his hand. "Hold up, wait just a minute." He pinched the bridge of his nose. She was relentless, burrowing under his skin.

Olivia's eyes narrowed. "Why? Need time to catch up? Not answering me is an answer, Lieutenant," she told him.

He studied her, considering her words. *Was she credible? Or crazy?*

"Think about it. A bike makes sense," she said.

"Who rides a bicycle to a murder?" Barry asked her.

"Someone who wants to blend in."

Chapter Three

Although Olivia didn't know the address, she was able to lead Barry back to the house. The bike was gone when they got there.

"It was right here. I swear," she told him.

Barry looked at his watch. It should still be there, at least if it belonged to neighborhood kids. School was just letting out. No one had been home long enough to move the bike. He was also sure it hadn't been there last night. He had come by this particular house himself.

"You're sure it was this house?" he had to ask despite the fact she was emphatic. He had to check all the boxes.

"Yes, I'm sure. I distinctly remember these bushes. They extended above the top of the fence. I felt like this was a pretty good hiding spot."

"Not good enough if you saw it from the road," Barry couldn't help but point out. He moved past her to get a look at the backyard. He peered through the slats of the wooden fence where he could.

Olivia took the most direct route and moved to the gate. "There's no lock and it's not latched," she told him.

Even better. Barry brushed past her, ensuring she was at arm's length behind him, moving into protector mode without even noticing. He pushed on the gate and leaned inside. "No bike."

"I wonder where the dog is," she murmured over his shoulder.

"What dog?" Barry asked, halting his forward momentum.

"The sign says *Beware of Dog*," she told him. Olivia wondered if the sign was supposed to make up for the fact there was no lock on the gate.

"And you let me just come in here? Without warning." Barry tried to sound annoyed. He was fighting an impulse, but he wasn't ready to succumb to it.

"I don't hear barking. The dog wasn't warning you. I didn't think I needed to either."

"Or it's not much of a guard dog," Barry said.

Olivia shivered involuntarily, reacting to energy, not weather.

Barry watched her quiver. "You okay?"

Olivia shook her head absently. "The food bowl is outside. The dog should be too."

Before Barry could really consider what that might mean, they heard a car. As they emerged from the backyard, they saw a silver hatchback pull into the driveway next door. Barry remembered the house from the night before. They had attempted a tap-and-rap at that house and the address where they were currently standing but had gotten no answer. He left his card at both houses but hadn't heard from either resident. "Maybe we'll have better luck next door."

Barry held forth the badge he wore on a chain around his neck as the driver exited the vehicle. "Lieutenant Barry Bartholomew of the San Antonio police department, ma'am," he said approaching in time to halt the woman's advance toward the house.

The neighbor looked at her house like she would much rather be inside, but there was no chance of that with the officer blocking her path. "Gail Wallace," she said without being asked.

"Ms. Wallace, may I have a minute of your time?" he asked.

Like I have a choice. Olivia caught a brief flash of the woman's annoyance as she joined Barry in the driveway. She couldn't shake the feeling that they shouldn't leave the other house. Something was wrong. *I'm in here.* This flash, and its origin, unsettled Olivia to her core.

"Have you seen your neighbor today?" Barry asked.

A slight frown crossed Gail's brow. Olivia guessed her to be in her mid to late thirties "I saw her come in this morning. She was pulling in as I was backing out." Gail was looking down, fidgeting with her purse.

She doesn't want to talk to him. She doesn't trust the police. Olivia tried to focus on the house next door, but Gail Wallace's agitation made it hard.

"So, you saw her this morning? Wendy is her name? Do you know her last name?" Barry asked.

"Wendy Florren. Yes, I definitely saw her this morning. She's a night nurse at North Central Baptist over in Stone Oak. She's usually getting in about the time I leave to take the kids to school. If she's working again tonight, she should be up soon."

Must be why no one had answered last night, Barry thought. Maybe she had already left for work. "Any kids?" he asked.

"One daughter, away at college."

Olivia and Barry exchanged looks. *So, who put the bike there?*

Olivia looked back at the house where Wendy lived. A flash went off in her head. *She might be there, but no one is home.* "What kind of dog does she have?"

Barry looked back at Olivia, caught off guard by the question and that she was even asking one at all. This was *his* investigation.

The woman looked from Barry to Olivia, obviously confused. Olivia felt the air between them change as the implications sank in. Annoyance gave way to concern. "Does this have anything to do with what happened the other night? The woman who was murdered at the end of the street?" the woman asked, looking at Olivia.

Barry answered quickly, attempting to regain her attention and his investigation. "Just some follow up ma'am. We were here last night canvassing the neighborhood, but missed you and your neighbor," he explained. He tried to keep his tone casual, non-threatening, but it wasn't working.

The woman ignored Barry despite his best efforts. "Schnauzer," she answered Olivia's question before addressing the lieutenant. "Last night was my turn to drive for the swim team. Today is Teresa's turn. She's my neighbor on the other side. She has the kids," Gail explained. "When I came back home last night, I found a card in my door. I think it was your name on it. Sorry I haven't called. Things have been hectic, you know?"

Olivia watched the woman's eyes stray to the ground. Gail thought the gesture made her last statement seem believable. It didn't. *She was lying.*

"Fu Manchu mustache?" Olivia asked. At least Gail had been honest with her.

"Yes."

"So, your kids aren't home yet?" Barry asked inserting himself back into the conversation.

Gail shook her head. "Kid. Just one. And no. Billy won't be home for at least another forty-five minutes."

"Tell me, Ms. Wallace, what does Billy like to do? Does he ride bikes with friends? Is your house the one with the big treehouse?" Olivia asked. She knew the answer already, but there was an unconscious reason the woman hadn't made the call to the police. Olivia wondered if Gail even knew what it was. It was the same reason that prompted her to lie. *Fear.*

"Is this about the bike I found in my yard?"

Olivia and Barry exchanged looks.

"It looked scuffed up. Billy said he found it. Kept asking if he could keep it, but I told him no. It's too dangerous. I told him to put it back wherever he found it," Gail explained. "It was gone this morning when I checked."

Olivia nodded sympathetically. "And the tree house?" she prompted. "Is it Billy's?"

"Yes."

"Was Billy home the other day? When it happened?" Olivia asked.

Billy's mom locked eyes with Olivia and shook her head slowly. "Monday is the only day we don't have practice." As a mother the nightmare was just starting to creep into her consciousness. She had yet to fully formulate the thought.

"Where's her husband?" Olivia asked, redirecting Gail from the mental road she was heading down. They needed her help and Olivia wasn't sure how much good she would be to them once she found her way.

27

Gail's brow furrowed again, and Olivia felt the realization taking shape. Gail was caught in thoughts of Billy and what he might have seen. Is that why she hadn't called? She didn't want to know?

"Whose husband?" Gail asked.

"Wendy's. Your neighbor."

"Wendy doesn't have a husband."

"Does she ever walk the dog?" Olivia asked quickly.

"Are you kidding? He hates the leash."

"We should go next door now," Olivia said, tugging at Barry's sleeve. He was still blocking Gail's route to her front door. Gail Wallace clearly wanted to be rid of them. Barry let Olivia pull him away.

"She has a boyfriend. His name's Mike. Does that help?" Gail said, beating a path to her door once the way was clear.

"You've been very helpful, ma'am. Thank you. We'll talk more, later." Barry nodded back at her as he rushed to keep up with Olivia. She was already at Wendy's front door.

"No, you won't," Olivia told him. "She won't talk to you again if she doesn't have to. She doesn't trust men. It's why she talked to me and not you," she explained.

Barry ignored the statement. He would have figured it out, but just like yesterday at the crime scene, she was one step ahead of him and he had no idea how he had gotten behind. "What the hell kind of questions were those? You're stepping on my toes and you're scaring the neighbor."

"She should be scared," Olivia snapped, her eyes focused on the door in front of them. Her breath was coming in short bursts. "I know I am. Her boy found a bike that clearly didn't belong to him. He hid it alongside the fence among the bushes, hoping to get it out of sight for safekeeping. He planned on riding it today. He wanted to keep it no matter what his mother said, just as you pointed out, but he didn't pick a very good hiding spot. The owner came back and found it, but that's not all he took."

Barry hadn't seen her so animated. Her words were coming in a rush. Her change in demeanor gave him pause. "And this Wendy woman knows something?" Barry asked, reigning in his territorial tendencies. She could help him if he would just let her.

Olivia shook her head and wrapped her arms around herself like a cocoon. *Not anymore.* "No. Wrong place. Wrong time. Wrong person."

Before knocking Barry decided to go take a quick peek in the garage. On tiptoes, he could see inside Wendy's garage just enough to make out the roof of what looked like a vehicle. He joined Olivia back at the front door. She hadn't moved.

"Car is in the garage. I hate to wake her, but if she is working tonight, it's time to get up." Barry reached out and rang the doorbell. They finally heard barking. Anxious little yelps came from the other side of the door.

Olivia imagined they originated from a schnauzer-sized dog.

No air stirred on the small, confined porch. The low overhang of the tree kept out the breeze. Barry's heart rate increased along with the bark of the dog.

Her words finally settled in his head. "What did you mean wrong place, wrong time? Wrong person?"

Barry looked back at Olivia when she didn't answer. She had gone silent. Standing still, rooted in place.

Olivia's eyes weren't looking at anything on the porch. They were haunted by some other visions, ones not of this place. She shook her head. Death slipped in quietly sometimes, but not this time. This time it came in the form of a screaming energy and the only thing muffling its crescendo was the door in front of them. Once opened, it could never be put back. Olivia struggled to brace herself, her fingers finding the tiny cross again.

Barry's pulse quickened and it had nothing to do with the yapping dog. "Olivia, talk to me. Where are you?" He reached for her, but she backed away.

"He stood right here. Right where we are now. He rang the doorbell." She was talking to him, but she was mesmerized by something else, maybe the scene she had just described. She shook her head as if trying to make it go away or alter the outcome.

"And then what happened?"

There was pain in her eyes as she looked at him. "She let him in."

"Why?"

"She trusted him. It's too late. We're too late."

"Olivia, I need you to stay with me. It's okay. It's going to be okay."

"No, it's not," she told him. Olivia shook her head again and backed away.

"I need you to stay right here," Barry said slowly. Gently he reached for her arm.

His touch steadied her. She was able to readjust her focus. Her green eyes were blazing. The man she met yesterday wasn't the real Barry. She was beginning to understand that he could be impatient, when he was tired, when he felt the need to protect, but the real him the one touching her now calmed her. Olivia felt the tug between them. The ebb and the flow. She wondered if he felt drawn to her because the darkness had touched him too. She nodded a promise to stay where she was.

Once he was convinced, she wasn't going anywhere, Barry turned back to the house. He raised his fist and knocked. On contact, the door slammed against the inside wall as if it had been jerked open by an energy inside the house. If the dog was inside the house, it was silent. Stillness closed in, stifling him. The hair on the back of his neck gave a slow rise. He looked back at Olivia and decided he was either all in or he wasn't. There was no turning back. "Wendy Florren? SAPD," Barry called out, never taking his eyes off Olivia.

She broke her promise and took a step forward this time. She wouldn't leave him on his own.

No answer.

All sense of space and time eluded him. All that mattered was right here. Right now. Both hands gripping his weapon, barrel down, Barry led with his left shoulder, pushing the door flush against the entryway wall, ensuring there was nothing lurking behind it. Crossing the threshold, Barry's senses swayed under an assault of sights and smells. Light-eliminating curtains disguised the fact that it was mid-afternoon outside. It was stifling inside, much hotter than it should be on this spring day, and there was an all too familiar smell: bodily fluids seeping into anything they touched. The much-talked-about dog appeared as a furry white object just on the edge of the entryway farthest from the door. He left a trail of crimson paw prints on the tile. He wasn't barking anymore. Either he had decided to trust the intruder, or he had no one left to protect. No more than two steps inside, Barry saw it. Crossing into the carpeted living room where the dog sat, he could just make out a figure on the floor. The dog was making his last stand. A lifeless pair of feet stuck out past the coffee table, the rest of the body was wedged between the table and the couch. It was a small space with no room to retreat. Sunlight snuck through the blades of the full-length blinds covering the sliding glass door out to the backyard where he and Olivia had just been, where the dog bowls were.

His weapon in his left hand, Barry used his right hand to remove the radio clipped on his hip. "This is Unit Twelve. I've got a one-eight-seven at 3524 Blossom Pointe. Ten-sixty."

"Wendy? Wendy Florren," Barry called softly, but knew there was no one to hear him. Olivia was right. She had been all along. They were too late.

A pop of static was followed by, "Units on the way, Lieutenant."

He hoped Olivia stayed put, but he forced thoughts of her aside. He needed to focus on making sure whoever killed Wendy Florren wasn't still in the house.

Chapter Four

Even with the windows and the patio door open, the odors of death permeated the house. Members of the CSU team milled about Wendy Florren's living room.

"Body temp is eighty-two. It'd likely be lower if it wasn't hotter'n Hades in here," Warren Meeks said. It was the second time in three days the Bexar County Chief Medical Examiner had been called to the same neighborhood, a fact not lost on anyone in the room. Meeks lifted Wendy Florren's left wrist, but not to check for a pulse. A broken watch would help pinpoint the time of the attack on the off chance it had been broken during a struggle. He was disappointed but not surprised when the digital minute display advanced.

"Any idea on time of death?" Barry asked.

"Body temp drops one point five degrees Celsius every hour until the temperature of the body reaches ambient temperature. Ms. Florren sleeps during the day. I don't reckon she's the one who cranked up the heat. At any rate, the unnatural warmth in here complicates things. I'm hesitant to estimate time of death until I examine her stomach contents," Meeks said as he packed up his bag.

"Come on, Doc," Barry said. "Hazard a guess?"

Meeks shrugged. "Preliminary estimation is six to eight hours." He nodded to two techs who had been waiting to remove the body.

"What're you thinking? Same guy?" Barry wanted to know.

"That's for y'all to determine, Lieutenant," Meeks said, stretching his back, which was stiff from kneeling.

Barry cocked his head, waiting for Meeks to offer something. "The staging is different, but..." Meeks glanced back as the two morgue techs lifted the bag containing Florren's body onto a gurney. They had been instructed by Meeks to take her out through the back door along the side of the house. The local station, WOAI, was still on the scene. It was almost Fiesta time. San Antonio was about to throw a two-week-long party and images of victims murdered in their homes were less than festive.

"The injury pattern is different. What isn't different, and what we don't see very often, is this level of frenzied violence. It's almost animalistic. Damnedest thing though, he sure as hell wasn't acting like an animal after the fact. He took the time to turn off the AC and turn on the heat before he left. The only reason for that is to accelerate the decomp rate. Things would look a lot different in here if we didn't find her within twenty-four hours."

"What was she wearing?" Mark asked. He was the fourth officer on the scene, summoned by Barry with explicit instructions to bring over the case file. Just the file, no photos. He wondered if his lieutenant was testing Olivia. If so, she would know it. And how would she feel about that? Mark had delivered the file to her, as instructed. She was outside now, sequestered in a squad car, reviewing it with the victim's schnauzer curled up in her lap as if they'd been friends for years.

"Yoga pants and a t-shirt, I think," one of the CSU

techs offered. "The logo on the shirt might be March of Dimes. It's hard to tell with all the blood." They would have to wait for confirmation until the body made it to Meeks's Morgue, the popular but unofficial name of the Bexar County ME's Office in the Forensic Science Center. The officer continued, "Her hospital badge is hanging on a key rack just inside the laundry room. Looks like she came in through the garage. According to the badge, she worked in the NICU. March of Dimes would make sense."

"Why are you interested in her sleeping attire?" another tech asked.

"Might tell us if she was working tonight and going straight to bed or staying up for a while to acclimate to having a couple of days off. There's no evidence of forced entry. That leads me to believe she let someone in," Mark said.

"If I'm single and alone, why would I open the door for someone I don't know?" one of the newer CSU officers asked. "It would have to be a pretty compelling reason." The officer had introduced herself to Barry earlier in the week, but it seemed a lifetime ago now. He was pretty sure her name started with a "K," Kelly or Katie, maybe.

"Someone she knew maybe. Someone she was expecting," Mark said.

"There's a lot of blood," Barry said, blocking the ME's way out. "She was alive when he started," Meeks said, suspecting the lieutenant wanted to know how much Wendy Florren had suffered before she died.

Barry shook his head.

"She took a powerful blow to the side of her head. There's a good chance she was unconscious during the worst of it," Meeks offered. "I'll do her post at nine in the morning. See you then."

"Wine bottle. It's likely what he used to take her down," Mark said, pointing to an evidence bag on the coffee table. "Looks like the knife he gutted her with came from her own set. There's an empty slot in the block in the kitchen."

Barry considered what that meant. The killer hadn't come prepared, or he liked to travel light. It made sense if he had come back for the bike. But how had he gotten to the house? And how had he left without being noticed? He had to have been covered in blood.

"Pay close attention to the bathrooms," Barry said to no one in particular. If the killer cleaned up before he left, there would be traces. Barry was sure he at least wiped himself off, otherwise, he would have looked like Jack the Ripper walking, or riding, through the neighborhood.

Barry was distracted by Kelly or Katie, who was kneeling at the threshold between the entryway and the living room.

Sensing his interest, she said, "The stain pattern looks like a print we casted at one of the other crime scenes."

Barry walked over and knelt down to get a closer look. She was right. The distinctive pattern was familiar: the shape of a spade from a deck of cards, with two dots above it that looked like a pair of eyes. "Katie, right?" he asked.

"Yes, sir. We'll cut this section out and get it to the lab," she said.

The ME and Captain Anthony Zavalla passed each

other in the doorway. Zavalla, or Big Tony as he had been called most of his career, quickly surveyed the space. He had seen enough murder scenes in his twenty-two years in law enforcement to know where the victim had taken her last breath. He ignored the large bloody area between the couch and coffee table and moved toward the fireplace, where CSU techs were still busy processing surfaces for prints, DNA, anything the UNSUB might have inadvertently left behind.

What interested Tony Zavalla more was what the killer intentionally left for them to find. The captain stood with his hands on his hips, gazing up at the wall above the fireplace, the space a bachelor would fill with a big-screen TV. Wendy Florren's choice of décor had been a large mirror. Dark red letters were scrawled across its surface. "What does it say?" Zavalla asked as he stared at the squiggles on the mirror.

"*'Father, forgive them, for they know not what they do.'* Luke 23:34," Olivia said, walking through the door just as Captain Zavalla asked the question. It was the literal translation. The crudely formed letters were not easy to read, but she didn't need to. She knew the verse.

Olivia didn't want to come inside, but even outside, within the confines of the police cruiser, she couldn't escape the remnants of death that lingered. Opening the doors and windows of the house was like releasing steam from a kettle. Like a flood, the dark energy had surrounded her in the car and sought cracks to penetrate. Inside the house, mixed with the energy of the living, it might lose some of its power. Maybe she could get some relief from the overwhelming buzzing in her head. Traces still lingered inside but the white noise of the human energy served as a buffer. She sought shelter in their proximity.

Getting inside hadn't been too difficult for her with the case file in hand, but Barry's nod to the officer guarding the perimeter had been the golden ticket.

"Is it written in blood?" the captain asked.

"Most likely," Barry said.

"Presumptive test was positive, though it's not necessarily human blood," Katie said.

"It's hers," Olivia said. "It's Wendy Florren's."

"Why does it always have to be Bible verses?" Zavalla shook his head and scanned the interior again. "Any other religious paraphernalia around?"

"It's the most widely-read book in all of Western civilization," Olivia answered for him whether he was looking for a response or not. "Makes it easily identifiable. He wants the attention at this point." *Or needs it.* Olivia looked across the room, carefully avoiding the space between the coffee table and couch, and noticed a crucifix above the sliding glass door. She turned to find one hanging above the front door she had just entered. The crosses were supposed to keep out evil. Maybe the owner had the house blessed, maybe she didn't. Either way, it hadn't seemed to work.

"You must be Dr. Osborne," Zavalla said, giving Olivia the once-over.

The lieutenant glanced at his superior officer and Olivia caught a flash of confusion.

It was clear to Barry that Zavalla knew about Olivia. He hadn't mentioned her to the captain. So, how did Zavalla know who she was? Had Mark informed him? Had Olivia herself? And what the hell did *Doctor* Osborne mean?

Before the lieutenant could seek clarification, Zavalla asked, "What's your take on this message, Dr. Osborne?" Her eyes returned to the scripture scrawled across the mirror's face.

"My first impression is that he's asking for forgiveness. He did this, but not because he wanted to."

"Setting up his defense already, son of a bitch," Zavalla muttered. Not exactly what she meant, but Olivia decided not to explain. He didn't know her well enough to get it and the lieutenant had taken a chance on her today. He hadn't stopped her from talking to the neighbor and he had turned over the case file. She wasn't going to rock the boat since the sea between her and Barry was calm, at least for now. She had the briefest touch of intuition about Zavalla. She'd learned to trust these flashes, but they weren't always complete. She would need to 'try it on for size' as her grandmother would say. Her brain was on overload, a quagmire of thoughts and images. She was sure the key was in there somewhere.

"Patrol just found our other victim's car," Mark told Barry. He didn't have to specify which victim. Only the last one had been found without her car. The call had come to Mark when Barry didn't answer his phone.

"Where?"

"McAllister Park." Eyes narrowed Barry looked at Mark. "You want to tell me how the hell Zavalla knows about Doctor Osborne's involvement in this investigation?"

"How about we discuss it on the way?" Mark suggested. Barry looked between Mark and Olivia. "Come with me."

Mark moved to join him.

"No," Barry said. "You stay here. I'm taking Olivia with me," he clarified.

Mark nodded, hoping to mask his surprise.

Olivia followed silently, mentally drained and eager to leave the house and the neighborhood. She wasn't looking forward to the car ride with the lieutenant, to the questions that hung over him like a cloud.

Barry looked down at her hand and then across the seat at her. "Zavalla knew about you." It was both a statement and a question.

"Mark spoke to him last—"

"Sonofabitch. What the hell is Mark doing? This was...you were supposed to be..." *What was she supposed to be? He still wasn't sure. He had only been humoring Mark. She was temporary, unofficial...*

"Don't blame Mark. I called him last night, and advised him to speak to his captain," she said.

"And what about his lieutenant? I'm just supposed be deaf and dumb, huh?"

"Lieutenant... Barry, this UNSUB, there's something..." *He won't understand.*

"Zavalla called you Dr. Osborne. You didn't correct him. What kind of—"

"Forensic psychologist," she said.

"Jesus Christ. Mark said you were a psychic, or something like one. Why would he lie?"

"He didn't. It's complicated. Look, I'll be glad to answer your questions, but all you need to know right now is that I'm here because Mark thought I could help. And we still need to talk to Billy," she reminded him, keeping her voice hushed because the dog had finally settled down. "A quick look around Wendy's house would've told the UNSUB she's not the one who stashed the bike." Olivia laid her hand on Barry's arm ensuring she had his attention. "I'm just saying, if he comes back, he'll go next door. Maybe the only reason he didn't start there is because no one was home."

The dog was snoring softly in her lap. Barry had forgotten about it. He radioed Mark. "I need you to go next door and talk to Gail Wallace. Her son's name is Billy. Ask her if—" Olivia furiously shook her head, "No, tell them they need to stay somewhere else tonight."

"Sure, boss. Before I do that, I'm going to have to calm down Miss Florren's boyfriend. Apparently, he's been waiting curbside to find out what happened to his girlfriend."

"Have him meet me at the substation on Jones. Call ahead and reserve me a room," Barry said. He didn't want the poor guy to have to drive all the way downtown.

"You got it. Just so you know, he's a big guy and he's not happy."

Well, that makes two of us.

****

Two units were waiting for them as they pulled to the back of the park.

"The vehicle was spotted by Officer Brad Harris," the uniformed officer pointed to his colleague standing off to the side of the black vehicle. "Harris is from the Jones substation. Their guys have been helping us out on patrols and we've been checking this park daily for cars." The park was a favorite of walkers and bikers due to the numerous trails, and it wasn't far from

41

Monday's crime scene.

Situated between neighborhoods, it was a narrow but deep stretch of real estate, surrounded by open land. Given all the coverage it provided, Barry wasn't surprised the UNSUB had chosen the spot to dump the car. He wondered why more crimes didn't occur there. Maybe it was the proximity of the middle- and upper-class neighborhoods. Barry recalled the only other murder case he had worked here almost two years ago. A fellow student shot a kid in the back of the head over a drug deal involving less than a hundred dollars just hours after his high school graduation. Such a waste. The shooter confessed less than an hour into the interview. They only brought him in because he had been annoyingly helpful.

"Today is the first time they spotted it." Another officer pointed to the small surveillance camera mounted on a nearby light post. "I've already asked the city to pull any footage they have."

Barry nodded his thanks and headed for the discovering officer. "So, tell me what you know, Officer Harris."

"You can call me, Brad, sir."

"I'll stick with your title. You've earned it," Barry said, noting that the kid couldn't have been out of the academy long. Harris was young and eager to please. Barry had a hard time remembering what that was like.

"Yes, Lieutenant. I came on shift at 1500. After roll call, I headed here. Even-numbered patrol cars have been instructed to make a pass through here every other day at the beginning of shift. Odd-numbered patrol cars pick up the days in between. Today was my day."

Barry nodded and made a note. "So how long

between the last check and yours?" He wanted a clear timeline.

"After roll call this morning. I already spoke to the officer before me, and she reported the lot was empty on her pass through just after seven this morning."

"Did you touch anything?"

"No, sir."

"How did you know it was our car?"

"BOLO, sir. It's taped to my laptop. I knew right away."

Barry nodded.

"I took a discretionary walk around the vehicle, shined a light inside just to make sure there was no immediate threat and then gave dispatch a call. I've been waiting for you here ever since, sir."

"Thank you, Officer Harris. You've been a big help," he said, dismissing the officer.

Barry walked over and gave the car his own once-over. The techs had finished their preliminary evidence collection and were standing by to tow the car in for further processing once Barry gave the word. Where had this car been for three days? And why was this the first time the UNSUB had taken a victim's car? Maybe he couldn't leave the same way he had come. Maybe Olivia was right. Again.

Chapter Five

Like a change in barometric pressure, the heaviness settled just behind her eyes. Some likened it to the birth of a migraine, but it was different. For her, it was the coagulating of residual energy trapped between this world and the other just after the cross-over. She felt it strongest where the veil between the two worlds was thinnest. The closer to the occurrence, the stronger the pull.

It started as soon as they entered the park, a gentle ping on the edge of her consciousness. Now, sitting next to the focal point, the energy slammed into her synapses like the banging of a drum. Olivia didn't need Barry to tell her the vehicle they had been searching for once belonged to Patricia Griffin. A nasty black ball of energy hung inside of it, and she struggled to block its force. First the house and now the car. She felt depleted as the barriers she erected between her world and the other buckled with fatigue. It made her more open, but also more vulnerable.

Olivia tried to concentrate on the case file still in her lap. She'd had to move the dog who was now curled up next to her in the front seat. Unconsciously, Olivia stroked his fur. The silkiness of it fed her need for comfort. She remembered as a child carrying a blanket trimmed in satin. She had rubbed the trim between her fingers when she tried to stop the dark from coming and she still reverted to what had comforted her in times of distress.

Barry opened her door. He squatted down to be on her level. "How are you doing?" he asked.

She couldn't respond. There was no way she could begin to describe the assault on her psyche. Beside her, the dog lifted his head but laid it right back down again when Barry's scent registered as friendly. "I need you to do something for me, if you can."

Olivia nodded. "Only if you do something for *me*."

"Shoot," Barry said without hesitation.

"Find out the dog's name. He's coming home with me. I've got to call him something."

Barry nodded.

Olivia climbed out of the car and prepared herself for what was to come. "This place was his original destination. He cut through the neighborhood," Olivia said. The information had not come from the case file, even if this UNSUB did have a proclivity for parks. She just *knew* things. Barry was starting to understand.

She followed him to the driver's side vehicle. He handed her a pair of gloves, which she quickly put on. He had snagged the smallest ones he could find.

"Can you just sit in the driver's seat?" Barry asked. "It looks too far back for Ms. Griffin. If I remember correctly, you are about her height." Secretly Barry was hoping for more than what the field techs found. People remembered to wipe down the steering wheel and door handle. Less conspicuous things, like the lever used to adjust the seat and the rearview mirror were easier to forget. At least that's what he was hoping for in this case.

Barry reached for the door, but Olivia stopped him.

"We should do this in the forensics bay, after the car has been fully processed. I'd hate to—"

"You're right, but that'll take hours. I'd rather not wait."

"You don't happen to have a Tyvek suit and booties handy, do you Lieutenant?"

He smiled, turned on his heel, and marched to his car.

Tentatively, Olivia grasped the door handle. A current of energy snaked its way up her arm. She gasped and released her grip as Barry returned with a plastic bundle.

"You good?"

She nodded but kept silent. Her process had tactile aspects he couldn't understand. She took the protective suit from him and got into it quickly, using his arm to steady herself as she pulled the booties over her shoes.

Olivia didn't let her hand linger on the handle this time. As she opened the door, she caught a whiff of Patricia's perfume. Something floral and sweet. No, not *Patricia*. She didn't like being called that. She preferred Patty. She had wanted to get home to make dinner. She had a life to live. It might not seem like a lot, but it was hers.

Olivia pushed past the residual memories and slid inside. The face of the steering wheel was messy with smears. She pushed images out of her mind, deciding to leave those details for the forensics lab. She placed her index fingers lightly on the steering wheel at the two and ten o'clock positions and settled back into the seat as if she was driving. Her feet didn't quite reach the pedals. Patty's wouldn't have either. She looked up at Barry and he nodded, signaling he had gotten the visual he needed. Patty Griffin had not been the last one to drive her car. It was the last thought Olivia had that was her own.

Like a cloud passing across the sun, grayness enveloped her, broken by lightning streaks of black. The air was electric. She felt charged particles collide against her face and heard them ping off the polyethylene coveralls. Her peripheral vision began to shrink as darkness enclosed her. She fumbled blindly for the steering wheel, but it was fathoms away, somewhere in the distorted depths. Her hands flailed, seeking something with which to ground herself. *He isn't alone. He is never alone, not anymore.* The thoughts rolled over her in dizzying waves.

Her intrusion on the other side sent ripples through the half-light. Dwellers there sensed her presence. Most only took note, but a rare few dared slither her way. Olivia wasn't safe, not like this. She was too open, too exposed. She needed to get back to the other side.

Her throat constricted as she tried to take a breath. Her lungs lay flat in her chest, deflated. Her innate fight-or-flight response sputtered to life, and she stumbled from that place, slamming the doors to her mind as she fled. She had no idea so many portals to her soul were open.

Struggling to break free, Olivia pushed back against the car seat solidly behind her, grounding her to this dimension. The upholstery hugged her. On the other side, darkness was coming, not for Patty, but for her. It was so fast. It would envelop her if she didn't retreat. Olivia managed to grab a breath that was heavy, dank, and acidic all at the same time. She coughed and felt bile rise as she struggled to sever the connection.

Barry was gazing over Olivia's head calculating if there was enough room in the hatchback to put the bike inside without folding the seats down when he heard her choking. He reached for her shoulder, shaking her, but she didn't respond. Desperate to make it stop, Barry grabbed her and pulled her free of the car. He had to do something. He had to bring her back. She didn't answer as he called her name. She was looking right through him. Once he freed her from the car, Barry eased himself to the ground with her in his arms. Olivia reached out. When she found him, she held on tight and didn't let go. He dipped his head and pressed his forehead to hers. He closed his eyes and breathed deep and steady until her breathing matched his. Her struggle for air subsided; the soft puffs from her lips sparking a ripple of goosebumps down his neck.

"Should I call someone, Lieutenant?" an officer behind him asked.

He recited Mark's number without looking up.

****

The room was stifling and filled with the anger that had drifted in from the living room. The turn of the fan overhead chilled her. Her clothes were damp with her own sweat and wisps of hair clung to her neck. Olivia tried to read the bedside clock, but her contacts were stuck to her eyes. She would have to peel them off. A lifetime ago, they used to freeze to her eyes, back when she helped the living.

Olivia vaguely remembered the trip to her house in Barry's car. He was on the phone taking directions from Mark. *He was worried. He thought I had a seizure or something.* Maybe that was what it looked like. She could count on one hand how many times she had lost herself like that.

The ceaseless onslaught of dark energy emanating from Wendy Florren's house had weakened her mental defenses; along with being out of practice, it was a crippling combination. She isolated herself for a reason. After almost four decades of struggling to cope, she had trained herself to manage the emotions of the living. Now they all but bounced off of her unless there were too many of them. Sometimes the energy of just one person could be too much if it was highly charged like the lieutenant had been the night they met.

The residual energy of a transition to the other side was a different phenomenon all together, one that played havoc with her psyche in a whole different way. It was predatory and unclean. It poked holes where the living couldn't. She forced the carousel of thoughts to stop. She needed to get off.

Mark must have convinced Barry she hadn't had a seizure because she woke up in her own bed and not at the hospital. If she wasn't mistaken, he also held her hand. Mark had been waiting for them when they arrived. The door had been open, every light in the house blazing. Someone had walked her to her bedroom and tucked her in, but she couldn't remember who.

Olivia looked over to find the little schnauzer curled next to her. He raised his head and she reached for him. He accepted a few feathery strokes before snuggling back down, readjusting himself firmly against her leg. She wondered how Daisy was taking to the newcomer. She wasn't yet excited or jealous enough to join them. Then again, Daisy couldn't jump up on the bed. Her legs were too spindly and probably, as a former racer, she felt more comfortable close to the ground. More importantly, Daisy was afraid to come into this room. Olivia wondered if Alice had also spooked Mark and that's why all the lights were on. Had Alice been startled by the intrusion? Her ghostly housemate was forever a child.

The curtains were still open in her room. Outside the shadows were long. It was really late or very early, depending on one's perspective. They were only three days past the full moon so the celestial body still offered its light. It was warmer than usual for this time of year, but the weather had nothing to do with the heat of the room. She sat up and fought the vertigo that came with the change in position. Her physical reserves were depleted. She needed nourishment.

Mark and Barry were in another room exchanging verbal blows. She couldn't make out what they were saying. She wondered what time it was but thought it must be late. Barry had to interview Wendy's boyfriend and finish up at the park. He probably left Mark to watch over her until he could come back and see for himself. Olivia stayed perfectly still and focused what little energy she had on listening.

Mark's voice broke through the fog. "You should never have taken her with you." Away from everyone else, he could let his true feelings show.

"You brought her to me," Barry snapped back. "Maybe if you'd given me a little more than that vague, bullshit explanation. Look, I get it now. She knows things. I only got as far as I did today because of her."

Twenty-four hours ago that was the last thing he would've said. Olivia shoved her feelings aside and concentrated.

"How was I supposed to know what would

happen?" Barry continued.

He had been impatient yesterday, but tonight he sounded unsure. Though she didn't think it was doubt that clung to his words; it was fear. Maybe he felt what she did—really scared for the first time in a long time. She sensed frustration there, too. He wanted to understand but didn't. Not yet.

"You're messing with things you know nothing about," Mark warned him.

"And why is that, Sergeant? Why is it that I know nothing about it, but our captain sure as hell did? He didn't question why Olivia was at the Wendy Florren crime scene. Why is *that*? What did you tell Zavalla that you didn't tell me? You've more than downplayed what she really does." Barry had seen what she was capable of, what happened in the car, the way she sized up people as well as he did a crime scene.

Olivia didn't need a heightened sense of perception to know the two men were on the verge of escalation. Both of them were short on patience and long on stress, and whatever was going on between them needed to stop before one of them went too far.

Selfishly, she needed them both to play the parts they had been cast. Olivia left her darkened cocoon and forged back into the light.

She found them in the kitchen. Barry saw her first, just over Mark's shoulder. He was relieved to see her looking much more like herself.

The change in his former partner's expression signaled to Mark their conversation was over. He turned to hand Olivia the glass of water he had intended to take her before Barry interrupted him. "Thought you might need this."

Olivia took the glass and drank until it was gone, thankful Mark knew what she needed. Her excursions today left her dehydrated. She was pretty sure before long Barry would know these things as well. He would figure it out sooner or later, or she would have to explain it to him. It might not be such an unpleasant conversation. She needed someone when she left the dark place and he had been there for her. She led a solitary existence, and his physical presence touched her in long dormant places.

"So, what's the dog's name?" she asked Barry, not wanting to dwell too long on personal thoughts. She was in no condition to deal with them.

"Alvin."

"Thanks," she said, heading toward the refrigerator. "Now I can give him and Daisy a proper introduction."

"I can get you whatever you need," Mark told her as she brushed past him.

"There is vodka in the freezer. I'd really like some of that."

"Okay," Mark said, putting a hand on the refrigerator door to block her. "But you need food first."

He had a point. Olivia leaned against the counter as he rummaged through takeout bags on the counter. She glanced through the open curtains of the window above the sink. Instinctively, she reached over and pulled them closed.

"How long was I out?" she asked.

"A couple of hours," Mark said and handed her a plate of chicken strips.

It was her comfort food, from a local place known

for their barbecue, but Olivia liked their crispy fried chicken best. It was just like her grandmother used to make, crispy on the outside and juicy on the inside. Gran would get the grease so hot it would ignite a match. Only when the smell of Sulphur tickled her nose was it hot enough, she used to say. And she liked their iced tea. It was spiked with pickle juice.

"There's more than enough," Mark said to Barry, who had not moved from his spot at the edge of the kitchen. "Just before closing they are very generous. There are some soft drinks in the fridge, or if you prefer something else," Mark held up his bottle of water as an offering.

"I think there's still a couple of beers in the back behind some stuff I need to throw out," Olivia said. *No, not beer. Liquor.* She saw a flash of amber liquid. His nerves were on fire. If he was home, he would have already had a shot. But tonight, she thought he would hold onto the fire a little while longer and douse the flames only when he was alone.

Barry took the water from Mark, and the three of them retreated to the dining room table with full plates. Olivia dunked everything in the gravy. Chicken strips, bread, French fries, green beans, all of it. She didn't care that it was cold. She caught Barry looking at her more than once. He was probably wondering where all the calories went. She had heard the comment before.

"I didn't have lunch today," she said between bites, but that was the easy answer. The cosmic cross-over really screwed with her metabolism.

They ate in silence after that. She was happy to note Mark had also snagged her an extra slice of coconut cream pie. It was waiting for her in the kitchen when she was done with what was in front of her. The sugar always helped recharge her before she began again. She looked across the dining room at Daisy in her bed, her toys surrounding her. She was what the animal behavioralists called a "gatherer." Daisy lounged there, content to accept what was to come, even if it meant a new roommate. She was just letting everyone know, the new one included, which toys belonged to her.

No one had anything to say, at least nothing suitable for dinner conversation. They all needed a little quiet time before they were forced to relive the nightmare again. It was going to be with them for a while.

For some of them, it might never go away.

Chapter Six

Thursday…"Thanks for coming in early to see me. I heard you had a late night," Zavalla said as Barry joined him in his office. Barry closed the door behind him without being asked.

The captain offered Barry a cup of coffee. Barry politely declined. Whatever the captain was drinking smelled like pralines and cream. One of Barry's ex-wives likened what he usually drank to jet fuel. He had already had two cups.

"I'm still doing some follow-up, but I can give you a quick rundown," Barry offered. He, Mark, and Olivia compared notes last night, but she was coming in today to go over some things with him in more detail. He had some CCTV footage he wanted her to see.

"That's not why I called you. We can talk about the case later. Right now, I want to talk about Olivia Osborne."

Barry was surprised. They had a serial killer on their hands. The post-mortem exam on their latest victim was due to start soon. Discussing Olivia was the last thing he expected this morning.

"Why did I have to find out you were using her from Sergeant Austin?" Zavalla wanted to know.

"You shouldn't have needed to know at all, Captain," Barry said.

Zavalla leaned back in his chair and crossed his

arms. "How's that, Lieutenant?"

"Sergeant Austin invited her; apparently, they go way back. She was just supposed to take a look at the scene, give us her thoughts, and head back to wherever she came from. Quick, simple, in and out. I wasn't expecting anything from her. I figured she's one of those psychics that, you know, touches a piece of clothing or something and says, 'I'm sensing the child is still alive. Look in a wooded area,' that kind of thing. But I thought, on the off chance she might be able to help us narrow our focus, she might give us something we don't already know. Hell, what's there to lose? Captain, I didn't tell you because I didn't believe it was even worth telling you. And truthfully, I didn't want you to think I believed in that stuff. I didn't want you to think I'd lost it."

"You're a lieutenant; you lost it a long time ago." Even Zavalla's attempt to put the officer at ease didn't break the tension in the room. "Now, please," the captain said indicating the vacant chairs in front of his desk, "Sit down and talk to me." The request finally slowed him. Barry had been unconsciously pacing the same trail from one end of the captain's desk to the other. He stopped and slid into the chair nearest the window. It gave him a view of the door. It was a cop thing; he always had to have an exit strategy.

"These cases are tough, certainly the worst since I got here, maybe the worst I've ever seen. I understand why Sergeant Austin thought to call her in. Serial killings are her thing."

Her thing? Barry held his tongue, unsure where the captain was going with this.

"So, tell me, has Dr. Osborne been helpful?"

Zavalla asked, waiting for a reaction. The look on Barry's face told him what he needed to know. His lieutenant had no idea who she really was.

"Until yesterday, I thought she was a nurse and a writer or maybe a psychic," Barry stopped talking since he really had no idea. Mark might have effectively evaded his questions, but Barry had pieced together enough details since last night that told him she was definitely not just a nurse or a psychic.

"She didn't tell you about the doctor thing, huh?" Zavalla nodded. "I heard she's not crazy about using the title." He shrugged as he chose not to comment on Barry's other guesses. The captain knew about the writing, but her forensic articles were a little too much for him, and her fiction was not his taste. The psychic or paranormal stuff certainly wasn't either.

"I was pretty sure she didn't work as a nurse anymore," Barry conceded. Though Mark hadn't mentioned it. The way she dressed and moved around the crime scene told him she was comfortable in that arena.

"Any idea why?"

"I thought she wrote books." Barry was still fumbling.

"Horror. Under some pen name, I'm sure. She didn't tell you?" Zavalla took a chance and asked. Just another part of his own personal investigation.

Barry shook his head. "No. Obviously not." Until yesterday he had never even been alone with her; Mark had been there as the intermediary or chaperone. Barry was currently a little fuzzy on what part Mark played, but he had already decided he needed clarification on Mark's place in her life sooner rather than later. He still couldn't believe Mark had discussed Olivia with Zavalla behind his back.

"Well, this is what I know," Zavalla offered. "She didn't have a lot of peer support as a nurse or during her brief stint at the Bureau."

"Wait, what? She was FBI?"

"For about a minute. Her theories aren't the most conventional. I understand her formal union with the Feds was severed after less than a year. For a while, she went freelance, testified for the defense at a number of high-profile trials. But she stopped all that a few years ago when she started consulting almost exclusively for the FBI."

Another surprise. She was full of them. "When she was freelance, you said she testified for the defense. So, she got the crazies off?" If so, that was quite a feat. Despite media coverage, only one percent of defendants in the criminal justice system used the insanity defense. It was a very tough argument to make, much less to win. The burden of proof was always on the defendant.

"Depends on your definition of *off,* and I'd say it's about fifty-fifty."

"So, she was only successful half of the time?" Somehow that didn't seem right. The confidence she exuded didn't come with a fifty-fifty rate. Then again, maybe that was as good as it got.

"No, if Dr. Osborne consulted for the defense, the defendant didn't go to prison. Overall, only twenty-five percent of insanity pleas are successful, but if she took the stand, the success rate was one hundred percent. The downside is only fifty percent of the defendants made it out alive."

Barry's eyes narrowed. He didn't understand what

the captain had just said, but it did shed some light on how she afforded the pricey real estate in Alamo Heights. Expert testimony.

"They didn't serve their time in prison. Where they went is probably worse. All were mandated to a state-run psychiatric facility, locked up on a ward designated for the criminally insane where only fifty percent of them end up staying. Think Hannibal Lecter," Zavalla suggested.

Barry didn't want to think about it at all. "So, they were eventually found to be sane and ended up at trial anyway?" Barry knew an insanity plea wasn't the magic loophole to avoid prosecution that some people thought it was. Again, blame the media for misrepresentation.

"No. Her remand rate was zero."

Barry leaned forward in his chair. "I'm still not following you. What happened to the other half if they didn't eventually go to trial?"

"They died in the psychiatric ward. Usually by suicide."

The weighty reality of this disclosure didn't have time to set in before the captain moved back to his original question. "So, you never answered me. Has she been helpful?"

Barry considered his words before speaking. Did he really want to share that Olivia, Dr. Osborne, had pinged on every one of his own gut feelings? "Currently, her bike theory is as solid as anything else we have." Of course, they had yet to recover the bike, but her version of events made sense. They had another dead victim at the last place the bike was seen. It had to be important to the UNSUB.

"Finding victim number three's car, once the bike disappeared, seems to have lent some credence to the theory," Zavalla agreed. "Does Dr. Osborne really think our guy pedaled up to his last victim?"

"I asked the same thing." Of course, Barry felt a whole lot different about the situation now than when he originally questioned it.

"Why the bike?" Zavalla wanted to know.

"She spotted some gravel covered in what appeared to be blood near some skid marks, which lead her to the bike theory. I have forensics checking the gravel now." Saying it out loud made the case seem flimsier than Barry felt it was.

"But no one, other than Dr. Osborne saw this bike?"

Barry cleared his throat. "The neighbor, Gail Wallace, did. Her son Billy brought it home. She got after him, said he had to return it, and assumed he had. I'll get the sergeant to get a detailed description of the bike from both Ms. Wallace and Billy."

"Fair enough," Zavalla said, his tone noncommittal.

Barry looked out the window of his boss's fifth-floor office. Below them, people were coming and going about their lives like there was nothing wrong. Like they were safe.

"So far, we've found nothing. How she puts this together, it's like she just knows. Like she's investigating on a whole other level. I can't explain it, the how or the why, but I trust her. I know that much. Her instincts are dead on," Barry said.

Zavalla assessed his lieutenant. Bartholomew's words weren't lost on him. It was high praise for an outsider. The fact he trusted Dr. Osborne made Zavalla more confident that he had been right in following through on her recommendation.

"She's not a psychic. What she is, or what she *has*, is called '*claircognizance*,' I believe," Zavalla said. "Exactly what that means or entails, you will have to ask the good doctor. But it is one of the many talents she brings to the table."

"You've worked with her in the past?" Barry couldn't help but ask. Damn Mark for not being straight with him.

"No. But I have been briefed on her abilities," Zavalla said. He didn't add that this briefing had been twenty minutes before the lieutenant walked through his office door. A member of the FBI's Behavioral Analysis Unit had provided a rundown of Dr. Osborne's talents just before boarding a flight to San Antonio.

Barry nodded. More to digest. "She assured me, unequivocally, we are dealing with a monster. From what I saw last night with Ms. Florren, and with the other three victims, I have to agree."

Zavalla knew for a fact Dr. Osborne's definition of monster and that of his lieutenant were different, but this was a detail Barry would have to discover for himself.

"Was that before or after she saw the bodies?" the captain asked.

"Before. She has the case file, but she hasn't seen the bodies," Barry told him. He didn't want to show her. He wanted to protect her in some small way.

"I think it's time she sees," Zavalla said, knowing why his lieutenant hadn't done it before now. Barry

Bartholomew might be hardened, but with Dr. Osborne, he was also chivalrous. There was no other explanation for his behavior. He trusted her professionally, but it also seemed he might feel invested in her on a personal level.

"Maybe she can tell us what kind of monster we're looking for," Zavalla suggested. "There's a blue moon this month, so if our boy keeps to it, we could have at least one more body on our hands before the end of the month. That is, if he hasn't escalated already."

Barry nodded and glanced at his watch. He got up from the chair ready to go.

"I know you've got the post and I've got another meeting, but I want to be clear, Lieutenant. There's a time to set egos aside and ask for a fresh perspective. Having said that," Zavalla reached into one of the drawers behind his desk and pulled out a folder. "So that you are fully aware of who, and what, you're dealing with." He handed Barry the file. "More on Dr. Osborne. Don't open it now."

"There's more?" Barry asked, taking the file.

"There's stuff in there I don't even want to try and explain. I don't want to sway your conclusion one way or the other."

Barry turned to go and then stopped himself. He thought back to something Mark had said. "Will what's in here tell me what happened to Mark's brother?" All Barry knew was that Mark's brother was dead because something he was working on went sideways. Mark never talked about it in the three years they'd worked together. He'd given no details whatsoever until the other night when he said Olivia had been there.

Zavalla shook his head. "You won't find it in this

file or any other that I'm aware of." From what the captain knew, it was *'don't ask, don't tell.'* "Trust me. No one in law enforcement will talk to you about it, so don't go poking around. Besides, it's not my tale to tell."

Barry had no idea where to start poking around, if he felt so inclined. From what the captain was describing, it sounded like things had gone more than sideways.

"Best I know, Dr. Osborne and Mark are the only ones who know the story, and I'm sure her version is different than his. She's the only one left alive who was there. Anyway," Zavalla felt he may have said too much already. "Once you take a look at the file, you'll see why I told you to show her the photos. If anything can scare her at this point, then we should all be afraid of whatever that is."

****

Barry was late. They had started without him but from the looks of things they hadn't gotten far. Mark, Dr. Meeks, and the photographer were gathered around Wendy Florren's head.

"What did I miss?"

"Confirmation of cause of death. Her head is full of blood. Wine bottle to the temple crushed her skull resulting in a subdural hematoma," Meeks told him. "There was a lot of power behind the blow."

"And?" Barry knew there was more. Meeks turned to one of the stainless-steel trays lined up beside him. "This," the ME said. He turned back to Barry. At the end of a pair of tweezers, he held up what looked like paper. "We just pulled this out of her mouth," Meeks told him. "I had to put it under the microscope to see myself," Meeks said, watching him squint. He wondered when the lieutenant was going to succumb to the reading glasses he'd been told he needed.

"So, are you going to make me guess what it is?" Barry asked.

"Business card," Mark told him. "One of yours. You left it the night you were canvassing. My guess is it's how the UNSUB got our victim to open her door."

Barry took a step back, Olivia's words echoing inside his head.

"She trusted him. She thought he was safe. That's why she let him in."

Chapter Seven

The time stamp read 02:32.

Twenty-four-year-old Addy Sullivan was just coming off her shift at The Dive, a small bar in the heart of Old Town Alexandria. She had bartended that night and was leaving with a nice wad of extra cash. Good thing because rent was due and she was running on fumes.

Her new coworker, Sharon Knox, parked on the other side of the building. Waitressing that night, she had come away with her own stack of bills. Briefly, the two girls toyed with the idea of going into the District for some of their own fun as the bars stayed open until 04:00 a.m. in the nation's capital. Ultimately, they decided against it because neither wanted to drive. All this information was supplied after the fact by Sharon, since the camera provided image only, no audio. They planned to do it another time. Except they wouldn't.

The two women said their good-byes at the corner of the building. Sharon was never actually visible in the footage. The camera was located on Addy's side of the bar. The owner only paid for surveillance for the side of the building where he instructed his employees to park. He actually cared more about their safety than his customers, the bulk of whom were tourists; his employees, he hoped, were there to stay. Addy had worked for him since before she was old enough to tend bar.

Thirty minutes after closing, the employee lot was empty except for Addy's old clunker.

Addy unlocked the driver's side door but never got inside. No one would ever know exactly why. The only thing they found in the back of her car was her purse. Inside was a cell phone. Maybe she wanted to make a call on the way home from work or maybe she wanted to put away the cash that was stashed in her back pocket.

Instead of opting for the safety of her car, Addy moved along the driver's side to the back. She inserted the key in the back and opened the hatch with her left hand. With her right hand, she reached to her right back pocket where she had stashed her tips. She didn't pull out the money or get the hatch all the way up before she turned and looked over her left shoulder. Judging from her facial expression something was moving along the sidewalk behind her. She hesitated, but just for a moment before shutting the hatch and starting for the edge of the dark. There was a look on her face that wasn't fear, but something closer to confusion or maybe even concern.

Addy headed for the perimeter of the lot and was obviously saying something. She still didn't appear afraid. She took another step forward, partially disappearing from the camera's line of sight. All that remained visible was her hair and one shoulder. There was a blur of movement just on the edge of the camera. Whatever it was moved too fast to be identified.

Within moments Addy staggered back into frame, her eyes wide, unfocused, her mouth frozen in an "o" of surprise or shock. She appeared to be trying to say something, but by this time she had lost all ability to speak. Her left hand was clamped to the side of her neck. Even in black and white it was easy to see the blood stream down her neck and spread onto her shirt. It seeped from between her fingers with every beat of her heart. It was astonishingly fast. She sank to her knees, then fell forward where she lie motionless.

There was only one blow. That's all it took. The body has three jugular veins: interior, anterior, and exterior. The system is part of the circulatory drainage structure for the head, ferrying blood to the lungs for resupply with fresh oxygen. As amazing as the external jugular vein is in its function and its vital importance to the body's circulatory system, its superficial location on the side of the neck leaves it vulnerable to outside forces. It has no hard structures like bone or cartilage to protect it. That's why Addy Sullivan bled out in less than sixty seconds. The entire camera footage lasted only a minute and thirty-five seconds.

On the other side of the building, just around the corner, Sharon Knox had not even pulled out of the parking lot to head in the opposite direction, oblivious to the fact her friend was now dead. It would be five more hours before she got the call.

A med student out for a post-shift run found Addy at 03:45 a.m., a little over an hour later. The blood around her had cooled by then. The four hundred dollars in small bills was still in her back pocket and her keys were still in the hatchback of her Ford Explorer.

****

"So, is this the guy you saw walking the dog?" Barry asked.

Olivia blinked and leaned forward in her chair, to get closer to the screen. Changing her position wouldn't help; she hadn't seen anything except the decade-old CCTV footage that lived inside her head. She had sat on this side of the viewing screen many times before. So why that replay? Why Addy? *Why now?*

Olivia cleared her throat. "Please play it again?" she asked Barry, unwilling to admit to him that she didn't see it the first time because she was somewhere else.

Barry sat next to her at the table, Mark across from her with a tape recorder. As a potential eyewitness, she would need to give an official statement. Barry commandeered a conference room because there wasn't enough room for the three of them and all the files in his office.

Olivia's purse was at her feet. Both she and Barry felt the vibration coming from within.

"That's the second time since you've been here," Barry commented. "Maybe you should answer it."

Olivia missed the first one. Must have been when she was in the past. She fished the phone out and checked the screen. No voicemail. Both calls from the same number with a 202 area code. Washington D.C. It was a private number. Olivia deactivated the vibrate alert and slid the phone back inside the pocket in her purse. She wasn't going to call back. She didn't have to. She would leave that up to her caller. It seemed like he needed her more than she needed him.

"We good to go?" Barry asked.

Olivia gave him a nod. She leaned forward and watched as the black hatchback pulled into the middle space of an open row. Maybe he picked the middle space because he wasn't so great at parking. He doesn't drive. The driver remained behind the wheel, but not for long. He didn't check the door to see if it locked. He never looked back. He fumbled with something in his right-hand pants pocket and disappeared from view. The timestamp in the corner of the screen read 08:12. The morning shift officer from the Jones substation probably just missed him.

Barry clicked it off again. "That's all there is. He never came back. The next person seen approaching the vehicle is the officer who called it in almost eight hours later. If this is our guy, it means he got to Wendy Florren's house on foot. So, is this the guy you saw walking her dog?"

"The sunglasses are the same. He looks to be the same height and build, but the clothes are wrong. He wasn't wearing jeans or that collared shirt when I met him, and he wore a different hat. That one has a logo on it. The other one was dark as well but had a different logo."

"Last night you said he was dressed funny. Describe 'funny'." Mark asked.

"Long-sleeve baggy t-shirt. Cargo shorts, cinched at the waist. They didn't seem to fit. Much too big," Olivia said. Her eyes were closed trying to find the snapshot in her head at the same time she wondered what the guy had stuffed in his pocket. "Same reflective aviator glasses. Same blondish non-descript hair. It looked like it needed to be combed. You can't see his shoes in the video, but he was wearing some weird kind of tennis shoes. They had straps instead of laces. And they were dirty."

"Anything written on the t-shirt?" Mark asked

hopefully.

Olivia shook her head. She remembered trying to read it, but the intensity of the stare she knew lurked beneath the shades distracted her. "Something was written on there, but I didn't get it all. Dogs, dimes, something with a *D*."

"Mike Stone, Wendy's boyfriend, is meeting us at her house. He's going to go through it to see if anything is missing. He said he kept some clothes there. I want you to come and meet him, just to rule him out as our dog walker," Barry told her.

"Does he want the dog back?" Olivia asked.

"Actually, no. He seemed relieved to know you had taken him. Apparently, Alvin didn't like him. He was jealous."

"After finishing with Wendy, the killer didn't use the shower. Cleaned up in the kitchen. Makes sense he would have been wearing other clothes when you saw him, but probably the same shoes," Mark said.

"Then it wasn't dirt I saw, but dried blood," Olivia murmured.

"The shoes would be harder to replace. Wendy wore a six, small for a woman, and Stone's a big guy. Makes sense why the cargo shorts wouldn't fit, either. Let's hope Stone is missing a pair. We just don't know what the UNSUB did with his clothes," Barry said.

"A city truck came around the corner while we were talking. Maybe he threw them out with the garbage," Olivia suggested.

"We checked. It wasn't garbage day, but it could have been recycle day or compost day," Mark said. *Damn.* He should have been more specific when he called or the city worker could have been more helpful.

Frustrated, he turned off the tape recorder and picked up his cell phone.

"You talk. I'll drive," Barry said.

****

Mark and Mike Stone, the bereaved boyfriend who had met Wendy Florren on a dating app a year ago, were waiting for them in Wendy's driveway. Olivia thought the boyfriend appeared pale and appropriately grief-stricken considering the circumstances.

Neither she nor Barry made a move to exit the car.

"Definitely not the man I saw yesterday," Olivia said. "You said he was a big guy, but I was not expecting him to be built like a linebacker. Makes sense though, given his line of work."

"How do you know what his line of work is?" Barry asked. "I don't think it was in the notes anywhere."

"Football coach," she informed him. "Let's just say I have my own set of notes." *If you only knew…*

"You okay to go back in there?" Barry asked. Olivia noticed Mark saying something to Mike Stone before he started walking toward them. Whatever he said, Mike did not move from his position. He was still leaning against his truck.

"Yes. I've gotten some rest. That always helps. Thanks for asking." The drive from downtown had given her time to prepare. Going back to a place she had previously visited was always easier, whether she chose to shut it out or open herself up. Today she opted to keep as many doors closed as possible.

When Olivia opened her car door and got out, Barry did the same.

"I think we should take him in through the

hallway," Mark suggested. "That'll be a direct route to the bedroom where he says he kept his clothes, and we can avoid the living room."

"Small mercies," Olivia muttered.

"Olivia says he's not our guy," Barry said

"Not even close," Olivia added.

Mark nodded. "You have the keys?"

Barry had confiscated Mike's key and garage opener to Wendy's place when he had interviewed him. He handed both to Mark but was distracted by Olivia who had walked around to join them but was focused on her phone.

"Need to make a call?" Barry asked.

"No," Olivia shook her head. "He'll call back."

Barry got the feeling whoever it was already had.

"If Mike's not our dog walker, then we need someone to get over to your house and process the dog's collar. If our perp took him for a walk, we might get a print." Mark could tell by the look on Barry's face, he hadn't gotten there yet.

"What about the leash?" Olivia asked.

"Never found it," Mark told her.

"Well," Barry said, "Shall we do this?"

The walk through the house went as planned. They avoided the living room completely, and Mike held it together, at least until he entered the bedroom. The sight of Wendy's personal items and the photos on her dresser hit him hard. He sat on the bed, trying very hard to keep his emotions in check.

"We'll give you a few minutes, Mike. Take your time. Check carefully, see if anything's missing," Mark told him. He motioned for Barry and Olivia to follow him into the hallway.

"Before y'all got here, he told me Wendy's daughter is due in from Colorado in less than an hour. Her parents are arriving from South Carolina shortly after. He's picking them all up from the airport," Mark said, briefing them on what they had missed.

Barry nodded. He was counting the seconds before he could start asking questions. He didn't have to wait long.

"Sergeant?" Mike called from the bedroom.

The three of them entered the room to find Mike standing in front of the dresser. One of the drawers was open. "A pair of khaki cargo shorts. A long-sleeve navy t-shirt," he said without being asked. "I got the shirt last week when I flipped burgers for a fundraiser. Wendy insisted on washing it before I wore it. Nurses," he said and had to stop for a minute. Once he regained his composure, he started again. "And a ball cap. I got it when we went to meet her parents last Thanksgiving. It was hanging on the bedpost. They're all missing."

Mark, Barry, and Olivia all looked at each other. Olivia had met their guy.

"When we get back to the station, I need you to meet with a sketch artist," Barry said to Olivia. He pulled his cell phone out to make the call. He was trying not to think about the implications of the meeting. So far Olivia was the only one to see their UNSUB and live to tell about it.

"Please, tell me this helps somehow," Mike said, trying awfully hard not to cry.

"Absolutely it does," Mark assured him and put a hand on his shoulder. Olivia nodded her head in confirmation.

Barry's phone rang in his hand before he could

complete his call. It was Zavalla.

"The Feds are here," he said without greeting. "I need you and Mark back ASAP. And is Dr. Osborne with you?"

"She is," Barry told him.

"Then bring her, too. He's asking for her."

Chapter Eight

He was dressed in the standard black suit, a starched white shirt, and a nondescript tie. Barry wondered if there was a class at Quantico on how to dress like a government agent. If so, the big guy waiting for them must have graduated at the top of his class. Barry would have known he was a Fed even without the head's up from the captain.

The agent stood at the front of the room while Zavalla, Meeks, Barry, Mark, and Olivia were all seated at a table in front of him like schoolchildren. Barry wondered if this was their call to the principal's office.

"I'm Special Agent Silas Branch with the FBI's Behavioral Analysis Unit," the agent said, surveying those before him. "You're all here at my request."

Barry wondered if they were supposed to thank him for the invitation. Then he looked down and saw the thin blue folder. They all had one. *Damn.* He had wanted more time.

"You should each have a packet with an overview of the case," Agent Branch said. "I'm going to need to know everything you know. It's the only way I can help you."

Barry opened the file in front of him and read only two words. They were all he needed. "Atascosa County," Barry said aloud. "I know all I need to know. This is not our case. Hell, it's not even our jurisdiction." He closed the file folder in front of him and looked up at the man who had just pulled him away from his latest crime scene. Barry didn't have time for this bullshit. "Sorry to disappoint, but you're in the wrong place."

The agent looked to Dr. Osborne. She looked back at him; they held each other's eyes for a fraction of a second too long and Barry saw everything. She and Special Agent Branch worked together. Maybe it was more than that. *Was the BAU here because of her?*

"They are unaware, obviously," Olivia answered even without a question. Her tone said Agent Branch should know this already. Unlike Barry, she had scanned beyond the first page and knew what this was about. It was the call that came to her cell phone yesterday right after she met a killer.

"So, Atascosa County is where?" Agent Branch wanted to know.

"About thirty miles south of downtown San Antonio," the captain told him.

"We live in Bexar County. The X is silent—pronounced *bear*, like the animal. Maybe you can look it up on a map," Barry suggested.

"I received a call from the sheriff over in Atascosa County just prior to being summoned to this meeting," Dr. Meeks admitted. "They are sending over the body of a fifty-two-year-old male who was impaled. Allegedly." In honor of the special agent, Meeks ended the sentence with his lawyer's favorite word. Meeks hated being dispatched from his basement world by the suits, especially Federal ones. Even more so when he had to contend with rush hour traffic.

"According to my sources, the victim was stabbed

with a pitchfork to the chest. Went straight through, pinning him to the ground," Agent Branch said.

"Your sources?" Barry asked. "Who might they be?"

"Have you wondered why the Texas Rangers aren't all over your investigation, Lieutenant?" Branch asked.

Barry glanced down at the case information in front of him. "I take it they're more interested in the Atascosa case."

"Oh, they're interested in Bexar too," he said.

But they have an arrangement, Barry guessed. Some kind of deal that involved clear territorial lines and the sharing of information. He had seen it before.

Meeks cleared his throat. "Impalement by pitchfork would take considerable force." He opened the folder for another look.

"Indeed," Silas agreed. "Dr. Osborne, do you have any comment?"

"I defer to Dr. Meeks since a medical opinion is his area of expertise," Olivia answered, keeping her tone neutral.

Barry caught a glimpse of what she must be like in court. Calm, cool, and collected despite the fact the agent was pushing some buttons.

"Do you care to provide *your* expert opinion regarding what this particular method of killing means?" Silas asked her instead.

"Certainly, Agent Branch. This unique signature may indicate a ritualistic killing."

Silas smiled. He was getting what he wanted. Not everything, but he was on his way. "Care to enlighten us regarding what kind of ritual? Why this specific method?"

Barry watched the banter between them. They obviously knew each other well.

"The cut to the throat was likely what killed him. Looks like it went all the way through to the trachea," Meeks commented out of turn. "You failed to mention that. The other part could have been theatrics."

Barry was reminded why he really liked the salty ME. He'd been in the room with Agent Branch for all of two minutes, and he had already decided he didn't like him. If Barry said anything that undermined Branch it could be considered insubordination, but the medical examiner enjoyed a certain amount of immunity.

"Thank you, Dr. Meeks," Agent Branch said.

"Dr. Osborne, do you have an opinion regarding Dr. Meeks' suggestion?"

Olivia hesitated. Her brief interactions with the medical examiner and observations at the crime scene told her Meeks was well respected. She would need to tread lightly. "I would have to refute the suggestion of theatrics. The attention to detail is too specific."

Meeks nodded, and Olivia interpreted the gesture as genuine interest. She hadn't pissed him off yet.

"The attention to detail leads you to believe this was what kind of killing, Dr. Osborne?" Agent Branch asked.

"A blood sacrifice ritual could be one," Olivia answered.

"It sounds like you have others in mind," Silas said.

Olivia knew what he was doing, even if his line of questioning seemed tedious. He was so used to being inserted into highly charged situations and his methodical quest for answers served to slow the room. He did everything with purpose. Maybe that was what had her worried.

"Is there a second or third type of ritual?" Silas wanted to know, snapping her back to attention. "We're on pins and needles."

The tone of his voice would have elicited an eyeroll from most, but Olivia was a master at controlling her emotions. This type of banter was typical Silas. He enjoyed showing her off like a prized pony.

"The method of killing could also be considered part of a ceremony involving witchcraft. Or it could be because whoever murdered the victim considered him to be a witch." Again, Olivia's tone was nothing but neutral, despite the fact she was seething inside.

Barry glanced at her and back to the agent. He felt left out, and he didn't like it. He really wished he'd had a chance to read the file Zavalla had given him earlier.

"How do you know this, Dr. Osborne?" Silas asked.

"Well, it's certainly not unprecedented. The so-called 'Witchcraft Murder' of Charles Walton in 1945 is a fairly well-known case. Any introductory paranormal influence course would expose even a beginner-level behavioral analyst to the concepts."

Silas smiled. He liked her when she was testy. And he did like showing her off. She made him look good, and she never gave herself enough credit.

****

"So, let me get this straight. You have four murders; two of them in the last four days. You have bible verses written in blood, and you've got

79

evisceration," Silas said, ticking each acknowledgment off on a finger like he was keeping score, which he undoubtedly was. "You've got a sexually motivated serial murderer here."

They remained in the same room, but the group had been whittled down to the captain, Barry, and Olivia. Those left behind were still in their seats. Barry watched and waited while the agent paced the front of the room. The way he moved was graceful for such a big guy, like a panther. He had to have been an athlete, well over six feet tall, yet nothing had gone to seed like Mike Stone, Wendy Florren's boyfriend. Agent Branch was a lean, solid mass beneath his FBI suit.

"Which is why I asked you here, Agent Branch," the captain said, glancing at Olivia hoping she would back him up. He missed the lieutenant's shift in body language that clearly conveyed this was news to him. "Dr. Osborne felt it was time to request BAU support due to the disturbing nature of these crimes."

Barry's focus shifted to Olivia.

What the hell? Agent Branch was Olivia's idea?

"It wasn't clear what we were dealing with until yesterday. Things have escalated," Olivia said, stepping in and doing just what the captain had hoped.

Agent Branch leaned in closer. "Things have most definitely escalated. I want to talk to Ana Lutz." That wasn't all he wanted, and he was pretty sure she knew that already. He just wanted the chance to be heard. Alone.

"Don't mix the two cases," Olivia cautioned him, giving him no indication as to what she knew or didn't know. His mention of the Wiccan priestess ruffled her. "Ana Lutz and the Wiccans have nothing to do with what's going on here in Bexar County. One case has nothing to do with the other." Olivia would cross the Ana Lutz bridge if and when she was forced to.

Silas slowly moved his eyes from her to the captain, but it took effort. Barry noticed if no one else did. His senses were finely tuned to the dynamic between the Special Agent and the doctor.

"So, do you think your people can brief me on your monster at say, nine a.m.?" Silas asked with a smile that was too bright.

Barry was probably the only one in the room who noticed the agent used the same term for their killer as Olivia did. *Monster.*

"Absolutely," Zavalla assured him.

Silas looked back to Olivia. "Dinner?" he asked.

She shifted in her chair very aware they were in a room full of people. Barry noted it was the only time he had seen her uncomfortable.

"Any recommendations?" Silas reframed the question, not missing a beat. If anyone had been paying attention, they might have noticed the fact he just invited her to dinner.

"A map might be helpful," she said.

Silas gave her a tight smile and exited the room.

"Is he always such a prick?" Barry asked before the agent was barely out of earshot. He also let out the breath he didn't realize he had been holding.

"We need to be ready. Get her the photos," the captain snapped, in full operational mode. The agent had spoken, and he intended to give him exactly what he asked for. Resistance was futile, both with this case and with the agent.

"Not until Olivia meets with a sketch artist. So far,

she's the only one that's seen the UNSUB." Barry left out the *'who's still alive'* part.

Zavalla looked at Dr. Osborne. He knew what Barry meant whether he was the one to say it or not. "If she's seen the UNSUB, then he's seen her." Zavalla was fully aware the stakes had just been raised.

Olivia knew what they were thinking, but her meeting the UNSUB was their biggest break so far. "There's no way he knows who I am. I know how to be safe," she assured them both. "Now, just point me in the direction of this artist you want me to meet," she said to Barry. "And don't take it personally. Silas has been a prick as long as I've known him."

****

The headlights of her SUV splashed across the driveway illuminating the vehicle waiting for her. *Double M Remodeling* was stenciled on the outside of the van. Owned and operated by Martin Mendoza.

Olivia eased out of the car. The fact Martin was waiting for her this late wasn't a good sign. If there had been a problem with the paint or supplies, he would have called, so this was a problem of a different kind. One that couldn't be left on a voicemail.

Martin stubbed out his cigarette and dropped it in the empty soda can beside him. He rose from the porch steps to greet her. "Ms. Olivia, I'm sorry to be waiting here like this, but I need to talk to you."

Olivia nodded. She was pretty sure what he was going to say before he said it. She joined him on the stone steps to hear it. "What is it this time?"

"Same as last time. The noises."

"Where?" Olivia asked.

"In the room that used to be yours." It was the

smaller of the two downstairs bedrooms. It had originally been her office, but now as their work progressed it had become her bedroom. It was the same room Daisy refused to enter.

She was familiar with the noises he was describing scratching, like something trapped inside the walls. Prior to construction, when she described the sounds to the contractor, he theorized it was probably rats or squirrels living in the walls; not uncommon for a century-old stucco house. But in the end, according to the inspector's report, all she had was bad wiring. She only told Martin about the noises when his workers started hearing them, too.

"It should've been squirrels," Martin said. "Your trees are full of them."

Olivia didn't interject. It wouldn't make him feel any better if she told him what it really was.

"This is my second crew," he confessed. His employees were simple men. They worked with their hands and asked very few questions, at least until now. "We're also having trouble with the water. It's coming on in the kitchen now." Olivia nodded. It started first in the bathroom with the shower turning on randomly. She knew it had moved. She just never mentioned it.

"And the dog, the greyhound, she spooked Ramon. She was barking at your room."

Olivia nodded, taking note he said *at* her room. As a general rule, greyhounds didn't bark. The notion had been a selling point prior to adoption. She wasn't looking for a guard dog. She was seeking companionship.

"I understand," Olivia said. She needed no further explanation. Just a game plan of how to get her house back in order. "So, what do we do now?" She could see the weariness in Martin's eyes. He needed this job as much as she needed it completed.

Martin shook his head. "I'll try to find some temporary workers. I'll get back to you as soon as I know something." At least his men would still work for him. Just not in this house. He grabbed the cooler, rose from the steps, and headed for his van.

Martin turned back, his eyes searching the rafters of her growing home. The bungalow was built in 1918 and still held its charm. Houses weren't built like this anymore; one of the many reasons Olivia wanted to preserve as much of the original structure as possible. Several old houses in the neighborhood had been leveled and replaced by new ones. She opted for refurbishment and built up, adding an entire new floor instead of tearing down. The craftsmanship Martin and his crew provided more than sold her on the fact she made the right choice by going with his small company, but now they were at a standstill. She very much needed order back in her life.

"Do you know why it's here? Does it want something?" Martin asked, trying to understand.

"They always do." He didn't want to know the real story anyway. It was tragic. Two girls, both six years old, one injured and one killed when they were run down by a truck taking the curve in front of the house too fast. At the time, the whole area was outside the city limits, and two thirteen-year-old boys had taken the "horseless carriage" joyriding. But that had been almost ninety years ago.

"You're not afraid?"

"No."

"Do you know what it is?"

"Something left behind."

"A spirit?"

Olivia shook her head. Alice Wilkes had been six years old when she died, not far from where remnants of her energy had settled. "It's an echo. Nothing to be afraid of."

****

"You brought an FBI profiler to my scene?" Barry yelled. "And you didn't think you should mention you were going to take your fantastic fucking idea to Zavalla?"

Mark had been on his way out the door with the case file he was supposed to deliver to Olivia. Barry had asked him to do it that morning, but now it looked like the errand was going to have to wait. He went over to close the door. Norma might be gone for the day, but there were other officers wandering in and out. They didn't need to hear this.

"It's not just your investigation," Mark reminded him. "We're all in this together."

Barry ignored the attempt to defuse him. He was running on adrenaline fumes.

"There was never any plan to bring in the FBI. Olivia came for the reason I told you: to help me. To help us," Mark said. "She went in blind. I told her nothing, just as you requested. I figured we needed all the help we could get."

Now that Barry had seen her in action, he understood what the captain had tried to tell him that morning. Taking a look at her file had helped bring it all together. "Instead, she called the Feds."

"She doesn't work for the FBI anymore," Mark

said.

"That's not what it looked like this afternoon," Barry said, vividly recalling her interactions with the vibrant Agent Branch. Not to mention the agent's inability to take his eyes off her.

"Consultant or not, she's a Fed."

"Don't let her hear you say that. Regardless, Branch being here means the Texas Rangers aren't. I don't know about you, but I'd rather deal with one asshole than a whole posse of them," Mark said. Barry was getting all worked up over something that didn't seem to have anything to do with the FBI commandeering the case. This felt personal. Not Barry's usual style when it came to women. He wasn't typically the pursuer, but Olivia had a way about her. She attracted attention whether she wanted to or not, but she didn't return it. At least not that Mark had seen in the two years she had been back in San Antonio. Personal relationships seemed to make her uncomfortable, but he held to the belief that still waters ran deep. If and when Olivia decided to let a man in her life, it would be because he was important to her.

Barry didn't say anything. Mark suspected his partner knew he'd said too much already, revealed a part of himself he hadn't intended.

"Are we done here?" Mark asked.

Barry looked at him, his face still clouded.

"Give me the file. I'll take it," Barry said.

Mark nodded and handed it over. So, that was it. Mark wondered if Barry was going to see Olivia or if he was looking for Agent Branch.

Chapter Nine

Barry chided himself for showing up at her house unannounced. After meeting Special Agent Branch today, Barry felt compelled to see who, if anyone, she spent her off time with. He wasn't disappointed when he found her alone.

Olivia opened the door before he could knock. He had a bag in one hand and a file folder in the other. "You don't seem surprised to see me."

"Your boss wanted me to review the photos. And I do need to see them before the meeting in the morning." Olivia knew he wouldn't leave the errand to Mark even before Mark called to say he wouldn't be by after all.

Barry nodded. He felt ridiculous. Who was he kidding? Not himself and certainly not her. "I could've sent Mark," he said.

"You could have. But you didn't." Olivia stepped aside, and he followed, caught in a hint of vanilla and spice. He also couldn't help but notice she had changed again, into something long and flowing this time. He knew if he touched the fabric it would slip easily through his fingers, and he would find the curves she was hiding underneath.

Barry followed her through the living room and purposefully redirected his attention. He noted the drop cloths and ladders and didn't see much indication of progress. The same could be said for the greyhound. She was still on her bed, surrounded by her stuffed toys. The little ball of white fur was curled up on the sofa. "How's he doing?"

"Alvin and Daisy are getting to know one another," Olivia said. "So, is this all business?" she asked, turning to face him.

She was direct. He liked that. Barry held the package in front of him as an offering. "I've asked a lot of you this week. The day we met, I wasn't so nice. I apologize for both."

"Murder can do that to a person," Olivia said and took the bottle-shaped bag from him. As she slid the wine out, she noted it was her favorite, a petit Syrah. There'd been a half-empty bottle of it on her kitchen counter the night before. At least he was paying attention and had put some effort into this. The wine wasn't overly expensive, but it was not always easy to find. "I still have vodka in the freezer," she told him as she headed for the opener and a glass.

Barry shook his head. Her assessment from last night was correct. He wasn't a vodka man. She retrieved a second wine glass from the cabinet. She filled her own glass and then held the bottle over his until he gave the nod to go ahead.

"Why didn't you tell me you worked for the Bureau?"

"I wasn't aware you were interested in my resumé," Olivia said. She slid his glass toward him and when he lifted it, she clinked hers against it. "And I don't. Haven't for a long time. I assist the BAU occasionally, that's it."

Barry responded with a nod of his head. They

sipped together.

"It's warm enough, want to sit on the porch?" Olivia suggested. She couldn't stand the mess inside. It disrupted her sense of order.

"Sure," he said and followed her. They took opposite chairs, both facing the road with the bottle of wine in the middle.

"So, the construction crew on strike?" he asked.

She nodded. "Did Mark tell you?" She was curious about the current status of their partnership. Had things smoothed over or were they still on shaky ground?

"He told me the other night you were redoing the house. Problem?" Barry asked.

He deflected her question with one of his own. He and Mark must still be on shaky ground. "It's not structural," Olivia said and sipped her wine.

"Does your work sometimes interfere with home?" Barry finally asked.

She smiled slightly. "Tell me, Lieutenant, does yours?"

Barry opened his mouth to comment and then closed it again. His eyes left her face to focus on the street. "I drove around your block a couple of times. It would make me feel better if you didn't have an alley and if this street didn't curve into the other one." It would have also made him feel better if he had convinced Zavalla to let him put some guys outside her house. Just at night if nothing else.

"I'll put in a complaint with the city tomorrow," Olivia said. She watched a rare smile almost reach his eyes. She knew no one would believe it, but it was Agent Branch who taught her levity was an important part of their job. She wasn't as skilled at it as Silas, but she had her moments. "Worried about me, Lieutenant?"

"Yes," Barry admitted, his eyes moving back to hers.

She held his gaze for a brief second before breaking the connection. "All of this used to be farmland. My great-grandfather refused to sell, so they just built around him," Olivia explained. Her street jutted out like an extra arm off the main thoroughfare. It contained only four lots.

"You own the whole curve?" He attempted to calculate how much the real estate was worth.

"Not anymore. My grandmother lost her husband to the Second World War. Not all at once mind you, but over the years. My grandfather never held the same job for very long after he came home. It seems no one knew much about PTSD back in those days."

"What did he do in the war?" Barry asked, curious. He didn't talk about his own family history.

"He helped evacuate France. Those he couldn't save, the Germans murdered while he watched. And they didn't discriminate based on gender or age. There are just some things you can't get out of your head." Olivia had never met her grandfather. He was dead before she was born, but she had heard the stories. "My Gran sold off pieces of the land to pay the bills. This one is all that's left. It's why I'm working so hard to preserve it. She was born in this house."

"Nice piece of history."

"History is all I have." Olivia took a long sip of her wine. "Don't worry about me, Lieutenant. I can handle myself," she assured him, done with her brief detour down memory lane.

Considering her background in law enforcement,

however brief, Barry knew it was useless to push the safety issue. They were still finding their way. Kind of like Alvin and Daisy.

In the back of his mind, he was pretty sure they should have informed Agent Branch regarding her probable encounter with the UNSUB. Then again, she said herself that she didn't work for the Bureau anymore. Barry was fuzzy on the inner workings of that "members only" club, so he was leaving it up to Olivia to divulge that tidbit to Branch. From where he sat it looked like she hadn't.

"Did someone come and take the dog's collar?" Barry asked instead.

"Yes."

"The captain gave me a file today."

"The one you won't put down?" Olivia asked.

"I'm to leave it with you, per his instructions. It contains crime scene photos," Barry said referring to the one he was still holding. "Zavalla gave me another file. It's in my desk and it's about you. I'm not sure I understood everything I read. Especially the stuff about demons and crossing over."

Olivia wondered what motivated Zavalla. Was he just making sure his lieutenant was up to speed on who and what he was dealing with? Olivia smiled. "Just so you know, even I don't understand it sometimes."

"I hope someday you can trust me enough to try to explain it to me," Barry said.

Olivia looked over at him. He was serious. "Then I'm going to need a lot more than this one bottle," she smiled.

Barry smiled back. "I'm sure that could be arranged. Just go slow. Your seven-second theory is a little over my head."

Olivia nodded. The bloody Bible verse scrolled across her thoughts. *Father, forgive them, for they know not what they do.* The killer might not have been referring to himself.

Barry put the file next to the wine. "See you in the morning."

"Mark never told you?" He had just taken the last step off of her porch when she moved from her chair.

Barry turned. With her, on the top step, they were almost at eye level. Her inviting scent invaded his senses again calling him to a warm comfortable place where he could easily lose himself. The urge to reach out and touch her was strong. He shoved his hands in his pockets so they didn't get away from him. "Not a word."

"Jason and I met in graduate school. We were there together when, you know. I think Mark has kind of looked at me like a big sister since then. I'm the last connection he has with his brother."

Barry nodded, digesting what she'd just told him. Not only the information, but the implications of the confession. She knew where he was heading, and she wasn't running away. "I needed to know that."

Olivia nodded back. "Thought so." Her memory wandered back in time…

****

"I can't believe I let you talk me into this," Jason said, wearing a wicked grin. Smiling, Olivia playfully elbowed him in the ribs. In fact, Jason—never short on ideas or persuasion—was responsible for their current situation. This particular idea had landed them both in the back seat of an Alexandria Police Department cruiser for what felt like an excruciatingly long three hours.

This had to be the most boring ride-along ever. A Saturday night in Old Towne Alexandria was not exactly the mean streets. They had followed a couple of cars on suspicion of DUI. Olivia thought she might, at the very least, get to see a drunk try to navigate a field sobriety test, but no. Jaworski or Nash, she couldn't remember who was who, had called it in, and another unit took over.

Other than that, their chauffeur's conversation had been limited to sports. Olivia knew the local football team, but the officers' conversation stayed focused on one of the local baseball teams, she was pretty sure.

"We might as well be in a cab," Olivia murmured.

Things weren't going as planned. Not that they had much of a plan. Jason's idea had been to chat the officers up, get them talking, perhaps learn something they hadn't discovered during their own investigation.

Calling it an investigation might be a stretch, but their quest had definitely extended beyond the assigned research project. This ride-along was supposed to be the culmination of a joint academic endeavor.

For Jason, the four murders over a six-week period were the subject of his final project for his graduate journalism program. The final segment of his documentary was to focus on the offender profile, and that's where Olivia came in. She believed the profile was all wrong. Not just believed it, she felt it. Jason wasn't sure where her instincts came from, but she'd been right more than once when the police hadn't been. He was the only one who knew that. They both thought maybe it was time for that to change. Olivia wanted someone to listen to her theory. Jason thought a debate would make for a more compelling story.

Olivia watched Jason take his video camera out of his messenger bag. He checked the setting before propping his elbow on the door to keep the camera steady. The camera was aimed toward the front seat, between the two officers. She leaned over to check the screen and saw Jaworksi and Nash's profiles in silhouette. The red record light was flashing.

"What are you doing?" she mouthed.

Jason grinned. He was bored. Jason was trouble when he was bored.

"Hey, guys, aren't we near the Divide?" he asked.

"Yeah, a couple blocks over," Jaworksi said.

"It has something to do with those murders, right? You guys doing extra patrols over there?" Jason asked.

"Yeah, some. Why?" Nash asked.

"Olivia is interested," Jason said. Olivia elbowed him again. This time, he winced.

"And why's that?" Jaworksi asked.

"She has a different perspective on the killer," Jason said.

"Oh, really? Let's hear it," Jaworksi said. If nothing else, it would help pass the time.

Olivia wasn't ready to share her theory, at least not with two patrol cops. She wasn't going to be goaded into it by Jason. She was a firm believer in the power of silence, a tactic she'd learned as a nurse. Maybe that's how she got her uncooperative subjects to talk. Most people don't like to be alone with their own thoughts.

"She thinks it's a woman," Jason finally said to break the stalemate. He didn't share Olivia's comfort with silence.

"Really?" Nash didn't even try to hide his skepticism. "Profile says male, twenty-five to thirty-five years of age."

"I know what the profile says," Olivia told him.

"You do realize over ninety percent of serial killers are men," Nash pointed out.

Olivia thought he probably picked that tidbit up on a documentary.

"Seventeen percent of serial homicides are committed by women, yet only ten percent of total murders are committed by women. Do the math," Olivia countered.

"So, you're into numbers. What about the victims? They were all female."

"I am thinking about the victims. That's why I think you should be looking for a woman," Olivia said.

It was exactly what Jason was hoping for. Maybe in the heat of the debate, the cop would give away some more information. Neither Jason nor Olivia had been privy to all the forensic data. There was something else up with these murders that no one was saying—at least not to outsiders.

"Never heard of a female serial killer targeting adult females," Jaworski said with a shake of his head.

"And I'm having a hard time believing a twenty-four-year-old woman, alone in a deserted parking lot at two-thirty in the morning approaches some man she doesn't know." She was describing the first victim, Addy Sullivan.

"What if she did know him?" Nash suggested.

"Your officers found no connection between the victims other than they all were in the Divide during the last twenty-four hours before they were killed. Old

Town is at the apex of the District, Virginia, and Maryland. A lot of people flow through here," Olivia reminded him. She knew the case backwards and forwards, at least the information she and Jason had been able to dig up. Jason had a couple of sources in the police department, but he wouldn't say who they were.

"So, she would approach a woman she didn't know?" Jaworski asked.

"It's more likely," Olivia said. "Inherently, we're less afraid of our own."

Jaworski gave a half nod to the suggestion. "The leading theory is that this guy is meeting these women in a bar, he flirts, gains their trust."

"You think a woman can't do the same thing? Who can mingle throughout a bar without people thinking about anything other than sex? If a woman is chatting up a man or a woman, isn't she going to blend in better than some guy who's maybe hanging around a little too long? Getting a little too close for comfort? A female doing the same thing could fly right under the radar."

Nash was considering the theory, but he wasn't ready to concede. "Maybe. But Addy is one of four victims."

"She is, but she's also the only victim who met her killer on camera. She stopped what she was doing and crossed the parking lot. Her face reflected concern, but not for herself. There was no fear there, and no sign of recognition."

"How do you—" Nash started to say before Jason cut him off.

"What do you say, guys? How about we drive by?" Jason suggested.

"You've never seen the Divide?" Jaworski asked.

"Not from this perspective. C'mon guys, it's not like there's something more interesting going on."

Nash apparently didn't have a counter for that one.

A couple of minutes later, they'd backed into a parking lot of the bar with a direct view of the front door.

"This is so much more thrilling than patrolling the streets," Olivia muttered.

"Are y'all criminal justice majors?" Nash asked, apparently ready to engage in something besides sports commentary.

"Journalism," Jason said.

"Psychology," Olivia said.

"She's a PhD candidate," Jason added.

"No shit?" Jaworski asked. "You gonna be a shrink?"

"Check it out," Nash said. The four of them watched as a couple exited the bar. The guy was steering his date to a dark convertible. It was slow going.

"She's wasted," Jason said.

"Hey, Scorsese, zoom in on that plate and call it out to me," Jaworski instructed Jason.

Jason did as he was told, excited to finally get to do something. The car was quiet as Jaworski ran the license plate, and they waited for the results.

"Joseph Tanner lives in Arlington," Nash said, reading the registration information.

There was some additional typing by Jaworski, and they waited for the subject's criminal history to display.

"And what do you know?" Nash said, looking over at Olivia.

"He's got a record. Likes to play with the ladies.

Solicitation of a minor and domestic assault. Care to change your theory, Dr. Olivia?"

Chapter Ten

Friday... "So, does everyone here think I'm a prick, or just the lieutenant?" Silas asked Olivia when she entered the murder room. He was in early.

"East Coast time," he told her when Olivia walked in and seemed surprised to see him. He had been staring at the board. It looked promising.

SAPD was closing in. Maybe not to the person, but at least to the area. Serial killers tended to kill, especially their first time, near their anchor point— the place they spent most of their time, where they were comfortable. The earlier in a series, the closer to the anchor point the crime scene was likely to be. Notes on the board indicated the UNSUB's most likely means of transportation was by bike. If that were the case, then both work and home should fall within the same radius. The bike theory was key. It limited their killer and thus kept his hunting ground small.

"Good morning, Olivia. How are you? Did you have a nice evening?" she replied. "Most civilized people start a conversation with a greeting."

"Most civilized people don't leave their colleagues to forage for food on their own."

Silas had a point, but he had been more annoying than usual yesterday. Maybe it was this case. Again, she was reminded how out of practice she was. The Bureau still occasionally asked her to consult, but it had been almost six weeks since she had been summoned or seen Silas.

Olivia slid her purse off her shoulder and took a moment to acquaint herself with the accommodations. She had never been in this particular room before. From the looks of the murder board, she could tell where Barry spent most of his three hours before he came to see her. He probably came back afterward as well. Not that she'd slept much, either. When she did finally give in, she was plagued by the occasional low growl from Alvin and the hum of bicycle spokes in her head. And the dream. Maybe it was because she had talked about Jason.

Olivia noted the sketch artist had posted the composite. She was impressed. She left here last night feeling like she had contributed nothing. The whole time during the interview she didn't think she had anything of importance to offer except how his shoes looked. It was hard being on the giving end instead of the receiving, yet the finished product looked like a real person even without the rendering of his eyes. The drawing was detailed enough to get some leads. Olivia was sure of it.

"I've been looking at that, too," Silas noted, his eyes trailing behind hers. "The question I keep asking myself is why did no one tell me there was a witness?"

Olivia poured herself a cup of coffee and settled down to sit next to him.

"Not answering me is an answer, Livie," Silas said quietly. He never called her that at work, certainly not in the murder room, but now was different. They were alone, and he very much wanted to push past the wall she had built between them.

Damn him. She knew she should have told him yesterday. She just didn't want to deal with him. Her standard mode of operation was typically full steam ahead, but on very rare occasions she ignored, denied, pushed things aside, or mentally packed them away inside a box. This was one of those occasions.

"I swung by the crime scene on Wednesday," she finally said.

"Before or after victim number four?" Silas asked. He had read the brief notes Zavalla provided via email last night. Due to the increase in activity, Silas concentrated his efforts on the events of the last week. He had at least a high-level overview so far.

"Before."

"So, you saw the Patricia Griffin crime scene?" Silas countered. Olivia wrapped her hands around her coffee cup and stared straight ahead. It was easier to answer his questions that way.

"I did. And Wendy Florren's."

"When were you going to tell me you were involved with this case? Imagine my surprise when I learned from the captain, of all people, that you were out with the officers yesterday. Are you going rogue on me, Dr. Osborne?"

"I didn't know they'd assign this case to you, but the way you showed up here," Olivia stopped talking and shook her head. "I would've gotten around to it," she admitted.

"I called. You didn't answer."

He's talking about now. Not then. "You didn't leave a message."

She had him there. "Okay. You're right. I surrender."

She sensed him stir in his chair next to her. He faced the murder board now instead of her. That was too easy. He wasn't done. They weren't done.

"We can talk about why I'm here later, away from the murder room. Right now, let's get back to the nastiness at hand. How did you get involved?"

"Mark called me. He asked if I would walk the scene and relay anything I picked up on. Apparently, they were feeling some heat."

Silas nodded. Before yesterday, he had never met Mark Austin, but he didn't need an introduction. He knew the back story, meaning he knew what the FBI knew. Only Olivia knew the details, and she wasn't one for sharing.

"I still had some questions, so I went back to have another look. During my surveillance, I encountered that guy," Olivia said, nodding toward the sketch staring down at them from the front of the room.

"I'm assuming events transpired that led you to believe he had something to do with this," Silas said for her.

"You could say that."

"You also know I'm going to say the encounter puts you in danger."

"And I'm going to say I think you're overreacting," she countered. "There's no way for him to connect me to the investigation."

Silas shook his head. She knew it without looking. "You don't know that. You have your own set of followers." She had testified in enough high-profile murder cases to anger family members and earn some fans from the dark side.

"Then why don't we just have some guys sit

outside my house twenty-four seven?" She stole a glance his way and noted the clench of his jaw. She was getting to him. He was genuinely concerned about her safety.

"I know how to take care of myself, Silas." It was the same argument she'd used with the lieutenant last night. "Besides, currently you don't have a strong enough case to convince your bosses to spend the funds necessary to put a protection detail on me."

"*Our* bosses," Silas corrected her. Whether she worked for the Bureau full-time or not, they still considered her a valuable asset. "And nothing says we can't at least do random drive-bys." He stopped short of offering to do them himself. They weren't there yet. "Unless, you need to tell me about some in-home security you have that I am unaware of."

And there it was. His first jab at Lieutenant Bartholomew.

Silas had done some reading up on him as well when he couldn't sleep last night. Bartholomew was a solid investigator. He had closed more than his share of difficult cases, but in Silas's book, he was just too rough around the edges for Livie. And Silas didn't like the way he looked at her like he wanted to sweep her off her feet and carry her away like some cliché jackass from a bodice-ripper novel. He hadn't asked about her evening because he didn't want to know if it included the lieutenant or not. Jealousy was unfamiliar to him, and he was struggling to get a handle on it.

Olivia stiffened. To the casual observer, it might have gone unnoticed, but Silas noticed. Her lack of a verbal response was encouraging.

"Sorry if I blew your cover yesterday. I got the

impression Lieutenant Bartholomew didn't exactly know your history. Hope that didn't mess things up between the two of you."

Olivia finally broke the stalemate and turned to look at him.

"I just call them like I see them." Silas was grinning.

"You can be a prick," Olivia told him.

"So I've heard. You wound me, but as for these locals, I wouldn't have it any other way." Silas took it in stride. He didn't care if he made friends. Hopefully, he wouldn't be here long enough to need any. With any luck, they'd catch their monster, and he would never have to see these people again.

A calm silence stretched between them. He and Olivia had found their peace for now. He knew better than to push her any further. He resumed his study of pinpoints on the map, avoiding the victim's side of the board. It was Olivia's domain. He hunted; she gathered.

With the arrival of the FBI, an unofficial task force was beginning to form. Eventually, the room filled with investigators and all eyes were drawn to the array of victim photos on the murder board. Barry had assigned Mark the duty of providing an overview of the victimology to ensure everyone was up to speed. Mark wasted no time.

"The first victim, Alicia Acuña, was a twenty-two-year-old EMT who had just been accepted to Incarnate Word Nursing School. A city maintenance crew found her in Blossom Park when they arrived to mow the grounds. The body was found lying on the hillside near the tennis courts, not far from the edge of the woods. No effort to conceal. Her car was found in the parking lot where she parked it the day before near the tennis courts where she was meeting a friend. Her cell phone and purse were found on the passenger's seat. She and the friend played tennis for an hour, and afterwards Ms. Acuña told her friend she wanted to go for a run. They parted ways at approximately 1830. As far as we know, it was the last time she was seen alive."

"Has the friend been checked out?" Barry asked.

"Yes. Kandace Leonard, age twenty-three. She's clean. We've verified her movements after she left the tennis court and we're able to exclude her. Ms. Acuña lived alone, had just broken up with her boyfriend, and had not been reported missing at the time her body was discovered. The ex-boyfriend is clean. It's important to note that the body was left wide out in the open. He could have dragged her a few more yards into the woods. He didn't. The injuries were grotesque."

Mark nodded at Dr. Meeks, his cue to jump in.

"Ms. Acuña was struck in the face hard enough to cause a complex zygomatic fracture," Meeks said, touching his left cheek. "The contusion pattern is consistent with a blow from a closed fist, which means the UNSUB is likely right-handed. The cause of death is exsanguination. Her abdominal organs were partially eviscerated, and I counted twenty-three deep lacerations." Meeks cleared his throat. "Of note, I observed no hesitation marks. Each of those cuts was purposeful and clean."

Mark let that sink in a moment before pointing to the second photo on the board.

"Twenty-nine days later, victim number two, Cindy Garza, was found in the creek bed of Hunter Mills Park. Ms. Garza was a twenty-five-year-old kindergarten teacher at Thousand Oaks Elementary. According to her roommate, Ms. Garza left to go for a walk around seven-thirty in the evening. The roommate returned home the next morning after spending the night with her date and realized Ms. Garza wasn't home. Concerned by the presence of Ms. Garza's car and purse and the fact that the dog had apparently not been fed or let out all night, she reported Ms. Garza missing. This was about the same time two eight-year-old boys cut through a drainage ditch on their way to school and discovered the body. Ms. Garza's cell phone and house key were still in her pocket."

Meeks added, "Cindy Garza also suffered a blow to the head. The injury suggests she was struck with a rough, blunt object, such as a rock or piece of concrete. She suffered a fracture of her suborbital foramen," he said, touching his index finger just below his left eyebrow near his nose. "The manner in which the bone shard chipped away from the skull suggests the blow was delivered in a downward motion. The killer was either much taller than the victim or was standing over her when he struck."

"Could she have been on her knees?" Barry asked.

"That is a possibility," Meeks said.

"Can you tell if that was a willing position?" Barry asked.

"Not definitively. The bottom of the ditch where she was found is rocky. She does have some abrasions on her palms, but that may be from attempting to break her fall after she was struck. Had she been forced down before she was struck, I would expect more contusions and abrasions on her knees."

"Cause of death?" Mark asked for the benefit of the

group.

"Same as Ms. Acuña, exsanguination resulting from over thirty penetrating wounds to the abdomen," Meeks informed them.

Nodding, Mark tapped the third photo on the board. "Thirty days later, Patricia Griffin, a single thirty-year-old nurse, was on her way home from work. She was found in the green belt of the Blossom Point neighborhood, this time within an hour of death."

"Estimated one hour, sergeant," Meeks added.

"Right. Ms. Griffin lived alone. She wasn't reported missing until the next morning when she didn't show up for work. Without a purse or car, she originally came in as a Jane Doe, but being a nurse, her fingerprints were on file, and we got a hit on her in IAFIS."

It was Meeks' turn. "In addition to the multiple stab wounds to the abdomen, her nose was fractured, and her two front teeth were loose. Based on my brief discussion with CSU, and I'm sure Frank will have more here, this was probably caused by the force of her face hitting the steering wheel of her car. This attack was more frenzied than the others. The wound pattern extended to her chest. I stopped counting at forty-eight. He may have stabbed her more times than that, but the wounds overlapped."

"Wendy Florren, victim number four, a forty-four-year-old NICU nurse was killed two and a half days later. There are differences in the UNSUB's M.O. with this one," Mark said and turned to Barry. This was where they ran out of steam. From here on, it would be up to Olivia.

The ME spoke up, "There are some similarities

though."

"Dr. Meeks let's hear your take on the nature of Wendy Florren's injuries and then Dr. Osborne can fill us in on the victimology," Silas suggested.

"Victim number four had expired or was close to it when the stabbing occurred. Again, the initial injury was blunt force trauma to the head, and again, on the left side— specifically, the parietal area." Meeks tapped the left side of the back of his head. "The wine bottle found at the scene is consistent with the type of object that caused this injury. The blow resulted in a subdural hematoma. The brain bleed had already started when she sustained the first stab wound. The blade used on Ms. Florren was larger than the others. The butcher knife missing from her kitchen knife block is consistent with her injuries. The attack was more frenzied. During the examination, I removed an object from the victim's mouth. It turned out to be Lieutenant Bartholomew's business card."

Silas and Olivia looked at Barry at the same time. "Why didn't you mention this yesterday?" Silas asked, addressing Bartholomew and not the medical examiner. Silas was sure it had been the lieutenant's call to withhold information.

"Unannounced visit. We were still processing," Barry told him.

Silas had heard it before. "I caution you, Lieutenant, if there is anything else to disclose, now would be the time."

Barry met the stare head-on. "There's nothing else."

Meeks waited a full minute for the alpha males to go back to their corners before resuming. "In general, all four women suffered a blow to the head prior to the stabbing. As a result, there are no defensive wounds. Fingernail scraping turned up no DNA evidence. The natural response to a knife attack is to fend off the attack and to attempt to grab the knife. When we don't see defensive wounds, it tells us the victim was incapable of fighting back. What I'm consistently seeing here is a blitzkrieg attack to disable the victim followed by deep penetrating stab wounds."

"Based on the description of the suspect, he doesn't seem to be particularly large or powerful. Maybe he lacks confidence in his ability to overpower these women, so he takes them down quickly," Barry added.

Meeks continued. "None of the victims exhibits signs of sexual penetration, and I found no semen on any of the victims."

Barry considered that. Most serial homicides were sexually motivated, but that didn't always mean sexual penetration. For some killers, stabbing or biting a victim was a substitute for penile penetration, and some needed to increase the violence each time to find sexual gratification.

"On our last two victims, however, I did come up with a positive amylase result on their necks. The presence of human saliva in that location suggests he is kissing or licking them. That there was enough present for a positive presumptive test tells me it's most likely the latter. It's possible we would've found the same on the other victims had the bodies not been exposed to the elements." Victim number one was drenched by the park sprinklers that went off at two in the morning prior to discovery, and a small thunderstorm passed over victim number two the night she spent in the ditch.

"The business card in the victim's mouth is a unique signature. It indicates oral fixation of another kind," Olivia added, not pleased with the implications.

Meeks kept moving. If he didn't, he would never get out of here. The ME's office was housed in the Forensic Science Center, not at police headquarters. He still had a drive across town ahead of him.

"The bladed weapon used on the first three victims is an inch wide and at least eight inches long. Ms. Garza had what looks like an errant blow to the upper thigh. It was a through-and-through, so based on that we have some indication of blade size. We're not talking about a pocketknife here. Based on the frenzied attack, and the depth of the wounds, I suspect the knife handle has finger grooves or rings, or a quill ion— a guard at the top of the handle. Wet blood is slick and the knife would have been covered in it. Without something to stop it, the attacker's hand would have slipped onto the blade."

"Like a Bowie knife?" Barry asked.

"Yes, or some other kind of non-serrated, dagger-type knife," Meeks said.

"Yet it's not what he used on his fourth victim," Silas interrupted. "Dr. Osborne, your thoughts?"

"He went there for another reason. Not to kill," Olivia answered automatically. "Killing was incidental when he saw no alternative."

"Any idea what that reason might've been?" Silas asked.

"Considering the bike was outside Wendy Florren's when I saw the suspect, and it was missing when the lieutenant and I returned, my guess is the bike. Also, it wouldn't have taken him long to determine that Ms. Florren had no connection to said bike."

Meeks cleared his throat. "If you will excuse me, I have an autopsy to tend to, courtesy of our neighbors in Atascosa County." Meeks closed the file in front of him and gathered his things. He leaned over and spoke softly to Olivia before leaving. "Agent Branch has assured me I'll see you again. It's been a pleasure."

Frank Tobias, head of Forensics, was up next. "So far, little trace evidence. Killing outside definitely has its advantages. I'll begin with the good news first, our biggest finding so far."

Frank held up an enlarged photo of a footprint with a distinctive pattern in the area of the ball of the foot. "We found a few incomplete prints similar to this one at the scenes of the first two murders, but given the fact they were found in parks with heavy foot traffic, we were unclear on whether they were connected. We also found another one at the Patricia Griffin crime scene, but again, given the foot traffic we were unsure. At Wendy Florren's house, we found the same imprint in blood on her carpet." Frank held up a picture of a photo taken from the crime scene.

"His shoes were unusual," Olivia interjected.

"What kind of a shoe would make this kind of a print?" Silas asked.

"A type of cycling shoe," Frank said and held up another photo that appeared to be from a catalog. "This type has a metal cleat that clips directly into the pedal."

"Would they make noise when you walked?" Olivia asked.

Frank nodded. "This type? Yes, due to the raised metal cleat. It would probably sound similar to tap shoes. We ordered a pair yesterday for examination."

"Any idea what type of a bike?" Barry asked. "I'm guessing with those shoes, it's not typical."

"Technically, a clip-in style pedal can be attached to just about any bike. But the type of cleat that these prints are compatible with is a two-hole pedal style typically used on mountain or touring bikes. We would be more likely to see a three-hole pedal and compatible shoes on a road or racing bike."

Barry's shoulders sagged. "So, you can't tell what specific model of bike we're looking for based on the shoes."

"No. Shoes pair with pedals, not with the bike. But, if we can match the print to a specific shoe's sole and cleat—"

"We can potentially tie the man wearing the shoes to the crime scenes," Barry finished.

"Right. And if you do find the bike, we can determine what type of shoes would be compatible with the pedals," Frank said. "Dr. Osborne is probably the best lead on the bike since she's the only one who saw it parked next to the Florren house."

"My view was from several yards away. I never saw it up close, so I'm not sure how much help I'll be," Olivia told him. "I suggest you talk to Billy Wallace, the ten-year-old who lives next to the Florren house."

Mark cleared his throat. "About that."

Silas stiffened, expecting another 'non-disclosed' piece of information. Olivia nudged him gently under the table. "*Don't*," she whispered.

"The afternoon we discovered Ms. Florren's body, on the advice of Dr. Osborne, we instructed Gail and Billy Wallace to stay somewhere else for the night just to be safe. Since that time, we have been unable to locate Ms. Wallace or her son. She's called off from work and an attendance clerk at the school said she called yesterday. The excuse she gave to both places is that she and Billy were going out of town.

"When I spoke to Ms. Wallace the night of, she assured me she would be staying with her aunt and even gave me her number," Mark explained. "Her aunt confirmed Ms. Wallace and her son stayed the first night. They left the next day, and the aunt swears she doesn't know where they went after that."

"Do you believe her?" Silas wanted to know.

"Not sure," Mark said. "I plan to talk to her again after this meeting. In person."

"I did reach out to Teresa Montez, the neighbor on the other side of the Wallace house. She shares carpool duty with Ms. Wallace for the neighborhood swim team," Barry said. "She believes Gail is in hiding somewhere. The Wallaces went through a nasty divorce and Gail is under the impression that any police involvement could jeopardize her ability to keep Billy in her home. The ex is a doctor and has made multiple threats to take custody of Billy, according to the neighbor."

"Any violence in the home? Any reason we should look more closely at the ex-husband?" Silas asked.

"No record of calls to the house for spousal abuse or domestic disturbance. According to Teresa, the neighbor, Dr. Wallace is more into verbal assault than physical."

"This impression came from whom? The neighbor or Gail Wallace?" Olivia asked, remembering the skittish woman wanting nothing more than to avoid the policeman blocking the path to her house.

Barry looked to Mark. "Neighbor."

Olivia nodded, filing the information away for another time.

"Since Ms. Montez's son, Alex, and Billy are friends, she agreed to let me interview Alex this afternoon after school. I would like Dr. Osborne to accompany me for the visit," Barry suggested.

Olivia nodded. "Of course."

"What else are you doing?" Silas wanted to know.

"BOLO out on Gail and Billy Wallace as well as her car. No hits so far. She has other family out of town, parents and a sister in Austin, a brother in San Angelo. We're working on running them all down. We'll have more on that after Sergeant Austin talks to the aunt in person. We're also conducting periodic patrols through the neighborhood to keep an eye on the house," Barry said.

Silas nodded, satisfied for the moment, and turned his attention back to the head of Forensics. Frank referred back to his notes.

"We were hopeful for more evidence in the house, but we found little except he's a lousy cleaner. Unfortunately, not lousy enough to leave prints or anything useful. Even with all the blood."

"How is that possible?" Mark asked.

"He brought gloves," Olivia said.

"Bingo," Frank agreed. "That's what I was thinking. The victim's dish gloves were next to the sink, but he didn't use those. After a thorough search, we didn't find any other supply of gloves in the house."

"What about the message written in blood on the mirror above the fireplace?" the captain asked. He remembered it was from the book of Luke but couldn't recall the words.

"The appearance of the message written on the mirror led me to conclude he brought his own gloves. The victim's dish gloves have textured fingertips. No sign of that texture in the writing," Frank said. "We picked up partials from the dog collar, but nothing from victim number three's car."

"He wears gloves during the kill. He also wore them when he drove Patty Griffin's car to Blossom Park," Olivia interrupted. "Video footage showed him stuffing something into his pants pocket when he exited the vehicle. It was a pair of gloves."

Barry was impressed. He'd been hung up on the movement of the UNSUB's hands as well but due to the grainy quality of the feed, it was unclear. The most likely conclusion would be he was putting car keys in his pocket except the keys to Patricia Griffin's car were still in the ignition.

"Considering the lack of prints, gloves make sense," Frank Tobias agreed. "Back to the car, we can confirm what Dr. Meeks said about the victim's head making contact with the steering wheel. We found her hair, nasal secretions, and blood on the wheel. After a thorough search of her car and her apartment, however, we still haven't located her cell phone."

"Any calls since?" Barry asked.

"Negative," Frank conceded. "The phone has been turned off. My guess is it's been disabled and trashed but the carrier is monitoring the number."

"If he was just going to trash the phone, why take it?" Olivia asked quietly.

"We ordered her phone records and received them

overnight. I have two techs trolling through them now. I'll get back to you if they pull out anything promising. I also have guys at the local dump substation at this moment, picking up a set of bloody clothes found in a can from the Florren neighborhood. Sanitation has the city divided into grids and with the addition of the new green compost barrel—which is what they were picking up the morning of the murder—the city's been pretty stringent about monitoring what goes into what barrels. In fact, they're planning to start fining people if they don't get it right. So, as soon as we examine the knife and the clothes, we'll get back to you on that as well."

"Look carefully for a dark baseball cap," Olivia instructed Frank. "He was wearing it in the CCTV footage from the park, but not when I met him walking the dog. Also, check the pockets for the gloves."

"Anything on the gravel we found near the drainage ditch?" Barry asked.

Frank's facial expression wasn't promising. "RSID test was positive for human blood, but that's all I can tell you at this point. There wasn't enough DNA to test."

"Mr. Tobias, you failed to mention the method of entry into Ms. Florren's house," Silas noted. There was an exchange of looks between the sergeant, lieutenant, and the head of forensics.

"We found no evidence of forced entry, sir," Frank spoke. He nodded to Barry indicating he had nothing else.

Barry leaned forward, prepared to answer, but Silas held up his hand, stopping him. "No. I want to hear this from Dr. Osborne." He recalled part of what the captain had sent him last night. Olivia was there for the discovery of Wendy Florren's body. Nothing about the scenario said the lieutenant should have gone inside. Olivia had been the reason.

"But first I want to know if someone can tell me if Ms. Florren was scheduled to work the night of her death?" Silas asked. "The fact she had just come off a shift said she should have been heading to bed. If she wasn't working again that night, she might have been opting for a nap later or forgoing sleep altogether."

"According to her supervisor, she was scheduled to work," Mark answered.

Silas nodded, slowly digesting the information. "Dr. Osborne, how did the UNSUB gain entry into Ms. Florren's house?"

"I believe she let him inside."

"Why? She should have been going to bed. A woman living alone..." Silas hung on to the thought because it also applied to Olivia. "Did she know him?"

Olivia didn't hesitate. "No."

"Then why did she let him in? What motivated her? How did he persuade her?" Silas asked.

Olivia looked away from Barry and directly at Silas. "SAPD canvassed the neighborhood the night before. No one answered at Ms. Florren's house. According to the grid search it was Lieutenant Bartholomew who left his card in her door. Because Ms. Florren used the garage as her entry point, I'm inclined to believe she never saw the card before the UNSUB used to it coerce her to open the door."

When she looked out the peephole, all she saw was the SAPD logo.

Chapter Eleven

Another well-placed nudge under the table told Silas they needed to take a break. He was waiting for Olivia before she could slip back into the conference room. He had her favorite soft drink in hand. "I knew you wouldn't get this for yourself," Silas said. He knew she drank diet, except when she really needed to recharge. Why she drank diet at all, he had no idea. She obviously worked out. He imagined yoga or something like it, both strenuous and meditative. Something to quiet her mind.

Olivia needed the sugar and the caffeine to combat the emotionally charged room and the war it waged on her psyche. She was a sensitive. She was empathic. She was a soda junkie. Olivia eagerly reached for the can as soon as Silas opened it for her. His role as caretaker was new. "Do you think you're being a little hard on the lieutenant?" she asked.

"You feel a need to protect him?" he pressed.

"No."

Silas nodded, relieved at the answer. "You're holding back." *On me.* "On this case. You're the reason he went in the house. I want to know what you saw or what you felt that pushed him in there."

Silas recognized Olivia's unease. She got that way when asked to explain her claircognizant abilities. Silas was trained to study evidence of behavior and use decades of collective understanding of what those behaviors mean to gain insight into an offender's psychology. The pieces fit together in a collage that became a picture of the type of person they were looking for. The things Olivia knew weren't based on training or experience, and they came without facts attached. She was an evolution of more than just the five senses. She didn't like talking about her talents, but Silas needed to understand.

"She thought she was safe. She let him in because she didn't see him as a threat and her guard was down. Knowing she was in there, dead, I couldn't leave her there. It wouldn't have been right."

Silas nodded. "You can be very persuasive. How did you get him to go inside?"

Olivia shook her head. "I didn't. He rang the doorbell and when she didn't answer he knocked. The door opened on its own."

Like an invitation.

****

"Before Dr. Osborne begins, I want to make it clear that we've found no connection between any of the four victims. Despite similarities in their victimology, nothing in our investigation has pointed to any of the victims knowing each other," Barry said. He was vaguely aware he was scrambling to regain his footing. Agent Branch didn't like him. It was obvious. The feeling was mutual, but that didn't mean he didn't know how to do his job or that it was his fault Wendy Florren was dead.

"So, to pick back up where we left off, our UNSUB is clever and crafty," Silas said. "Dr. Osborne, what's your take on him? Would our guy do the

119

Wallace woman and the kid?"

The break had tempered the agent's mood—some. Barry wondered if that had been the intent. He had seen the nudge under the table.

"At this point, I think our guy is capable of almost anything. However, he is limited geographically. The bike is important. It is his sole means of transportation. That means his anchor point is somewhere within these few miles," Olivia said with a nod toward the board. "His hunting ground is limited because he lives or works, probably both, within this radius. And that is our only real advantage."

"Organized or disorganized?" Barry asked.

"Both," Silas and Olivia answered in unison. Olivia glanced at Silas, hoping he would be the one to explain.

"Every offender falls somewhere on a continuum, exhibiting some behaviors that are more organized, and some that are disorganized," Silas said.

"He cleaned up, wore gloves," Frank pointed out. "That indicates organization."

Olivia spoke up. "Yes, but his choice of victim and attack location are opportunistic. He used a knife and bottle from Wendy Florren's home rather than bringing a weapon with him. He's spontaneous. Those behaviors would push him toward the other end of the spectrum."

"Both organized and disorganized? That's not helpful," Barry said.

"I agree, Lieutenant," Silas said. "That's why the BAU no longer relies on those terms as classifiers."

"What *is* helpful," Olivia said, "is examining the relationship between offender and victim, his approach and method of attack. Does he approach and kill at the same location? Does he transport the body or leave it at the murder scene? Is there any effort to conceal the body? Is there evidence of sexual activity? Is it ante or post-mortem? Those aspects give us much more insight."

"Can you give us any *specific* insights, Dr. Osborne?" Barry asked.

"Disposable gloves are a part of his everyday life. I would expect him to work in healthcare, or possibly food service. In health care, he would be a non-licensed employee, an orderly or nurse's aide. He's of average intelligence and has a basic understanding of human anatomy. Based on my direct observation, I would estimate his age to be mid-twenties to early thirties."

So, the agent did know she was the witness. Barry wondered how that conversation had gone and how Branch had handled her. Clearly, Olivia was more to him than just his consultant.

"He's younger than I originally suspected," Olivia admitted. "He exhibits characteristics of someone significantly older than his age. He was possibly raised by grandparents, or older extended family."

"He's a planner, and he's in control. He deliberately adjusted the thermostat in Wendy Florren's house to accelerate decomposition. He took her dog for a walk around the neighborhood," Silas pointed out.

"These are indications of learned behavior. He saw an opportunity and took it. Nothing more. Nothing less," Olivia said.

Silas interrupted. "The front door being left unlocked also bothers me. I'm with you on how our UNSUB persuaded Ms. Florren to open the door. A request from law enforcement is pretty compelling," Silas reiterated, glancing toward the lieutenant. "But if he went to the trouble of adjusting the thermostat, why didn't he lock the door behind him?" The killer granted them easy access to the house. Why?

"From reviewing photos of the door, I think it was probably a recent upgrade to the house. Aesthetically pleasing, yes, but also practical for a woman living alone." Olivia knew this because she had selected a similar door lock and key arrangement for her own house. "It's also a perfect solution for someone who uses the garage as her primary entrance. She couldn't lock herself out of the house by accidently pulling it closed behind her. You would need the key. I'm betting the UNSUB didn't know that. Either that it didn't lock behind him or he didn't know where the key was and didn't want to stop and look for it once he decided to leave."

When no one questioned her, Olivia continued. "I think he was walking the neighborhood because he was hoping Gail Wallace would return. Based on the timestamp of the CCTV footage from McAllister Park, and the time it would take a healthy adult to walk to the neighborhood, in all probability he saw her pull out of her driveway on her way to drop Billy off at school. The treehouse in her backyard is hard to miss. I can't be the only one who saw it. He learned fairly quickly, Wendy was not the one who took his bike. Therefore, he knows there's a potential witness. I also think he wanted to make sure his bloody clothes got picked up by sanitation."

"So, Gail and Billy Wallace are in danger?" Mark asked.

"They always have been," Olivia assured him. "Until now he's been a lazy killer. It's one of the reasons he kills outside. He has also learned that leaving a mess has consequences. He uses the environment to his advantage. The elements wreak havoc on forensics. And he's not done. He won't stop."

"If he's stalking Gail and Billy like the others—" Silas said.

Olivia shook her head. "Gail and Billy are different. They're possible witnesses, and he sees them as a threat. He doesn't stalk."

"He's limited, because of the bike," Barry said.

"Absolutely," Olivia said.

"So, the UNSUB's activity area is limited to a ten-mile radius," Silas said as he studied the grid. It was still a considerable number of potential suspects in a city of more than a million people. They needed to limit their focus somehow. He looked to Olivia.

"He could work night shift, which would explain the time he dropped off the car. He was off in the morning, in the middle of the week," she said.

"He has also been active in early evening and mid-morning," Barry said.

"Flexibility of schedule. No personal obligations. He lives alone. No one to check on his comings and goings," Olivia said.

"So how does he select his victims?" the captain asked, eager to cut to the chase.

"He doesn't. They select him," Olivia said.

"He told us as much." Silas turned to look at her. There was a familiar tingle at the base of his neck. It happened when Olivia homed in on their subject. Her instincts played havoc with those who were guided by logic alone. He had learned to put it aside. "You're going to need to help us along with this one, Dr.

Osborne," Silas said for the benefit of the others.

"He's resourceful," she said. She had sensed something. Olivia paused. "Recently acquired traits, inconsistent with his chronological age." She stopped there, hesitant to move forward.

"You can come back to it," Silas told her, gently squeezing her wrist. The lieutenant noticed her shift in demeanor. It reminded him of how she acted at the crime scene when she seemed to be listening to something only she could hear. The contact from Silas brought Olivia back the same way Barry had when he pulled her from Patricia Griffin's car. Feeling grounded, she resumed her previous course.

"He uses what's available to him. While not having a car probably didn't win him any friends in high school and since, he's now using it to his advantage. He might have toyed with the notion of taking up racing, it brings a certain 'coolness' to the bike. But more than that he wants to *appear* that he has, thus the shoes. Maybe even going so far as to shave his legs."

"If he races that would narrow the search," Mark suggested.

"I doubt he actually does. He's playing a part," Olivia said. "For his new purpose, the bike allowed him to go unnoticed at the parks where he met his first two victims. He wouldn't fit in among real cyclists. He probably doesn't wear all the proper attire. His bike may not even be appropriate for racing."

"Meeks said there were no hesitation marks on the first victim. What you just said leads me to believe you don't think he has killed before this series," Barry said.

"I don't believe he has, not people anyway. There were probably several cats missing in his neighborhood during his adolescent years," Olivia said. "To me, the frenzied nature of his attacks says he's new at this kind of killing, and he's enjoying it. Also, he's local, probably lived here his entire life, and this type of brutality couldn't have stayed under the radar. If he'd done anything remotely close to this before now, SAPD would've known about it."

"The third victim wasn't killed in a park," Silas pointed out. Olivia was smart, but sometimes she was a little scary. He looked over at the lieutenant. Was she scaring him as well? Silas watched him watching her. The lieutenant knew there was more to her than anything she could have learned from the BAU. But Olivia hadn't let him in. At least not yet.

"I'm getting to that," she assured him. "The parks are his hunting grounds. On the bike, the park is probably the only place he blends in. I think he uses it as a ruse, fakes a fall, gets his victims to see him as vulnerable and let their guard down. It's simple really. It worked for Ted Bundy."

"How do you know this?" Silas asked. It was a compliment, not a challenge.

"Who doesn't know about Ted Bundy? I believe our guy was probably on his way to McAllister Park in search of his next victim. Only this time, he actually hurt himself. He targeted Patricia Griffin when she stopped to help him." Olivia paused, giving the room a chance to catch up with her. "Look at the occupations of all his victims. We have an EMT, a kindergarten teacher, and a nurse. What do they all do? They care. They help people. And our guy makes them pay for it."

"You said he told us why he was doing this," Zavalla pointed out. "When exactly did he tell us?"

There was a soft knock at the door. Mark answered. There was a flurry of rushed whispering causing the sergeant to step outside, closing the door behind him.

"The writing on the mirror. Luke 23: 34; *'Father, forgive them, for they know not what they do.'* He's not asking forgiveness, Captain," Olivia said. "He's telling us he's punishing his victims."

"Why?" the captain asked.

"For helping him. He's not worthy of it." Silas let out a breath. "Bible verses are never a good sign."

"No, they are not," Olivia agreed. For a moment, she thought about the dark place she glimpsed while in Patricia Griffin's car and when she stood at the place where she bled out. What had the blood sacrifice lured to the surface?

"So, what's the sexual component?" Zavalla asked. "The way he kills stems from some sort of sexual motivation, correct?"

"Yes, but not in a sexual act type of way, like penetration or dominance. He's obliterating their sex. It may be motivated by anger he holds against a person close to him, a person who once helped the wrong person. I'm thinking a mother figure. Thus, being raised by grandparents or aunts or something of that nature. It drives his need to punish those who help."

"Does he want to punish himself?" Barry asked.

"Does he want to die?" Olivia was intrigued. She had not considered this. "He might. But he's not ready. He's not done."

"And the oral fixation," Silas reminded her. "You specifically commented on the card placed in the mouth of the last victim, the one belonging to Lieutenant

Bartholomew. Tell us your thoughts on the significance of that." Silas didn't appreciate the lieutenant keeping that piece of information under wraps. He had taken an unnecessary risk.

"The licking, as suggested by Dr. Meeks, could be motivated by the premature cessation of an oral connection, such as the loss of his mother at a very young age. However, the card between the teeth says something else. It has been suggested that the nursing relationship between mother and infant changes at the time the infant begins to grow teeth. Breastfeeding can be painful. During teething the baby learns they have the ability to inflict pain on the mother, giving them power for the first time. Oral sadism in adulthood is driven by a perverse desire to cause others harm or pain. In this case, I think, given the opportunity, the killer would very much like to cause you pain, Lieutenant Bartholomew."

"Why the lieutenant in particular?" the captain wanted to know.

"He left his card at Wendy Florren's. He knows who's hunting him now," Olivia explained.

The door opened and Mark returned. "I apologize for the interruption, but I have news. I got a call from Frank. Forensics found a bloody knife matching the set on Wendy Florren's kitchen counter. It was wrapped up in the bundle of bloody clothes retrieved by CSU at the dump. Also, we just got a call from a woman who says she was on the phone with our third victim, Patricia Griffin. She says Ms. Griffin saw a guy fall off his bike. She got off the phone to help him."

"Congratulations, Sergeant," Silas said. "You've just confirmed Dr. Osborne's theory."

Chapter Twelve

Once everyone but Mark, Barry, Silas, and Olivia had cleared the room, Mark punched in Tiffany Kelly's phone number on the desk phone. Tiffany, Patricia Griffin's best friend, had told him during their brief phone chat that she and Patricia had been on their weekly "phone date." At that point, Tiffany wasn't aware their conversation ended likely no more than a few minutes before Patricia was killed.

"Today's Friday, so where has Miss Kelly been?" Silas asked before Mark connected the call.

"She flew from Corpus Christi to Atlanta after talking to Patricia. Said her mother had surgery and she had been cooped up in a hospital room. She got worried when she never heard back from Patricia after letting her know her mother's surgery went well. She claims it wasn't like her friend to not call back."

Tiffany Kelly picked up on the first ring. Mark introduced those in the room and let her know she was on speakerphone, and that the call was being recorded.

"I can't believe it. I'd just talked to her," Tiffany said. She sounded stuffy like she had been crying. "It felt weird that I didn't hear back from her after she got off the phone so quickly. It's not like Patty not to call me back. I thought about checking on her, I really did, but I took an evening flight to Atlanta. And then I just got busy." There was a pause as Tiffany tried to get herself together.

"Any idea why she was in that neighborhood?" Barry asked. The subdivision wasn't a straight shot between Patricia Griffin's work and her apartment. It was one of those little things that nagged at him. Also, he thought if he could get her to start from the beginning, she might stay calm. She had learned that her friend was dead less than two hours ago. In a last-ditch effort, Tiffany had called her friend's employer when she couldn't get Patricia to answer her calls. The receptionist at the medical office was the one who broke the news.

"Okay," Tiffany paused and cleared her throat. "She started regularly cutting through that neighborhood when they were doing construction at the elementary school. She liked the neighborhood so much she was thinking about looking for a house there. She went through a really nasty divorce and was just trying to put her life back together, meet a nice guy." They could hear the tears in her voice as she trailed off about plans Patricia would never keep.

Sensing Tiffany was close to pulling back, Olivia spoke up. "Tiffany, it's obvious you and Patricia were close. I know this has to be difficult for you, and we appreciate you talking to us. The best way you can help her right now is to tell us everything she said to you about why she stopped her car."

"Okay, I'll try." Tiffany paused to blow her nose. "It's Patty. She didn't go by Patricia."

"Thank you for telling us, Tiffany. It's important we get it right because we want to take care of Patty too," Olivia said.

"Do you think he did it—the guy she stopped to

help?" Tiffany asked.

Olivia looked to Barry.

"It's possible he was one of the last people she encountered. That's why it's very important we find him." Barry thought the woman had been through enough for one day. She didn't need any more details.

"Okay. I understand. So, we'd been talking for a little while about my mom. Patty was so helpful since she's a nurse. We talked about her job. She liked it but was a little bored. She said she was circling the block again. She thought she'd seen a *For Sale* sign in a yard, but it was just a sign for a roofing company. She was turning around in the cul-de-sac when she said she saw some guy fall off his bike."

"Did she say anything specific about him?" Barry asked. "Take your time and think about it."

"At first, she thought it was a kid, but then when he got up, she said it wasn't. She could tell he scraped his knee pretty good. That's why she thought she should stop."

"What made her realize he wasn't a kid?" Mark asked.

"She said when he bent down his cap fell off. He was bald."

****

"Doesn't mean it wasn't our guy," Olivia said. Silas had a rental car, but since it was her town and they both had to be back at police headquarters later, she drove them to see Meeks.

"There could be two of them," Silas suggested as he watched her weave in and out of traffic. One older. One younger. He knew that aspect of the profile was bothering her.

Olivia shook her head. "No. It doesn't feel right."

Silas shook his head too and resumed looking out the window. When Olivia got something in her head, there was no stopping her. Maybe because odds were, she was right. "Tell me, would you, as a nurse, stop and help this guy?" Silas asked.

"I don't think I'm a typical nurse."

Silas smiled. "You're not, but just humor me for a second."

Olivia considered it but not for long. "At this point in my life I *might* stop and help you. Depends on what day it is," Olivia said. "But I think they were inclined to. They probably felt safe. In a park in the middle of a neighborhood, you're supposed to be safe with so many other people around. What they failed to realize is those *other* people, the ones that used to make you safer in numbers, aren't paying attention. They're too absorbed in their own lives, the music blaring through their headphones, texting, or looking at whatever social media they're scrolling through. There is no situational awareness anymore."

"Thank you for the social commentary," Silas said. She was either feeling cynical or she was still unhappy about the UNSUB being bald.

"Am I wrong?" she said.

"No, you're not," Silas said. "So, what makes the UNSUB do what he does?"

"Something wants him to hate," Olivia answered without hesitation.

"I don't know why I ask you questions," Silas said. "It makes me nervous when you talk like that."

"What? You asked a question, I answered. What more do you want?"

"I'd prefer it if you'd said some*one*, not some*thing*." Olivia rolled her eyes and didn't even offer him a glance.

"You've been thinking about it. I know you have. The comment you made about his chronological age," Silas prompted her. She didn't always want to follow where her gifts took her. But more and more they ended up in the same place. He had worked with her enough years to see it.

"There's not enough evidence to suggest there is anything at work here except the UNSUB," Olivia told him.

Silas nodded. "I trust you on that. I have to. But as with any other piece of evidence I don't want you to discount it just because you don't want it to be so."

She didn't answer him.

"So, have you heard from Ana Lutz?" he asked changing the subject. He wasn't going to get anything else out of her on the other subject.

"I thought you didn't like asking me questions."

"I think I might be safe on this one. I'm not asking for an opinion," Silas said.

"I told you, she called me on Wednesday. The day I stopped in the neighborhood and bumped into the killer."

"And what did she say?" Olivia had already told him, but Silas wanted to hear it again.

"She said she was going to lie low for a little while."

Silas didn't verbalize his thoughts on the matter, but it was clear he didn't believe Ana Lutz. Olivia didn't know what his issue was with the woman, so she was just going to have to take a stab in the dark and play the odds. "The Wiccans are a religious order, nothing more."

"So you say."

"You would also know this if you bothered to educate yourself. Take one of my cultural sensitivity classes," Olivia suggested. "As for the Wiccans, think along the lines of Native American mysticism."

"Still sounds *other worldly* to me."

"She wanted to know if I had heard from Father Dominic." Olivia hated revealing the little detail, but she knew she had to. She couldn't keep things from Silas, especially since there was a dead body involved.

"*Father.* You still call him that?"

"It's a title. He earned it," Olivia said.

"Doesn't matter that the Catholic Church doesn't recognize his title anymore?" Silas reminded her. "Excommunication and all that."

"He wasn't excommunicated," Olivia corrected.

"He's not a priest anymore, am I correct?"

"Priestly ordination remains valid forever, so a priest is always a priest."

"Those Catholics have a way around everything, don't they?"

"Aren't you Catholic, Silas?" Olivia asked.

"Notre Dame, alum—so you tell me. Was thinking of changing to Episcopalian though," Silas said just to get a rise out of her.

"Catholic-lite, then." Olivia shook her head. She knew when he was baiting her. "Father Dominic left the priesthood of his own volition, like resigning from a job. I'm technically still a nurse just like he's still a priest. He just doesn't work as one anymore."

"All this happened after that thing he got his hand

slapped for though, am I right?"

Olivia refused to comment.

"Do you still practice?" Silas asked, genuinely curious this time. "Catholicism? Still receive the Eucharist, go to confession?" He noted she still wore the little silver cross.

"I believe wholeheartedly in the teachings of the Church, but I am also of the mindset one doesn't have to worship at the altar to be counted among the believers." It was true, even though she subscribed to some of the older ways. Besides, churches were full of emotion, and she avoided them for the most part.

"Fair enough."

"You also cannot believe in the existence of evil without also believing in the existence of good."

"Interesting order in which to list those concepts," Silas commented. "So, what did you tell Ana?"

"That no, I haven't heard from Dominic in a while."

"Give him a call," Silas suggested. "For me."

Olivia didn't respond, but Silas knew that was as good as a *yes* from her. They rode the rest of the way in silence as Silas concentrated on the scenery. According to the passing billboards, Fiesta was coming. It was San Antonio's signature event with an economic impact of close to three hundred million dollars. He'd read about it last night when he'd grown tired of Captain Zavalla's notes, and sleep wouldn't come. It was a two-week-long celebration that began as a single event to honor the memory of the battles of the Alamo and San Jacinto. Part of it now included a four-night block party in the market square of downtown dubbed NIOSA— *Night in Old San Antonio.* Even if the UNSUB was limited by his transportation needs, there was always the local VIA bus system. It might be worth it to him. He would have larger crowds from which to choose, crowds that could be good cover if he thought they were on to him.

"I've decided the lieutenant shouldn't be at the press conference this afternoon," Silas said. "I don't want the UNSUB getting eyes on him, especially after what you said about the card. The captain is going to do the talking, but no introductions of local police."

"I think that's an excellent idea."

Silas was glad they finally agreed on something.

****

"Meet Ferdinand Roche. Fifty-two-year-old male, resident of Poteet, Texas," Meeks said as he unveiled his latest arrival. He had completed the autopsy before they arrived.

"I'm assuming Poteet is located in Atascosa County," Silas said, walking around the stainless-steel table.

"You are correct," Meeks told him.

"Found it on a map," Silas said with a wink Olivia's way.

"Poteet is the birthplace of the one and only George Strait, and home of the Strawberry Festival," Meeks said.

"The festival is part of the Fiesta celebration," Olivia told Silas. "They have a pageant, elect a queen, and there are floats and a parade. You would hate it."

Silas continued to circle the table. He noted no defensive wounds and concluded it had been a surprise attack. "From his name, I'm guessing he's not a native of these parts." Roche sounded French to him.

"You are correct, again," Meeks agreed. "Relocated here from New Orleans after Hurricane Katrina. Worked as a day laborer, mainly installing laminate flooring, and doing some landscaping. He was working outside when this unfortunate event occurred."

"Let me guess. You practiced a little voodoo on the side as well?" Silas said, pointing to the markings on the deceased Mr. Roche's shoulder.

"That does appear to be a pentagram. Poorly constructed in my opinion but given the canvas..." Meeks said. If it had been a tattoo and not a carving directly into flesh, it might have looked better. "He was known by the locals to engage in a few ritualistic goings-on. Cited for vagrancy at an abandoned building and known by the local authorities to be partial to marijuana. A couple of arrests within the last year for possession and suspicion of dealing." Meeks handed the police folder he had been reading from over to Silas.

"Cause of death?" Olivia asked. She was chilled, and it had nothing to do with the temperature of the room. She was ready to leave.

"Singular cut to the throat. No hesitation. One cut severed both the jugular and the carotid. Bled out in under a minute," Meeks told her.

"And these wounds here?" Silas asked, pointing to the four evenly spaced holes across the chest.

"According to the sheriff's report and the photos in the folder I just handed you, they are the result of a pitch fork. He was impaled after his throat was slit, so he was already a dead man. The tines did go all the way through to the ground, pinning him in place," Meeks clarified.

"Ritualistic killing," Silas said, glancing at Olivia.

Something was wrong; something had spooked her, and she was hovering by the door. Though as far as body identifications went, this was one of the mild ones.

"He seems to be a very fit guy for fifty-two. How did they disable him?" Olivia wanted to know.

"They?" Meeks asked.

"If you were frightened enough by someone to carve a pentagram into their shoulder, you wouldn't approach them alone," Olivia explained. "Looks like there was bleeding at the site, consistent with a beating heart."

"Correct. The pentagram was carved after the blow to the back of his head and before his throat was cut. I pulled some wood particles out of the scalp, which indicate he was probably struck with a branch or log," Meeks said.

"So, we're looking for more than one perp. Excellent," Silas said.

"You might be looking for more than that," Olivia said. "Can we go, please?"

****

She waited until they were back in the car to tell Silas the rest. "That was no ordinary pentagram."

Silas sighed. "Of course, it wasn't. I guess it was too much for me to hope we were just dealing with poor artists."

"The pentagram was inverted. One point was down. It's a sign of subservience to something *otherworldly*," Olivia said. "It represents the dark side."

Chapter Thirteen

Olivia managed to dodge a private lunch with Silas when he got a call on his cell phone. Silas stepped away to take the call, and Olivia headed for the food truck parked in front of SAPD. Street tacos sounded good, and since she never came downtown, she decided to indulge. Before Olivia was even in the car, she could tell Barry wasn't happy. He accepted the tacos she handed him but didn't seem interested in eating.

"What's up?" she asked.

"I can't believe he asked me to leave."

"It's for your own protection," Olivia assured him, glad for the distraction.

"You're sure he doesn't want the investigation for himself?" Barry tried not to sound bitter, but he did even to his own ears.

"Silas would very much like to not be here hunting," Olivia assured him.

The agent might not want to be hunting a killer, but Barry was convinced Branch was in town for other reasons, whether Olivia was ready to acknowledge it or not.

"We would both like to be doing something else," she said, gazing out the window. At least she wasn't driving this time. She finished her taco as Barry navigated traffic.

"Where are we headed?" she asked.

"To interview Alex Montez. If we can't find Billy, maybe his buddy can tell us something."

"One can only hope," she said. "You never know with kids."

"You and Agent Branch seem to have worked together quite a bit. How well do you know him?" Barry asked before he could stop himself.

Olivia was glad she was looking out the window and not at him, otherwise, he would have seen how much his question amused her. "Tell me, Lieutenant, is that a personal or professional question?"

"Are you going to think less of me if I say personal?"

"Answering a question with a question. Kind of a rookie move, isn't it?" Olivia looked over at him and smiled.

He *felt* like a rookie. At least where she was concerned. *Where was this urge to protect her, the urge to keep her safe, coming from?*

"No, I won't think less of you." It might even score him some points because it might mean he wanted to do more than just sleep with her. "Silas and I have worked together for many years. Seen a lot. Been through a lot."

"All of that work related?"

Olivia nodded. *Of course, it was just work. Right?* How could she answer that for the lieutenant when she couldn't even unwrap the answer for herself? It was still stuck in the little box where she kept it. She was glad it hadn't popped out during the car ride to see Meeks. It was the first and only time she and Silas had been alone, but they had been working. They were particularly good at keeping things separate. She would have to deal with Silas eventually, but not today.

The silence stretched between them until Barry couldn't take it anymore. She was the tougher one. He wondered how long it would be before he admitted it to her.

"Can you tell me how you do it? How you do this?" Barry asked. He never developed personal relationships with women he worked with. He had never known a woman who was truly aware of what he dealt with on a daily basis. "From what I've read, you've met some pretty nasty predators."

Oh, yes, the infamous file. Olivia wondered what he had read. It wasn't everything. She knew that much. "Those cases weren't normal," she said.

"And this is?"

"It's your first serial case, isn't it?" Olivia asked.

"Yes."

She nodded. That was the real reason he felt like he had been kicked off the team. "Welcome to the club, but this case isn't on the level of the cases you read about. At least not yet. Probably not ever." *Hopefully not ever.* Silas had asked something on their way back downtown that still nagged her.

"Do you ever think this kind of thing follows you?"

"You went to see some of them, afterwards," Barry said bringing her thoughts back inside the car.

"I did," Olivia confessed.

"Why?"

"They asked to see me."

"Why, do you think?"

Olivia shook her head and looked away. "They were looking for answers."

"To what?"

"In the end, they thought I was the only one who understood."

"Understood why they did what they did?" Barry asked. "How could you? How could anyone?"

"They lost their motivation," Olivia said. "The force that drove them to commit the acts that landed them behind bars was gone. You've read my dissertation, right? This goes back to my seven-second theory."

"Yes, but I don't fully understand."

"They were abandoned and they didn't know what to do with themselves." Olivia closed her eyes with the memories. Thankfully, there were few.

"So, what happened then?"

"They killed themselves."

****

"Thanks for talking to us, Alex. I'm sure there are other things you would rather be doing on your Friday afternoon," Olivia began. Barry asked her to take the lead. A fourth-grade boy was more likely to respond to her questions than his. She had a softer disposition. And she was prettier.

Alex didn't even look up. "Billy isn't here so I guess there really isn't anything to do."

"I know. I heard he hasn't been at school." These boys were more than friends. They were neighbors, classmates, and teammates. At ten years old, that meant that they were each other's world.

Alex nodded.

"Do you know where he is? Have you heard from him?" Olivia asked.

"No. He's not answering his phone. He has it turned off."

"You've been calling him?" his mom asked.

"Don't freak out, Mom. I know I'm only supposed to use the phone for emergencies," Alex said. "But talking to Billy is kind of an emergency."

Teresa Montez looked across the table at Olivia and Barry. "Gail and I both got the boys phones, but only to use if they needed them after practice," she said as if she needed to explain why her ten-year-old son had a cell phone.

"Was there something important you needed to talk to Billy about?" Olivia asked.

Alex shook his head. "No, I just miss talking to him."

"I bet. He's your best friend, right?" Olivia asked.

Another nod from Alex.

"Alex, Billy's mom said he brought a bicycle home. Do you know anything about that?"

Alex looked at his mom who reached over to smooth his hair. It was a gesture meant to comfort.

"Did someone give it to him? Did he find it somewhere?" Again, another look to his mother.

"Go ahead, Alex. Tell them. Billy's not in any trouble. They just want to know," Teresa Montez encouraged him.

He looked at Olivia, avoiding Barry. "We both found it. I have one. Billy doesn't. His mom says they're too dangerous."

Olivia nodded and smiled. "That's what she said. Do you remember where you found it and when?"

"We found it Tuesday morning before school. We saw the policemen were gone and we wanted to go take a look at where they had been, but we chickened out. We were hanging out by the curve when we saw it in the drainage ditch."

Olivia and Barry exchanged looks.

"You know you're not supposed to go down there," Teresa reminded him.

"They mowed last week, Mom," Alex told her. "It's not like we're going to get lost."

Teresa took a deep breath and Olivia was glad to see she chose to table the subject of the drainage ditch for another time.

"Do you remember anything specific about the bike?" Barry asked. "Did you or Billy ride it?"

"It was fancy. Billy and I both tried to ride it, but we kept falling down. It was too hard to balance."

Barry nodded. The bike would have been too big for the boys to handle.

"If we show you some pictures, do you think you could pick out what kind of bike it was?" Olivia asked.

Alex shrugged. "I guess so." He was starting to fidget. He practically vibrated with energy. Maybe if she got him up and moving, she would get more out of him.

"Just one more question about the bike, Alex, I promise," Olivia said with a smile. "Do you know what Billy did with the bike when his mom told him to get rid of it?" Undoubtedly, he knew some version of what happened to Wendy Florren, but hopefully, he had no idea the bike had anything to do with it.

"Billy didn't want to get rid of it. All he told me is he put it somewhere his mom wouldn't find it," Alex admitted. "We were going to try and ride it again after school, but when we got home his mom said he had to stay in for the rest of the day."

"I guess it is kind of boring around here without

him. I heard you and Billy like to spend time in the treehouse. I saw it. It looks pretty cool. I would really like to see what you can see from up there. Do you think you could take me up inside?"

Luckily the gate to the Wallace yard was unlocked.

"We thought about putting in a connecting gate," Teresa commented as they all four trudged over together. "The boys spend so much time together."

Barry nodded, evaluating the treehouse ahead. Alex scaled the sturdy ladder with the agility expected of a ten-year-old.

Olivia paused to take off her shoes, which she handed to Barry, telling herself she apparently needed to stop wearing skirts when she was working.

"Need a boost?" he asked, only half joking as he took an appreciative look at her legs.

"I got this, Lieutenant, but you're going to need to back up and turn around," she told him with a smile.

She had no problem ascending and only looked over her shoulder once to see if Barry was watching her. She noted his head was down and he was grinning.

"Wow, you can see everything from up here," Olivia said, taking a quick survey of the neighborhood. She had an unobstructed view of the kill zone.

"Pretty cool, huh?" For just a moment Alex seemed to forget he was missing his best friend.

"You and Billy could be the neighborhood watch patrol."

"We thought about it."

"You said you watched the police officers, is that right?"

Alex nodded. "Until it got too dark."

"Billy's mom told me you all didn't have swim

practice on Monday. Were the two of you up here before the police came?"

"Yeah," he admitted sheepishly.

"What did you see, Alex? It's very important. Maybe if we knew we could help get Billy to come home," Olivia suggested.

"I was late. Stupid math homework was really hard that day. By the time I got here it was all over. Billy is the only one who saw it."

Olivia bent at the knees, putting herself on Alex's level. She really wanted him to look at her. "What exactly did Billy see?"

"The man and the lady."

"What were they doing?"

"They were on the ground. He thought they were about to make out or do something gross, but they didn't. They were fighting. Billy said the guy was hitting the woman in the stomach."

"Did he tell anyone? Did either of you?" Olivia asked gently. The question finally earned a look from Alex.

"No. He said when stuff like that happened, he was supposed to go somewhere else and not look and especially not tell."

Olivia nodded. Gail Wallace was more abused than anyone knew.

"He didn't want to tell his mom?" Olivia asked.

"No. Especially not her. It was his dad. It's always his dad. That's why he made me promise not to say anything."

"What do you mean? He thought it was his dad?" Olivia asked.

"The guy hitting the woman in the stomach. He

was wearing doctor clothes. Billy's dad is a doctor. He wears those scrub things."

Olivia felt the need to offer him some kind of comfort since his mother was twenty feet below them. "A lot of people wear scrubs, Alex. It doesn't mean it was Billy's dad."

"I told Billy that too, but he said he'd seen his dad do the same thing before. And he's bald, like the guy who hurt the lady. Billy was afraid it was him."

****

"I'm going to need Billy's cell phone number," Barry said. Once back in the house, Alex was excused to his room and Teresa Montez was left alone with Olivia and Barry.

Teresa turned on Alex's phone and handed it over. Barry hadn't known Billy had a cell phone and certainly didn't have the number. The second phone hadn't shown up on Gail's cell phone bill. Maybe Dad paid for it. They could track Gail's phone if it ever turned back on, and now they could do the same with Billy's. If they were lucky, maybe Billy, like Alex, would feel the need to talk to his friend.

"So, you have no idea where Gail would go?" Barry asked.

Teresa shook her head no. "That night, you asked her to go somewhere else, she told me she was going to her aunt's house. Since then, I haven't heard from her. I'm sorry."

Olivia and Barry exchanged looks.

"Is Gail afraid of her ex-husband?" Olivia asked.

"I think so," Teresa said, "but I don't really know." Olivia wondered if she told Mark she didn't think it was physical because she didn't want to think about it or because Gail was really good at covering it up?

"They were divorced by the time we moved in. He's pretty controlling. He never thinks what Gail is doing for or with Billy is right or enough. He seems like a real asshole. They were high school sweethearts, you know. She put him through medical school, and now look at him."

"Do you know what kind of doctor he is? Where he works?" Barry asked.

"He's an OB-GYN at Stone Oak Methodist." Barry and Olivia retreated outside to his car, but Barry made no move to leave.

"We need to know where Dr. Wallace was Monday evening," Barry said as they sat in his car, still in Teresa's driveway. "I don't want him to know we're on to him just yet," Barry said, studying the Wallace house. It looked as empty as he knew it to be.

"On it," Olivia told him. She had looked up Kurt Wallace's office number, briefly spoken to the receptionist, and had been placed on hold. Before Barry could ask her what she had in mind, she was put through.

"Oh, hi, this is Vickie from the hospital. I have some charts Dr. Wallace needs to sign off on." Olivia stopped and listened for a moment. "Oh, I wasn't sure if he was gone for the day or not. Well, these charts are from Monday afternoon. Can you tell me when I should expect him to come by and sign them?"

Olivia listened some more. "Oh, so you're telling me he wasn't scheduled for surgery Monday afternoon? Oh, shoot, you're right. My mistake. I must've read the date wrong. I'm sure he was seeing patients, right?" Olivia stopped to listen again. "Oh, Dr. Wallace was out of the office that afternoon? Oh, ok, thanks, hon. Sorry to bother you."

"What did you just do?" Barry asked.

"I'm a nurse, remember? You have to know how to talk the talk. If they think you're in the club it's amazing what you can learn."

"I'm curious about that, by the way. I'm assuming that was before you joined the Bureau."

"Yes. A lifetime ago."

"Why forensic psychology?"

"I think I got tired of not understanding why people do the screwed-up things they do. Pursuing answers, really. Speaking of, I guess you're going to have to check Dr. Wallace out sooner rather than later. Billy's dad wasn't in the office and he wasn't at the hospital Monday afternoon. His office staff just told me he cancelled his afternoon patients at the last minute."

Barry made a call to the station for someone to start looking for Dr. Kurt Wallace, OB-GYN. They needed to chat.

"He was wearing scrubs. He either works in healthcare, or he's wearing a costume again," she said. "A clinical setting, but not a hospital. A job that requires minimal training, like a personal care aide or an orderly."

"And bald. That's the second time we've heard that description today. First Tiffany Kelly and now Alex," Barry said once they were on their way back downtown. "I saw the CCTV footage. You saw the guy. Both had hair."

Olivia nodded. "I'm aware. The profile is right. The picture is wrong."

****

Barry dropped Olivia at her car once they returned to headquarters. "I have a pass to get out of the parking garage free," he offered.

"I was going to expense it," she told him. He opened her car door for her, but she didn't get in. He was reluctant to let her go even though he knew the captain and Agent Branch were probably waiting for him. "Can I bring you dinner?"

"No. I would like to eat tonight and you have no guarantee when you'll get out of here." Olivia smiled. "Besides I have a standing date every Friday night at the fancy grocery on Broadway. Their deli is awesome."

"It is," Barry agreed.

"I didn't know we were neighbors," Olivia said. "Or are you an interloper?" The upscale supermarket attracted San Antonians whether they lived in Alamo Heights or not. It was known for its chef-prepared meals in the deli as well as pastries, breads, and wine selections. They even offered valet parking during the holidays.

"I'm in the condos on Hildebrand and 281. Across from UIW."

"Fancy," Olivia said.

"Hard to get to me on the thirteenth floor, and no yard to mow."

Olivia nodded. "Now I see."

"Fabulous view, especially on the Fourth of July. Or any time really."

"I bet. Do you actually sit out on your balcony?" Olivia asked. "Somehow I don't see it."

Barry smiled. "Okay, I have a couple of balconies. I don't sit on either one of them. But I'd like to."

"Fair enough," Olivia smiled. "I always buy plenty at the deli," she said. "But I don't have a balcony."

Barry leaned in and stopped whatever she was going to say next. It was an impulse he could no longer control. Her lips were softer than he imagined, and it wasn't the quick kiss he intended. "It could be late," he whispered when he was finally able to pull himself away from her.

"Dinner will be waiting," she said.

Chapter Fourteen

Past memories flooded back to Olivia...
They tailed the convertible to Grace Mansion.

"I heard someone won this place in a poker game," Jason said.

"That's one story," Nash confirmed.

"I'm just going over our guy's info. Wonder if he's a member of the Grace clan," Jaworski said, looking at his computer screen.

"That could be why we weren't given all the info," Jason whispered to Olivia. "If this guy's part of the Grace family maybe someone is protecting him."

Olivia shrugged. Somehow, she didn't think it was something that simple. Nash and Jaworski didn't seem to recognize the guy. The problem was forensics. Some pieces were missing.

"Are you going in?" Jason asked. "I think I just saw the guy close the curtains in the front window."

"No crime against that," Nash told him.

"No probable cause either, but there's nothing that says I can't take a walk around the area," Jaworski said.

Jason slung his messenger bag strap over his shoulder, ready to follow.

"Slow your roll kid. You two are staying in the car," Nash said.

He had just opened the door when a scream pierced the night.

"Shit! You two stay here." Before Jason could protest, the two officers were out of the car and sprinting toward the house.

Olivia and Jason were alone in the quiet car. A moment later, the radio came to life.

"Unit three-seven-one, code four-six. 14238 Tobin Place." It was Nash's voice.

"What's a code four-six?" Jason asked.

"How the hell would I know? Can't be anything good. Happy now?" Olivia asked. She had hoped listening in would keep him in the car.

Jason removed an extra battery from his bag and slid it in his jacket pocket.

"You are not going in there," Olivia said.

"You'll be fine, Liv."

"It's not me I'm worried about."

"Look, I don't have your brains. The camera has to do the work for me," Jason said. "I'll be careful, I promise."

When he tried to open the door, he realized it was locked. The doors had to be opened from the outside. They were locked in the car; Olivia felt relief wash over her.

For a moment. Until Jason grinned, reached out the open window, and opened the door from the outside.

"Shit. Jason, please stay in the—"

"I'll be right back, Liv. You won't even know I'm gone."

And then he was gone, and she was alone.

A pop of static from the radio startled her. "Unit three-seven-one, status?"

Olivia waited for a response from Nash and Jaworski. Nothing. Just more static.

Why aren't they answering? The static came in and out. Olivia thought she heard…

"We're not going to hurt you." It was Nash's voice, but it wasn't coming from the radio. Was it? Olivia wasn't sure.

"O-liv-eve-ah." Her name was a hiss. Not the radio, she was sure of it.

The smell of something dank and earthy filled the car. A dark, closed-up place.

"There's so much blood." Jason's voice.

"She's shaking like a leaf." Nash.

Olivia heard sobbing.

"Where's the man who brought you here?" Jason asked.

No, something's wrong. Olivia felt it. *Get out!*

"Stay with her. We've got to—"

"Proximare," a female voice said.

Olivia was frozen, held in an icy vice. *Getoutgetoutgetout.*

"Proximare."

Olivia shook her head violently, even though no one was there to see her.

"I just want to help you. Come back out. I can't see you," Jason said.

"Jesus, is that him?" Nash. "His throat is gone."

"Proximare." The female voice was no longer whimpering. It was insistent.

Jason, don't. Don't go in the dark. Olivia was desperate for him to hear her somehow…

And she knew, beyond any doubt, that her profile had been right.

****

Present day…

Silas predicted it. "Leading our local news tonight, Captain Anthony Zavalla of SAPD's homicide unit took to the steps of police headquarters to alert the public that his officers are actively pursuing a serial killer in the local area. Captain Zavalla warned citizens to use the buddy system in all parks and neighborhoods, and especially when helping strangers. The captain stopped short of asking citizens not to help one another. A composite sketch was promised as part of the press kit but was mysteriously absent. It left this reporter wondering, how can we be alert when we don't even know what the killer looks like? If the police know, why are they not sharing the description with the public? This is Jessica Tate with Channel Four News."

Zavalla snapped off the broadcast. He had heard enough. It had been three hours since the press release, and already the vultures were circling. It had been his last-minute decision to yank the sketch, all because of what Tiffany Kelly told his officers. Now it seemed she was not the only one who had contradicted Dr. Osborne's description.

"First Miss Kelly says her friend, Patricia Griffin, identified the guy on the bike as bald, and now you're telling me the neighborhood kid said the same thing?" he asked his lieutenant. Captain Zavalla shot a glance Silas' way, as if it was somehow his fault.

"Olivia maintains the profile is correct. It's the sketch that's wrong," Barry said. "She pegged the guy from the CCTV footage as one and the same. The guy in the video has hair."

"So, does she believe the kid or not?" the captain asked.

"Alex Montez is a ten-year-old boy repeating what

his friend told him," Barry explained.

"Are you a politician or a police officer?"

"Whoa, Captain," Silas said. Zavalla had taken some intense questions from the press. It had been an exceptionally brutal week; tensions were high, and nerves were frayed. As part of the BAU, Silas was accustomed to working under these conditions, but the other two officers were not. "What the lieutenant is trying to say is that everyone is just repeating what they were told or what they think they saw."

Barry looked at Silas. He was surprised at the unexpected intervention by the Fed, but then realized it was Olivia he was really defending. He felt compelled to do the same. "What is consistent is Olivia's belief in what she saw. She's confident the dog walker is our guy, hair or no hair."

Zavalla let out the long breath he had been holding. Today was the first time the citizens of San Antonio, and more importantly, the city leaders who hired him had seen him front and center in a situation directly affecting their safety. He had wanted it to go smoothly, but it hadn't because he had failed to deliver what he had promised.

"What do you suggest I do about the press, Special Agent Branch?" Zavalla asked. "The public wants to see what this predator looks like. They're waiting for the sketch I promised them." Zavalla didn't give two shits about the press, but they could make or break him. He had family in Texas. He had a kid in college at UTSA. He wanted San Antonio to be his last career move, one that culminated in a fruitful retirement.

"Tell them we've had another witness come forward. It's the truth," Silas reminded him. "Tell them, based on this possible new information, the composite drawing is pending an interview with the witness. It makes you look cautious as well as thorough." Silas didn't point out that had the captain discussed his decision not to release the sketch, he could have spared Zavalla the misstep.

As much as he liked being in control, Silas typically did not like to take center stage. The presence of the FBI usually signaled to the UNSUB that he was important, and Silas hated handing out that kind of satisfaction. He crossed the room and took the seat next to Barry, across from the captain's desk. He leaned forward.

"One last thing," Silas said. "I've worked with Dr. Osborne for years. My best advice is to trust her. Sometimes it just takes the rest of us a little time to catch up with her. Give it twenty-four hours."

Zavalla gave the agent a conciliatory glance before directing his next question to Barry. "In the meantime, what are we doing?"

"I'm waiting to talk to Sergeant Austin about his meeting with the aunt," Barry said.

"I already did. He made it back in time to be in on the press conference," Zavalla informed him. Mark and Silas had flanked him on the steps of police headquarters for the press release and photo op, but as agreed, no introductions were made. "Sergeant Austin believes the aunt is telling the truth when she says she doesn't know where her niece is. He is following up with some other relatives. The aunt thinks Ms. Wallace is in hiding from the husband. Consensus is he's a prick. I told him to continue the random patrols on the house."

"I'm looking to talk to Dr. Wallace, the neighbor's ex-husband, myself. Frank promised me an update on the clothes they pulled out of Wendy Florren's recycle bin. Billy Wallace's phone account is under the neighbor's name. They didn't want Dr. Wallace to know about the phone, and had Teresa Montez set up the account, apparently. Ms. Montez is monitoring the phone via an app. All I can do at this point is hope he uses it."

"Good." Calm, at least for the moment, the captain surveyed the mound of papers on his desk. "I need to make it home tonight before ten, or I won't hear the end of it. Touch base with me the minute there are any updates," he told Barry.

Barry nodded and exited the captain's office on his way to forensics.

Silas caught up with him at the elevator. "A little tip, Lieutenant, just for future reference. Regardless of what you call her in private, anytime we're in there, or anywhere that involves this case, she's *Doctor Osborne*."

The elevator pinged. Barry stepped in and instinctively reached over to hold the door. Silas smiled.

"No, thanks. I'll take the stairs."

Chapter Fifteen

When Olivia arrived home from her shopping trip, Martin's van was parked in front of her house. She had become so accustomed to working from home that being gone most of the week had disrupted her routine. Olivia missed her house, even if it was a mess. She also had a couple of inquisitive emails from her agent regarding the status of the new book, which she consciously ignored. Lenore would catch on soon enough when her production stopped. Before the interruption, Olivia had been churning out a chapter a day. It was hard for her to concentrate on fictional monsters when there was a real one in her life. Normally, fiction was a safe place, a good hiding spot from reality. Real monsters left her no place to hide.

"Two nights in a row, Martin. Please tell me this is good news."

The painter smiled and reached over to take some of her packages. He already had the front door unlocked, and even before she made it inside, Olivia could see the dining room was clear of clutter.

They deposited the bags in the kitchen, and she eagerly followed Martin through the house while he showed her his progress. He seemed almost as relieved as she did. "One of my guys came back and I found a couple of new painters who were looking for some temporary work. They both have other jobs, but one of them was able to stay and help finish this room today."

"Looks like he did a good job," Olivia said, pleased with what she saw. Just seeing the dining room all one color made a difference. Now the only room left to paint downstairs was her temporary one.

"Ramon is coming back tomorrow to touch up the tile in the second bath upstairs. He said the master bath is good to go. We finished the crown molding upstairs and covered the floors in the bedrooms and hallway in preparation for paint tomorrow. Both of my new guys will be back in the morning to paint upstairs. With those rooms done, it'll give you a few days to settle in the master and free up the little bedroom down here. After that, we should be done."

Olivia smiled. "I can finally sleep in my new room." It also meant she could have her new bedroom furniture delivered. She had been using her grandmother's bed since she moved in more than two years ago. "It's been a rough day, Martin. I really needed some good news. Thank you so much."

"I'm glad I could do it." Martin wasn't exactly sure what she did, except a lot of typing on her computer. Something serious must have come up to get her out of the house. "I want to get an early start tomorrow if that's ok, say around eight? I'm going to come over with the guys for a couple of hours since they're new, and because it was the only way I could get Ramon to come back."

"I see," Olivia nodded but knew something else was coming. Martin's smile was gone.

"I just need to let you know something. It's about the new dog."

"Oh, where are the dogs?" Olivia asked. She felt

bad for just now realizing they weren't around, but she had been distracted by thoughts of making her house a home again.

"They're in the back. I left them there. I hope that's okay."

"Sure, you do what you need to do. What about Alvin?"

"The little one was fine with me and Ramon yesterday, but today he wouldn't stop barking. Once the new guys showed up, I thought he was going to bite them."

"I'm so sorry. It's been a rough couple of days for him. He unexpectedly lost his owner. He's probably going through a hard time. Maybe just too many new people all at once. But he was okay with you, though?"

"He was fine with me," Martin assured her. "My wife always says I have a way with dogs and babies. Maybe after being here a couple of days, he feels like it's his home now. He was just letting us know who is boss."

Olivia smiled. "Maybe. Sorry about Alvin. I'll take him and Daisy for a long walk when you get here tomorrow and then figure out what to do with him the rest of the day. Maybe he can just run errands with me." Alvin did great during the car ride the other night so Olivia suspected the dog was used to it. Since he didn't like the leash, Wendy must have carried him. Olivia didn't see that happening so they were going to have to find a compromise.

"Ok, see you in the morning. If everything goes well, we should be out of your hair by early next week."

"Thanks, Martin. I know it hasn't been easy for

you either." Olivia closed the door behind him and took a deep breath. Maybe she was back on track to getting her house in order.

****

Barry never made it to forensics. Instead, he met Mark outside the interview room as requested. "Kurt Wallace, MD," Mark said gesturing to the man on the other side of the glass.

"That was fast."

"Don't thank me. I just put him in a room. He made it easy on both of us. He was looking for his ex-wife. He's supposed to have the kid this weekend and she isn't returning his phone calls. He showed up to file a complaint. Someone in dispatch knew we were looking for him and routed him here. Don't ask me who knew what or how, except that everyone in the building is all over this case," Mark explained. "Now that all of San Antonio knows we're hunting a serial killer it seems everyone wants to be a detective."

Great.

****

Norma didn't really want to stay late on a Friday night fielding calls but the city was paying her overtime and what else did she have to do? She had decided this call would be her last.

"This is Jessica Tate with Channel Four News and I need to speak with Lieutenant Barry Bartholomew."

"He's unavailable at the moment, may I take a message?" Norma asked. She could recite the line in her sleep.

"Well, who can I speak to?"

"Regarding?" Norma asked. She knew who the reporter was. After her critique of Captain Zavalla aired less than an hour ago, everyone in the building knew who she was. Given her statements regarding the department, it wasn't going to take much for the sassy brunette to get on Norma's last nerve.

"I need someone from the San Antonio Police Department to confirm whether or not investigators on the serial murder case are working with forensic psychologist, Dr. Olivia Osborne."

"I'm going to have to take your number and have someone call you back." Norma knew she wasn't going home any time soon.

After the third call from Norma, Barry handed Mark his phone. Barry was in the middle of questioning Dr. Wallace on his whereabouts on Monday afternoon and didn't want to break his rhythm. Mark took the phone and stepped outside the interview room. Before he could return the call, the phone rang again. This time it was from the captain's office.

****

Silas hadn't known how he would feel about seeing her again, but after spending the day with her, she did what she always did to him; she took his breath away. In the past, it had been his own failings that kept her from looking at him the way he wanted her to. The trip to San Antonio was proving to be more difficult to manage than he had expected, and it had little to do with the case. The lieutenant's insertion into the mix was messing with his head. Silas needed to step outside for a breath of fresh air.

He left the building. If he couldn't see Livie, then he wanted nothing more than to be at home in Virginia, but since neither of those things was on the horizon he decided he needed to attend to some basic needs. He was hungry and he might as well enjoy some local cuisine. The captain recommended a little place down the street in the market square called *Mi Corazón*. The brightly lit restaurant reminded Silas of Christmas, even though it was only spring. The food was excellent and according to the menu they were open twenty-four hours a day; which explained the place's popularity with cops. It also meant he could return for breakfast if he wanted. Although he hoped they didn't have the strolling musicians, or *los troubadours*, as the locals called them, at that hour of the morning. Two sips into the margarita and Silas decided that tequila itself might make up for staying in Texas.

The call from the captain torpedoed his plans.

Silas arrived at Zavalla's office just behind Sergeant Austin. Silas brushed past him, his cell phone at his ear, and headed to the farthest corner of the room.

"Yes, I am aware of the First Amendment, Ms. Tate," Silas said. "While I'm a fan of the Constitution, I take Dr. Osborne's safety very seriously. Unless you want the full wrath of the FBI to rain down on you like ash from hell, you will give me twenty-four hours to secure her."

The captain motioned for the sergeant to close the door.

"Jessica Tate and the station's attorney will be here in thirty," Silas said, taking the phone from his ear but keeping it in his hand.

"I've already called our legal counsel," Zavalla assured him. "He's on his way."

"Where's Bartholomew?" Silas asked Mark.

"In an interview room with Dr. Wallace, sir."

"Then tag, you're it. I'm assuming you know

where Dr. Osborne lives. Get over there and secure her," Silas said, not waiting for an answer. "If, in your professional opinion, you aren't satisfied we can protect her there, bring her back here and I'll find a place."

"What's going on? What's happened?" Mark asked.

"Jessica Tate from Channel Four News identified Dr. Osborne from the crime scene the other night. She wants to run with the story that we're using her for this case," Zavalla explained.

"So, the UNSUB will have a name to go with a face. Damn," Mark said. He had noticed Jessica Tate loitering with the other vultures just outside the perimeter of the Wendy Florren crime scene. She must have watched him deliver the case file to Olivia, and asked around until she found out who the woman sitting in the lieutenant's car was.

"And it's not *if*, but *when*. I can only hold them off so long," Silas admitted. "Ms. Tate said she did us a favor by keeping this information to herself for as long as she did. Unbelievable." Silas put the phone to his ear and stalked back to the corner.

Zavalla looked to the sergeant. "Norma should still be out there somewhere. Give her the lieutenant's phone. She can take it back to him. If he knows where you're going and why…" Zavalla didn't finish the sentence.

"Got it."

"Answer the damn phone," Silas cursed with each passing ring.

****

With her master bath complete, Olivia was enjoying her first bath in the new sleigh-shaped porcelain bathtub. She initially considered staying true to the era of the house and going with a claw foot tub, but she found the antique style lacked the roominess she wanted. Ultimately, she decided on a modern, more comfortable style. The black and white octagonal tile downstairs was her only nod to the original style of the home. It had taken some time to get the onyx for the tile, but she thought the result was definitely worth the delay. Gran would approve.

Olivia sipped wine and soaked up the view from the bathroom's picturesque window. She missed the setting sun but relished the remaining streaks left behind as they disappeared into the night. It had been a long week, and at the end of it, she found herself facing the fact she actually had a date. At least, that was how she was taking it. The kiss in the parking lot sealed the deal.

The buzz of the phone interrupted her attempt at peace. Her phone was plugged in on the counter, but to answer it, she would have to get out of the water. She ignored it the first time and listened for the ping of a voicemail instead. When all she got was more ringing, she grabbed a towel and tiptoed over to answer the phone before the ringing stopped.

Silas. "This better be good," she answered. It was just like him to interrupt her perfectly tranquil Friday night. The soak wasn't so much about solace this time as celebration. If he had called to ask her to dinner all of that would be lost. She wasn't ready.

"Where are you?"

"Home."

"Are you secure?" She knew from his tone this had nothing to do with dinner. Olivia immediately switched gears and mentally inventoried all exits and entries. All doors and windows were locked. The three gates to the backyard were bolted, as was the little house in the back. The dogs were inside. "Yes."

"Still know how to handle the gun?"

"Just because I've never had to use it doesn't mean I don't know how," she assured him. The gun was downstairs, loaded, and stored inside the drawer of her bedside table. There was another one in the kitchen. "Why are we having this discussion?"

"Sergeant Austin is on his way to you now."

"Why? What's happened?"

"Jessica Tate."

"That "*News You Need to Know*" woman from Channel Four? I saw her at the crime scene the other night." Olivia remembered wondering if the UNSUB was there as well. Silas had to be playing those same odds.

"It seems she saw you too. Apparently, she's a fan of yours."

"I'm assuming you're not calling to tell me she wants an autograph."

"Wish it were that simple. She's going to go public with your involvement in this case and lead this bastard right to you."

"Could be our best chance to catch him."

"Don't even think about it," he told her.

Chapter Sixteen

"Dr. Osborne was right about him wearing gloves. We checked the pants pocket and found an unused pair of latex gloves inside. No sweat, no DNA inside. Interesting, but still nothing that will give us any more information about who he is," Frank Tobias said. The forensic chief paused a moment before delivering another bit of disappointing news. "Unfortunately, we found no DNA on the knife we recovered, other than Wendy Florren's."

"Did you find the dark hat, the one Dr. Osborne mentioned?" Barry asked.

"Not at first," Frank admitted. "It didn't come in with the jeans and the shirt. I called back and sanitation found it two barrels down. The UNSUB specifically separated it from the other articles."

"Somehow the hat is important," Barry said. Who was this guy? Did he get off on crime shows? Outsmarting the cops? He was doing everything he could to stay one step ahead of them, but they were catching up. Thanks to Olivia.

"We wouldn't have known to look for it, if Dr. Osborne hadn't told us," Frank said, echoing Barry's thoughts.

"So? What did you find in the hat?" Barry asked.

"Hair," Frank said, holding up a strand with a pair of tweezers. "Synthetic. Upon close examination, we see there is no root, no follicle. The texture is similar to fine thread or fishing wire. I suspect it's from a cheap wig. We're verifying, but I'm thinking it's something you can pick up at any party store."

"So, our guy is bald," Barry concluded. It all made sense.

"I think that's a safe assumption at this point, given the evidence," Frank agreed. "The picture is wrong, just like Dr. Osborne said. By my count, she's three for three today."

On his way to the captain's office Barry called the police artist and ordered a sketch of the UNSUB without hair. He was mildly curious as to where Mark had disappeared to, but his thoughts scattered when he passed Jessica Tate coming out of Zavalla's office. SAPD counsel Jim Webber passed him as well, and another guy in a rush to catch up to the reporter.

"Are we consorting with the press now?"

"We have twelve hours," Silas said.

"Twelve hours?" Barry didn't like the vibe he was getting from the room.

"Twelve hours before our UNSUB knows who Olivia is."

****

Within ten minutes of arriving at Olivia's house, Mark was walking the property with her, reviewing the entry and exit points. By the time they made it back around to the front, the two officers assigned for night duty had arrived. They all went inside together.

"Looks nice," Mark commented as she showed them around. He had seen the house in the beginning and had watched the slow, steady building process. She had been living under construction for months. "Happy to finally have the end in sight?" Mark asked.

"God, you have no idea."

"Any work scheduled for tomorrow?" Mark asked the question, but the other two officers were paying attention. They needed to know who to look for.

Olivia nodded. "Martin Mendoza will be here around eight with his tile guy and two painters. He'll be driving a white van. *Double M Remodeling*," she told them.

"Make sure you include that in your report and pass it on to your relief detail," Mark instructed.

"Any firearms on the premises?" one of the officers asked.

"I have a gun in my bedside table. Another in the kitchen, top right-hand drawer."

"Loaded?"

"Not much good if it's not," Olivia told him.

Mark took the officers around to the back and repeated the perimeter review. When they returned to the front, Olivia was sitting on the porch, glass in hand.

"Care to join me for some wine? Or a beer?" she offered as the two officers headed to their car.

"Not if it's the red stuff that tastes like dirt, or the fruity girl beer in the fridge." Mark could tell by the look on her face those were his only options. "Never mind. I have my own in the car. I'll get it."

"Suit yourself." Olivia noticed Mark came back with only one. He had already decided he wasn't staying long.

"The place really does look nice," Mark said after a long swig from the bottle. "I had my doubts a couple of days ago."

"I think it was the prospect of another delay that

gave me the most grief," Olivia admitted. "But it was all for nothing. Martin came through in the end." She owned her obsessive-compulsive nature when it came to her personal space. She found it hard to concentrate when things were out of place. There was already enough going on inside of her head, so disruption in her physical surroundings made it nearly impossible to maintain the status quo.

Mark nodded. Olivia thought he seemed content to let her talk, but she could tell he also had something to say. If it was about what she thought, she didn't know if she was ready to hear it. She was ill-prepared for the barrage of personal issues piling up around her.

"We talked to Dr. Wallace. He came in on his own, but only because he was pissed that his ex-wife wasn't returning his phone calls. He's supposed to have Billy this weekend and instead of asking himself where his ex-wife and kid were or being worried about their safety, he wanted to file a report so he could sue her for contempt of the judge's visitation order or some bullshit like that."

"Wow," was all Olivia could say. Just when she thought she had heard it all there was always a new version of an old story. "Did he fess up to where he was on Monday afternoon instead of seeing his patients?"

"Didn't get to stay for that part," Mark confessed. "Things got a little testy upstairs, but I do know that Agent Branch definitely has your back."

Olivia nodded. "Silas has his good points." She looked over to see Mark had already finished his beer. "Quick visit?"

"You have plans," he said. It was a statement, not a question.

He knows. Olivia noted he was careful to look at the street. She wondered if that was because he couldn't look at her or if he didn't want her to see him.

"I know I've probably asked you this before, but did he know it was coming? Jason, I mean. Did he know he was going to die?"

The question was not at all what she had been prepared for. They hadn't discussed Jason in years.

"I just got to thinking about it while we were going through the offender MO today. At least our guy disables them quickly before the real killing begins. I guess if you have to go, that would be preferable. Is that how my brother went? Was it quick or did he know?"

"It happened fast," she assured him. It wasn't a lie.

By the time she had gotten out of the car and ran into the house, he was already gone. She knew it when she looked into his eyes. And when she saw the blood. "He didn't know."

None of them did...except maybe her. When she told them they were looking for a woman, no one believed her. They wanted easy, explainable answers. They always did. Something that fit their understanding of things.

Mark nodded, satisfied. "You have a good night. Hopefully, he won't be much longer."

Mark suspected it the day before at Wendy Florren's place when she and Barry walked into the house together, and then there had been the discussion about the agent. He was certain there had to be a woman involved when Barry turned down his offer to grab a beer after work, only this time the woman was Livie. It was going to take Mark a little while to process, but he would work through it. She had never been on the same page with him, though that had never stopped him from hoping things might change.

"He really is a good guy. Just lousy at picking women who can deal with him and his crazy life. I think this time he might have gotten it right."

Olivia didn't know what to say.

****

She was in her new bedroom considering decorating options when she saw the splash of headlights outside. She decided this was an added bonus of her new bathroom, having already made the decision not to cover the window. Now she just needed to have the glass treated so no one could see inside, and she could enjoy the long baths she planned to take in her new retreat.

"Wow," Barry said, the one word slipping out when she opened the door.

He could get used to seeing her like this. Her hair, usually swept back and tucked away, hung loose on her shoulders, falling freely in waves. The dress was long and made for comfort. Unlike last night's attire, this one hugged the curves he'd known were there. The crimson she was wearing now was a head-turning departure from her conservative navy and black.

Olivia smiled at the compliment. "Glad to see you, too," she said, letting him pull her in for a quick kiss. "I don't know about you, but I'm starving," she whispered and steered him to the dining room. Dinner was simple but good. Grilled chicken breast with fresh Parmesan cheese, black olives, and fresh spinach paired with bread and wine.

"You didn't have to wait," Barry told her.

"I said I would. I wanted to." They weren't empty

words, and she wasn't saying them just to please him. She waited for no other reason than she wanted to share a meal with him.

"Thank you. That's sweet," he said, and she knew he meant it. They hadn't discussed it, but Olivia believed they shared very similar private lives. Spending so much time alone, it was easy to forget the little pieces of daily life that went missing when there wasn't another person around to share them with. Meals were one of those things. Maybe it was part of the reason Silas wanted to have dinner.

"I have good news," Barry said when they pushed the dishes away. "You were right about the profile and about the picture. Forensics found the dark hat. The fibers inside weren't real hair. It seems our guy could be bald after all, because he was wearing a wig."

Olivia was pleased to hear the news but not surprised. "And Dr. Wallace? Mark said he left before you got to the good part. Like where he was on Monday when he should have been seeing patients."

Barry shook his head. "I thought we were going to come to blows across the table, but he finally gave it up, said he spent the afternoon shacked up with some drug rep. Pulled up the receipt for the hotel on his phone. He's a real class act."

"I'll make sure to not recommend him to anyone I know."

Barry reached over and took her hand in his, linking them together. He liked the way it felt. "So, how are you doing with all of this?"

"I'm assuming you mean the cops camped outside my house?" Olivia asked.

Barry nodded.

"I won't say I'm used to it, but it's not the first time. These are not uncharted waters. Can we shelve the shop talk, just for a bit?"

Barry agreed and followed her up the stairs to sit on the floor in her new bedroom. She had another glass of wine, and he sipped the Canadian whiskey she picked up on impulse at the liquor store. He'd been more amused than surprised she had pegged his favorite.

"The bathtub seems to be a pivotal part of the room," Barry commented.

Olivia had a sliding door installed between her room and the bathroom. It was open, so she could take it all in. "It's my favorite part." Olivia smiled.

"Is there a story behind it?" He wanted to know more about her. Sitting on the floor of her empty bedroom was bringing several things to mind. He was working on using restraint.

"The water soothes me, calms me." Beneath it, she could almost block out the things that went bump in her head.

"Is that purely a solo activity?" he asked, eyeing her bathtub.

"Has been so far," she said, trying to hide a smile.

"So, do you think that thing holds two?"

"According to the advertisement," she said. "The only prudent thing to do would be to try it out, but not tonight."

Barry smiled. "I'm a patient man," he told her, his finger gliding down her jawline just before his lips found their way to hers.

Chapter Seventeen

*Saturday....*A text woke her.

"Hm," Olivia said, reaching for her phone, silencing it before it could ping again. She squinted at the words on the screen.

—*We need to talk*—

Damnit. She still had seven minutes before her alarm.

Barry stirred behind her. He had been nestled like that most of the night. He had wanted to stay, and she wasn't exactly sure she wanted him to leave. But Olivia also knew she wasn't ready for anything more than that. So, they slept, fully clothed, in her grandmother's bed.

"I should go," Barry said, his face buried in her hair. He hoped the scent of vanilla would linger the rest of the day.

"Mm," Olivia responded, settling back into him. The warmth radiating off him was comforting. She just wanted to close her eyes and not think for a little while longer.

"Doing that isn't going to make me want to leave," Barry warned. He pulled her closer, but not for long. Last night had been good. To sleep, truly sleep with someone was a surrender. Barry knew he had never appreciated the meaning of it before. It was also the best sleep he'd had all week.

Olivia sighed contentedly. She savored a few more

minutes wrapped safely in their cocoon— tucked away, monsters forgotten for a moment.

"I have a swim meet to get to," Barry told her. "Alex and Billy's team. I don't expect Billy to show, but Frank is sending one of his guys over with some pictures of bikes for the kid to look at. Once we narrow down a type, I'm going to want you to take a look."

"Okay," Olivia sighed, but still didn't move.

"So, you can do more than purr like a cat in the morning?"

Olivia rolled over on her back so she could look up at him. "Don't tell me you wake up and immediately start talking?"

Barry gazed down at her, enjoying the view. "I can be eloquent if I need to," he said, a flood of other options filling his head.

Olivia smiled up at him. Barry reached across her to thread his fingers through hers.

"Call me about the bike, but I do have to tell you I'm not as good with inanimate objects as I am with people," Olivia said.

"Noted."

"The painters are coming, and I have a date with my dog friends," she said.

"These two?" Barry asked. Alvin was curled up between their feet and Daisy was in the hallway on her bed, her nose barely breaching the doorway.

"Plus, one," Olivia said. "Silas says he and I need to talk."

Barry felt an instant change in his mood. "Atascosa County?" he hoped.

"I'm sure."

"I want to see you again, later," Barry said, kissing

her cheek and trying to dismiss all thoughts of what Agent Branch may want to talk to her about. Barry was quite sure the agent wouldn't have been happy about last night's sleeping arrangements.

****

Olivia sent Barry away with a giant mug of coffee and managed to leave the house just as Martin and another vehicle arrived.

She texted Silas the address of where she was taking the dogs. It was a baseball field open to greyhound owners when the field wasn't in use. They closed the gates, muzzled the dogs, and let them run free in their own friendly competition reminiscent of their racing days. At least that's what they all told themselves. Olivia doubted Daisy missed her days on the track. The brindle female had only been eighteen months old when she was retired. Since retirement came young, it meant Daisy had not been successful. At least she had fewer behavior problems than most greyhounds, and her trainer had done more than prepare her for the track. Olivia knew, because Daisy liked to play fetch. Daisy might not have been a winner on the track, but she was definitely one of the lucky ones. Olivia wondered if she ever missed her other life.

Silas showed up with a bag under his arm. He had to go with her second choice since her favorite bagels were back in Virginia. Silas would have preferred to go back to the place he discovered yesterday, but since he requested the meeting, these were her terms. He came armed with a cappuccino and an almond croissant. He knew they were her favorite.

"The little one yours, too?" Silas asked, joining her on the bleachers.

Alvin was snuggled next to her. When she sat him down after putting Daisy on the field with the other greyhounds, she didn't even have a chance to slip Daisy's leash on him before he was off, circling the field where the greyhounds were. Instinct kicked in and the larger dogs followed in hot pursuit. He probably resembled the little white rabbit they chased in their racing days. Olivia was glad he did so well without the leash. After a few laps around the field, Alvin made his way back to her side without coaxing. He barely stirred when Silas arrived.

"He is now."

Silas nodded and handed over breakfast. "There was an attempted break-in at the morgue last night. I'm thinking it leads back to Roche." He got down to business before she even unwrapped the croissant.

"Patty Griffin's body is still there as well," Olivia said. "But you're probably right." She indulged in a long sip of her cappuccino.

"Meeks called me late last night before the break-in."

"Really? I'm surprised you waited until this morning to share."

Under any other circumstances Silas would have called her, but something about the lieutenant's demeanor last night told Silas he wanted to get out of there, and that was even before they heard from Jessica Tate. He didn't have to wonder why or where Barry wanted to go. Silas confirmed it when he drove by Olivia's house later and saw the lieutenant's car in the driveway. He tried to tell himself the drive-by was for security purposes, but Silas knew it wasn't. If he had the same option as the lieutenant, he would have done the same.

"Figured it could wait," Silas said. "Meeks found some red and white substances on Roche's body yesterday during the post. He said he didn't mention it when we were there because he assumed it had something to do with the land Roche was clearing when he was killed. The forensics lab identified the substance as red pepper and salt."

"An odd find. Hence your call to me," Olivia added. "You know me well. Or maybe I know you."

Silas was looking at her, but she refused to meet his eyes. "Something like that," he confessed.

Olivia pinched off a piece of her croissant and handed him the peace offering. He wanted her attention, but she wasn't ready to give it fully. "I'll have to verify this, but I think it's used to keep a witch from returning to his or her body. Meaning something has been done to drive it out."

"Such as?" Silas wanted to know. He accepted the bite and wanted more.

"Death."

"So, someone was very serious about disposing of Roche. What worries me is they didn't stop there."

"Me too," Olivia agreed.

"The captain wants to talk about Roche around noonish today. He's not happy about his neighboring county bringing their problems to him. Can you talk to Father Dominic before then? We can keep that conversation between the two of us. I'll even spring for lunch."

Olivia held Silas's gaze. Reluctantly, she pulled out her phone and initiated a reunion she had been avoiding. There were a lot of bad memories tied up in

Father Dominic and this part of her life. She wanted to trade those for more like the ones she collected last night.

"You and Dom have a falling out?" Silas asked.

Olivia shook her head. Despite the oversized sunglasses she wore, her face told him something was wrong. Silas was a damn good behavioral analyst. Couple that with the years they had spent working together and there wasn't much she could hide from him.

"No, we didn't have a falling out. Just sometimes I wish I wasn't the go-to girl for 'What do you get when you combine a dead body with red pepper and salt'?"

She sounded wistful. He wondered if the lieutenant had anything to do with it. "Sounds like some messed up trivia game," Silas said and patted her knee. "Sorry, but someone has to do it. I'll include drinks with lunch today if it will make you feel any better," he offered. He had gone back to the restaurant after his drive-by of her house last night and could say with authority that the margaritas were definitely worth another try.

Silas wasn't burdened with the extra baggage she carried, but he knew how she felt when it came to what they encountered on a daily basis. It's why he was quick with the sarcasm. The banter kept what he was really feeling at bay. They had a lonely, solitary job, sometimes full of horror. So many times, he wished he could discuss his day at the office with someone, even share some feelings about what it did to his psyche, but none of it would resemble a normal conversation, so he kept it all in. This banter with her, this familiarity was one small part of what had drawn him to San Antonio.

"Since we're talking about things we don't want to talk about, I guess you and I should have this conversation before I bring it up with the captain today."

Olivia actually sighed this time. "What now? I don't want to know, do I?"

"Probably not," Silas said, "but it's non-negotiable. Frank in Forensics is getting a description of the bike. The lieutenant has the sketch artist working on another drawing showing our UNSUB without hair. I'm assuming you know about that development." Silas tried to sound casual.

"I do," Olivia said, fully aware Silas was cleverly probing what she did last night and disguising it as work.

"It's not a criticism, but any idea how you missed that? Frank said it was a pretty cheap wig."

"He distracted me." Olivia shook her head. "Something about his eyes, even if he was wearing shades. Bringing me in after three victims has thrown me as well. I know I keep saying he changed with Wendy, but what if he changed before that? With Patty Griffin instead?"

"You're creeping me out a little bit," Silas said. He had watched her stare down some nasty perpetrators in her time. For one to unsettle her so much made him uncomfortable. "Is this going to change the profile?"

Olivia shook her head again. "Just for me, and how I perceive him."

"Still not making me feel all fuzzy inside."

"I'll be sure and share later," Olivia promised.

"Okay. Until then, we'll move forward to release all three sketches at once, two of the UNSUB, and one of the bike. We promised to release them to Jessica Tate first. It's how we held her off as long as we did. At the same time, we'll target VIA bus drivers assigned to the routes between our kill zone and your neighborhood, ASAP. If any one of them remotely IDs him, you're out of there and off to somewhere else, somewhere safe."

Olivia knew better than to argue. Besides, Silas had a point. She knew he was thinking Wendy Florren represented a potential threat in the UNSUB's mind and look what he did to her. Patty Griffin's phone still hadn't been found. Neither of the other women's phones were missing, though both of them carried them at the time of the attack. It could be the UNSUB saw Patty on hers, and he was trying to figure out who she was talking to. Fortunately for Tiffany Kelly, her number wasn't local, so even if the UNSUB did try and track her down, he couldn't get to her. And as much as everyone wanted to know the whereabouts of Gail and Billy Wallace, Olivia was glad they weren't home.

"I've got a bad feeling about this guy, and I think there's a pretty good chance he's coming for you. I want those drivers on alert. He obviously doesn't like to take chances, and I intend to catch him before he catches you."

****

Father Dominic texted Olivia back just after Silas left the park. Could he postpone their talk until tomorrow? After leaving the church Dominic gained employment as a social worker with one of the local health plans focused on geriatric patients. After hours Olivia knew he spent his time volunteering, which in reality meant visiting patients who had little or no family. He also did some work with the local boys' club. He knew that a priest whose ties with the Church had been severed was bound to raise some eyebrows for volunteering at a boys' club. The decision to leave his position had been entirely Dominic's and involved no wrongdoing on his part. But he didn't want to have to explain the real reason for his choice any more than he wanted to deal with baseless insinuations.

In the meantime, Olivia reached out to Ana Lutz, who neither answered her phone nor responded to Olivia's text. Probably because she knew it concerned Roche's death. The fact that the Wiccan priestess didn't want to talk about it gave Olivia some answers. None of them good.

Olivia returned to the house to see Martin's van gone, but the other vehicle was still there. She decided not to go in, just in case Alvin had another barking attack. She let the dogs in the backyard instead, unloading her passengers before her trip to an official government building that wasn't exactly accommodating for canines. The dogs had free range in the large yard and even their own retreat. The structure was smaller than a garage but larger than a shed. It was where she did her laundry prior to the expansion. Since then, she had upgraded the door to include a doggy entrance to provide shelter from the elements. Olivia wasn't sure if she was going to keep the structure or not. It was one heck of a doghouse, but she needed a garage instead of just a carport. Yet another item on her home to-do list.

By the time Olivia got downtown it was almost noon, so she wouldn't have had much time with Father Dominic anyway. Dr. Meeks and Silas were waiting for her in the captain's office along with the sheriff of Atascosa County.

"Care to enlighten me on what we're dealing with here, and why the hell I need to get this Texas Ranger on the phone?" Zavalla asked, doing little to mask his obvious annoyance with the situation. It didn't matter that the attempted break-in of the Bexar County morgue had been unsuccessful. What mattered was the timing. That it came the day after the announcement there was a serial killer on the loose didn't exactly bolster public opinion.

"Let me start by saying you're not going to like it," Silas said.

Chapter Eighteen

"This has something to do with the pentagram, doesn't it?" Meeks asked.

"Pentagram?" Zavalla repeated. This was the first he had heard of it. Zavalla cast a glance toward Atascosa County Sheriff Jim Tennent, who expertly avoided eye contact. "Jesus," Zavalla said when it was clear both the sheriff and the medical examiner had chosen not to inform him.

Local politics was one of Silas's biggest pet peeves about coming onto other people's turf. Even in the best working environments, there was usually some tension seething just below the surface, and he never knew when he was going to step in it. He didn't have time to deal with a turf war. They could pick up the pieces when he and his team left, but right now he needed them all to play nice.

"Since Dr. Osborne is the expert on this subject. I'm going to let her explain," Silas said, turning to Olivia.

Olivia looked at the three men seated across from her, which included a police captain, a medical examiner, and a county sheriff who was even wearing an actual cowboy hat. Dialed in on the captain's speakerphone was gravelly-voiced lawman Herschel Gaines, one of the Texas Rangers covering Atascosa County. Though Olivia didn't have a visual, in her mind's eye he looked like Sam Elliot and chain-smoked for the duration of the call. The sheriff didn't want to look at her or hear what she had to say. Not because he didn't believe her, but maybe because on some level he did. The police captain was tired and irritated, and this was just one more item stacked on the growing pile of shit rolling downhill from the FBI to him. The medical examiner was genuinely curious. He was a man of science but had been around long enough and seen enough in his career to know some situations defied the natural order of things.

"If you will just let me take you through what we know, then I'm open to questions," Olivia said.

Silas liked her use of the word "we." He liked to think she was circling the Bureau wagons, but she wasn't really a part of the Bureau, and there was no "we." Silas had heard what was coming before, or some variation of it. It was for the non-believers and the fence sitters, as he liked to call them. They wouldn't willingly talk about what she was about to discuss, but they would know that there were things they didn't really want to understand. There was another world that existed beyond them whether they accepted it or not. They would trust what she told them but leave it to her to navigate that shadow world. They would follow her lead because without her they would be left to face it on their own, and that was a far more frightening prospect.

"The manner in which Mr. Roche was killed is suggestive of a ritualistic killing. Starting with the cut to the throat. This was a bloodletting, an offered sacrifice." She could see Captain Zavalla had a question already, but he closed his mouth, doing as she had requested, and held it.

"Impaling Mr. Roche to the ground with the pitchfork demonstrates that the perpetrators believed Mr. Roche to be a witch. It was a message. The sprinkling of red pepper and salt on his skin was another. According to some literature, anointing the skin in such a way makes it too painful for a witch to return to their earthly body. I think this move was done as insurance. A fail-safe in case the extent of Mr. Roche's abilities exceeded their initial assessment.

"You were correct to recognize the pentagram didn't look right," Olivia said, speaking directly to Dr. Meeks. She gave credit where credit was due because she wanted those she worked with to trust their gut no matter what. Trusting one's own instincts saved lives. "The pentagram carved into Mr. Roche's shoulder isn't your traditional pentagram."

"One of them new-fangled pentagrams, was it?" the Ranger chimed in. "What constitutes 'untraditional' in this context, ma'am? Help me out."

"That's not quite what I meant, Ranger Gaines. This pentagram was drawn inverted, with one point down. This signifies evil in its purest form. The antemortem carving of the symbol was meant to send another message, one beyond this realm of existence," she clarified.

"Excuse me? No offense, ma'am, but this sounds like a load of horseshit. Next you're gonna be telling me we need to get a shaman out here," Ranger Gaines said.

"Your skepticism is well founded, Ranger. I get that," Olivia countered. "What we're dealing with here is definitely fringe stuff. The attempted break-in was one last attempt to get to Mr. Roche. Incineration is the only way to make sure the witch is completely obliterated."

The three men in the room were speechless. Ranger Gaines was not.

"Folks, now y'all look here. I've seen some screwed up stuff, Santeria and whatnot. These goddamn cartels do some pretty horrendous shit to each other, so I'm not sure why we're leaping to this witchcraft business. That said, I'll go along for the ride and withhold judgment as best I can, but you'll forgive this old Ranger his incredulity for now, will you?"

"Absolutely, Ranger Gaines," Olivia said, warmed by both the frankness and the long Texas drawl in the faceless man's voice.

Silas smiled. He enjoyed watching them squirm. "Questions?"

"You said the killers were offering a sacrifice. A sacrifice to whom?" Captain Zavalla spoke first. "Or what?"

"It would depend on their motivation. Did they kill Roche to stop him and his influence, or to take his power?" Olivia's eyes crossed to the sheriff, but he continued to avoid hers. "The manner of the killing sends a message of power across this world and into the other." There was no follow-up question to her response.

"You mentioned killers, plural, before," Meeks pointed out. "You're sticking with that?"

"Given the amount of diligence put into this murder and the fail-safes, no one person would have dared approach Roche alone. Even if the persons involved don't believe any of the mumbo jumbo I just laid out for you; they still recognized Roche was a powerful enough player in something that they didn't want to approach him alone."

" 'Mumbo jumbo' is a good word for it," Gaines said.

Zavalla looked to Sheriff Tennent, but he didn't appear to have a question. "You mentioned another message. One that had to do with carving the pentagram prior to death versus after. What was the other message?" The captain wanted to know, or at least thought he did. The longer he listened to the question in his head the more he wished he never asked it.

"Friedrich Nietzsche said, 'When you gaze into an abyss, the abyss also gazes into you.' By acknowledging Roche's evil, his killers either drew the pentagram to say, 'We're done here. I have killed the witch' or 'I see you and now you see me.' Let's hope it was the first message."

"And if it's not the first message?" Meeks was the only one who dared to ask.

"Then Roche won't be the last murder." Olivia looked to the man seated next to the captain. "Sheriff, I recommend you share everything you have on what's been going on in your little corner of the world. I just laid out the worst possible scenario. Let's pray it's not that."

"If you choose not to take Dr. Osborne's suggestion, or if you decline to be forthcoming with Ranger Gaines," Silas said, wanting to make sure the sheriff got the point, "things won't go well for you. You can ask Captain Zavalla. He'll tell you. You do not want me in your county."

"Sheriff, you and I are gonna get along just fine. I know you agree," the Ranger said. "Peas and carrots,

Sheriff. Peas and carrots. Now, if y'all don't mind, I'm going to hop off this phone and go load up my Colt with some silver bullets. Y'all take care now, y'hear?" A click on the line confirmed the Ranger's departure.

They took a break between the Atascosa County business and the local UNSUB. Tennent asked for a moment alone with Zavalla and Meeks headed back to whatever he did on Saturdays when he wasn't working. Silas and Olivia walked to the vending machines where Silas sprang for a real soda for both of them.

"You scared the shit out of me," Silas said. "Please tell me you played it up for the locals."

"I was completely honest with them on what it could mean, but I know nothing about the reality of it," she admitted. "I can't see Father Dominic until tomorrow, and Ana isn't responding. Someone out there knows their *other worldly* stuff, as you call it. That alone is enough to make me uneasy. Whatever it is, the murder was overkill. I don't like it because when you start at the top, the only place left to go is over."

"Do you ever wish you didn't know this stuff?" Silas asked.

"All the time."

"The Rangers think drugs are involved," Silas said. "That's why their focus is in Atascosa and not Bexar County."

"They're probably right," Olivia said. "Drugs mean money. Money motivates greed. Greed leads to murder."

Five minutes later they were back in the captain's office. The sheriff and the medical examiner had been replaced by the head of forensics and the lieutenant, the latter of whom Olivia noted must have dashed home after leaving her house because he had changed his shirt and shaved.

Frank handed Olivia a picture. "Popular Road Bike. The kid was able to give us enough details to identify it. It might not be this exact model but should be similar to the UNSUB's."

Olivia stared at the image before her. In her mind, she saw the bike leaning against the fence, under the honeysuckle. She handed the picture back to Frank.

"All I can confirm is that the bike was dark in color and blended in with the surroundings, which might have been why Billy decided to hide it there. He didn't want his mother to know he still had it, and next to Wendy's house was the best hiding place he could come up with on short notice. If this picture fits the description Alex gave you, then I'll have to say yes. I never saw the bike up close. Alex did. And as I explained to Lieutenant Bartholomew, I'm not as good with inanimate objects."

"We got our hands on a pair of the cycling shoes. They do sound like tap shoes when you walk in them. We're pretty confident the UNSUB was wearing this type of shoe."

"He was," Olivia assured him. She avoided eye contact with Barry while she said it. She had been avoiding him since her first glance. She recognized the fact she felt uncomfortable with him and Silas in the same room. She hadn't noticed it so much the day before. She had been focused on the case. But last night spent with Barry, and her alone time with Silas this morning begged her attention.

"How much does a bike like this cost?" Olivia asked. She needed to push whatever personal feelings she was having aside.

"Somewhere in the mid four-hundred- to low six-hundred-dollar range," Frank said.

Olivia nodded. "He could afford it. If he saved up, which I'm sure he did. He had no other choice."

Frank continued his presentation. "According to victim number three, he fell off the bike. If he left it behind, there's a good possibility it might have been damaged."

Barry added, "If it was, maybe that's why he deviated from his plan and took the victim's car. There're a couple of bike shops, one on Wetmore and one on Thousand Oaks. We'll need to check them out."

"Good work," Zavalla said. He would take good news anywhere he could get it at this point. "We'll add the bike picture to the press release."

Barry handed Zavalla another picture. "The artist's rendering of the UNSUB without hair."

Zavalla gave it a quick glance, glad to move forward. "Run with it," he said.

Barry nodded. "I also think we should have photos of the bike to show to VIA bus drivers assigned to the route between Dr. Osborne's house and the kill zone. I want them to report any passenger that loads their bike on the bus."

Silas looked to Olivia, and she gave a slight shake of her head letting him know she had not shared their conversation with Barry. She wouldn't. Something else was up.

"Lieutenant Bartholomew, please tell me why I should send patrol officers out on a Saturday to question VIA bus drivers that are outside our kill zone." No matter what the situation, manpower, and money were always factors in Zavalla's decision-making.

"This UNSUB might not have picked his victims in the beginning, but he specifically targeted Wendy Florren because he thought she was the one who found his bike." Barry looked only at Olivia. "I went back to the notes I took on your statement. The suspect point-blank said he thought you were there about the murder. You knew he didn't believe you when you said you were house hunting. Once he knows who you are, he'll come for you."

Silas leaned forward in his chair, a curious questioning look on his face.

"All that sounds plausible, Lieutenant, but didn't Dr. Osborne herself tell us this guy doesn't stalk?" Zavalla looked at Barry and then to Olivia.

"Let me clarify," Olivia rushed to say. "He didn't stalk his first three victims, but he deviated with Wendy Florren. She was different."

"The UNSUB is different now too, apparently. What you'd call an escalation, I believe," Zavalla said.

"I think you need to explain that statement," Silas said before Olivia could.

"Tiffany Kelly called me just before I walked in here. She woke up to a voicemail that came from Patricia Griffin's cell phone," Barry said.

"Hold up," Silas interrupted. "This is the phone you said had not been recovered?" He wanted to be perfectly clear before he digested the information the lieutenant was about to share.

"Correct," Barry said, his eyes finally sliding Silas's way. He was trying to stay one step ahead of the agent.

No matter what Olivia said, Barry felt it was a competition between the two of them.

"What was the message?" Olivia asked.

"Patty says hello from Hell."

Chapter Nineteen

For a moment, everything went quiet, like when she laid her head back in the bath and the water rushed into her ears and silenced the world. But she couldn't go to that place. There was yelling instead. It was what brought her back.

It was Silas's voice she heard first. He was on his feet, towering over her. "So help me God, you better be telling the truth when you say you just took that call."

Olivia had seen Silas angry before, but not like this. He was a whirlwind of rage. Barry was on his feet before Silas finished, and the two stood inches apart. Testosterone flooded the room, making her feel very small, caught in the middle of these two equally strong men.

"Of course, I just got the call. Why would I keep it from you?" Barry snapped.

"You should have led the conversation with that information," Silas bellowed.

"Silas," Olivia said. She reached out for his arm, but he met her halfway. He gave her fingers a squeeze and then let them go.

"Agent Branch," Zavalla snapped. "You may be the agent in charge, but I am still captain of this unit. This is my office, and this man is a lieutenant under my command. Stand down, now." The captain said it all from the comfort of his chair with no need to stand. The tone of his voice said it all.

Silas looked at Zavalla. He might be volatile, but Silas knew when to follow orders. Olivia noted a slight loosening of his shoulders. Silas took a breath and let it out slowly.

"We still would have needed to review the bike description before we released it to the media or the VIA bus drivers. Nothing would have happened any faster," Zavalla said slowly.

"This guy doesn't like loose ends. Dr. Osborne could be considered a loose end," Silas replied, his words measured and purposeful. Controlled. "The fact this guy is escalating puts her in danger. Olivia's with me until you talk to those VIA bus drivers. I want to know what you know the minute you know it, Lieutenant Bartholomew," Silas said, never taking his eyes off Barry. "Don't hold back on me again."

"You got it, Agent Branch," Barry assured him. He hadn't relaxed his posture at all. At least not that Olivia could see.

Silas looked to Olivia, and she silently followed him out the door.

Barry watched them go. The agent had been ready to take him on, but Olivia had backed him down. "Shut the door, Lieutenant," Zavalla said once the others had cleared out of his office. "And take a seat."

Barry pushed down the silent rage inside of him and did as he was told. He had done it for the first fifteen years of his life, so it was nothing more than muscle memory. He knew how to play the part.

"I'm only going to say this once. I'm not sure what that was all about, and while I can appreciate the implications of the case, I think it had more to the do with the good doctor than the investigation."

Barry looked at him.

"I don't want to know details. I just need you to handle it. Somewhere outside of my office, by doing something that does not prompt a call from whomever Agent Branch calls boss. No matter how big of an asshole he is, he is very well respected within the FBI. You do not want to tangle with him."

"Yes, I understand. I would like to be dismissed, if there is nothing else, sir. I would very much like to go talk to some bus drivers," Barry requested.

"There is one more thing. I suppose now is as good a time as any. I need to let you know Sergeant Austin has asked to be reassigned." Zavalla knew Mark's request also had to do with Dr. Osborne, but maybe in a different way.

At least he hoped so. Besides, the sergeant was proving himself. Maybe he was ready to take a step forward.

"They're forming a task force in Atascosa County, and Mark will be helping out over there. It seems the Rangers think they may have a bit of a drug problem."

****

"What the hell was that?" Olivia asked once they were alone in the elevator. She couldn't wait until they were outside.

Silas looked over at her. The elevator ride wasn't long enough to explain the list of problems he had with the lieutenant, the majority of them she wouldn't want to hear because they had nothing to do with this case. The doors opened on the street level, and Silas got out. He held his hand out to her and she ignored it.

"Where are we going? I parked in the garage,"

Olivia told him.

"I promised you lunch. And drinks. They are both down the street, and I very much want you to come with me."

Olivia stepped out and followed him. They were a block away before she tried again. "You need to talk to me."

"Right now, I need a drink." Two more blocks and they arrived at *Mi Corazón*. The hostess greeted Silas as if he was a long-lost friend. But that was Silas. He never met a stranger. He had been popular his whole life. Olivia wasn't surprised he had already made friends with the locals.

They were seated at a table on the market square side. Silas immediately ordered margaritas on the rocks. Easy on the salt for Olivia. He didn't even have to ask.

"I don't like it that the lieutenant is such a cowboy," Silas said once they were alone.

"This is Texas. Everyone's a cowboy," Olivia said.

"You know what I mean."

"I don't actually. How, specifically, is Lieutenant Bartholomew a cowboy?"

"He has not been forthcoming on this case since the beginning."

"Silas, this was his case until you showed up," Olivia reminded him.

"Until *we* showed up," Silas corrected her.

"The lieutenant has been working this case from the beginning. He's not accustomed to being told what to do," Olivia said.

"Are you defending him?" Silas wanted to know.

Olivia's eyes narrowed. She wasn't used to this type of behavior from Silas. Seizing control, yes.

Jealousy, no.

Silas turned away to look at the waitress delivering their drinks. Maybe she had sensed they needed them sooner rather than later. They both shooed her away when she asked what they wanted to eat.

"That's the second time you've asked me that. The answer now is the same as it was the first time. No, he doesn't need me to protect him, but he does need you to let him do his job. They all do. This is San Antonio, Texas, not some dirty little place in Florida."

Silas's eyes narrowed at the mention of Florida, but now was not the time. "He might not be concerned for his own safety, but I sure as hell won't let him jeopardize yours."

"Silas, didn't you hear the captain? Whether Barry told us about the phone call at the beginning or the end, it changes nothing. You cannot control everything. All you did in there was cause a scene."

Or mark your territory, Olivia couldn't help but think. She kept the thought to herself, but the look she gave Silas told him she knew what he was doing.

"I got the lieutenant's attention," he said.

"And you're quite happy with yourself about that."

Silas raised his glass to Olivia. "As a matter of fact, I am," he agreed and took a drink. He watched her, but she didn't do the same. "Just taste it, please. It's good."

"I'll taste if you're ready to listen." She had his attention. Maybe it was the tone of her voice or the look on her face, but Silas knew she had just changed the subject. "I know the UNSUB has Patty Griffin's phone and is the one who made the call. But how does he know she goes by Patty?"

Silas shook his head. She had a point. He was

pretty sure he wasn't going to like where this was going. "He doesn't talk to his victims," he said.

"You're right. He doesn't. That's not what they're for." Olivia finally took a sip of her drink. "I've heard the message before," she told him and took another drink. Not a sip this time. "The message wasn't from the UNSUB. He's just an intermediary."

Silas's bravado evaporated.

"I'm going to need more than this one drink. Maybe three or five."

****

Olivia didn't make it to five drinks. Silas stopped her at two. He tried to get her to walk the market with him and sober up, but it wasn't happening. She never explained the story, just kept dousing it with tequila. Whatever it was had spooked her was like nothing he had ever seen before, and he was powerless to stop her from unraveling. When she started crying, he knew it was time to go.

Silas got her back to the parking garage and poured her into the car. He was glad she was asleep. That way he didn't have to explain how he knew how to get to her house. He could check out the surveillance for himself. And taking Olivia to her house was safer than taking her to his hotel room. She was going to need comfort when she woke up.

Olivia was still snoozing in the seat when they got there. He waited while the truck pulled out of the driveway. She had said something about painters. Luckily, it looked like they were done for the day. Silas unlocked the front door, carried her inside, and deposited her on her bed. It was unmade. He didn't want to know if she'd been the only one in it when she woke up this morning. He went to the fridge and got her a bottle of water. He noted there were only dinner dishes in her sink. *That was a good sign, right?* Hopefully, it meant the lieutenant hadn't been around for breakfast.

Silas took the water and sat it next to the bed. She was going to need it when she woke up. He was on his way back to the front door when he saw the officer on the porch. Silas opened the door before he could knock. He didn't want to wake Olivia. They both had their IDs in hand.

"Lieutenant Bartholomew wanted me to check on Dr. Osborne," the patrolman said. He tried not to show it, but he felt a little intimidated as the agent sized him up.

"How do you know the lieutenant, Officer Harris?" Silas asked. The kid barely looked old enough to be out of the academy. They kept getting younger every year.

"I was the one who found Ms. Griffin's car in the park. The lieutenant said he would remember me, and he was true to his word."

"Good job," Silas said. "You can tell Lieutenant Bartholomew I'm here with Dr. Osborne. But first, if you don't mind stepping inside while I go take a look around?"

"Of course, sir."

Officer Harris had readily accepted the extra duty. Silas figured he needed the overtime pay.

Silas took a walk around the block and into the alley. He didn't like what he saw. He didn't like the accessibility of the alleyway, the large amount of yard, or the layout of the street. Silas liked the ladder resting against her house in the back even less. It was a tall expandable one. Why would the painters leave it behind? It looked expensive. The house looked almost done. He went to the shed in the back. It was unlocked. He stowed the ladder inside and locked the door. At least the gate beside the driveway was locked. He went out through it, making sure to lock it behind him. He was pleased to find it secure from the other side. Back in front of the house, Silas took a peek at the other side, the one without the driveway.

He was glad he did. He found a third entry to the backyard. He wouldn't have noticed it except the sun was coming through the trees, and there was a gleam off the gate. It was ornate, with vines snaking across the top. It was also unlocked.

Silas heard the front door open. He locked the gate and went back around. Officer Harris was on the porch. Silas nodded at him, busy taking inventory of what he found. He hoped Olivia woke up soon. He didn't like it, but it might be nothing. He had no way of knowing.

"I didn't want to wake the doctor, but I had to come out and ask how you kept the little dog from barking. He's been yapping a lot today."

"What?" Silas asked.

"The dog, the little white one."

The dogs weren't in the yard or the house. They were gone. Silas's phone rang.

"I'm coming to you."

Barry hung up before Silas could respond.

Chapter Twenty

"I found this one running down Austin Highway," Officer Brad Harris told Silas as he led the greyhound up the steps of the house. Luckily, she headed for home when he called her name because there was no way he could have caught up with her otherwise. The little white schnauzer fell in line behind her.

Silas was relieved. Olivia's day had been bad enough already. He didn't want to add to it by telling her the dogs were missing.

"Where do you want them?" the officer asked.

"Leave them in the house for now," Silas said. Daisy immediately went to her bed, and Alvin headed for Olivia's room.

"Were the gates secure when you came on duty this morning?" Silas wanted to know.

"Yes, sir. I checked them myself. Did you find one unlocked?"

"The one on this side," Silas said referring to the one next to the kitchen. The old gate he had spotted at the end. Had the intent been to get rid of the dogs?

"Painters, maybe?" Officer Harris offered.

Silas shook his head. "Doesn't make sense." The painter's ladder was leaning against the house under what was Olivia's new bedroom suite. It was on the other side of the house from the unlocked gate. If the painters did it by accident, the gate by the driveway is the one that should have been unlocked. Instead, it was the gate that was easy to miss, also the one they didn't appear to be using. Leaving the gate unlocked was intentional. Silas was sure of it. He really needed to talk to Olivia.

"No one's been here except the painters, sir," Brad told him.

"Do me a favor, officer, get your computer and find out everything you can about this Martin Mendoza. He's the one doing the remodeling."

"Yes, sir. I'll let you know as soon as I find something," Officer Harris said and headed for the car.

"Where is Dr. Osborne?" Barry asked, passing the young officer on his way in the door.

"Sleeping," Silas told him from the porch.

"Sleeping? It's the middle of the afternoon," Barry said, obviously waiting for Silas to explain.

Silas looked back at the house. He had to close the door to keep the dogs inside, but he didn't want Olivia to wake up and think she was alone. "Come inside but keep your voice down. She's had a rough day. She had a few too many margaritas."

"What?" They went drinking after what happened in the captain's office?

"We have bigger problems than Olivia day drinking," Silas said.

"We do," Barry confirmed.

Silas looked at him.

"VIA bus driver Guillermo Lopez identified our UNSUB as a passenger on his bus route to this neighborhood two nights ago."

Silas began to pace. "Two nights ago? That doesn't make any sense. How could our guy have known?"

Barry showed his agreement with a shake of his head. He thought the same thing.

"Any other positive IDs?" Silas wanted to know.

"Not so far. Mr. Lopez didn't work last night. We're trying to track down the driver who worked his route."

"How could the UNSUB have known where to find her?"

"Olivia mentioned she wondered if the UNSUB was outside Wendy Florren's house the night of the murder," Barry offered.

"Has anyone reviewed the media footage from that night?" Silas asked.

"There wasn't a lot," Barry said. "Most of it was too dark. The shots we did get, the camera was focused on the reporter only."

Silas pulled out his phone and punched in a number. "Ms. Tate, at this time, I'm going to need you to turn over all of your footage from the Wendy Florren crime scene to the SAPD. This request will fall under the same binding agreement we made last night. This is not arbitrary and definitely not up for discussion. I'll be at police headquarters within the hour. Don't argue and don't keep me waiting. Bring the lawyer if you think you need to."

Barry watched Silas, hands on his hips. Did the FBI make him like this? Probably not. He had been this way his whole life. Silas Branch was used to getting what he wanted when he wanted it. "You want to tell me why Olivia was day drinking?" Barry asked.

"I told you she's having a rough day," Silas said.

Barry continued to stare him down.

"She says she's heard the message before," Silas

revealed. "The one the UNSUB left on Tiffany Kelly's phone."

The statement made Barry pause. "How is that even possible?"

"Do you have any clue what Olivia can do?" Silas asked.

"I'm starting to get an idea."

Silas shook his head. "She knows things. Other worldly things I call them."

"She soaks up residual energy," Barry said. He remembered her saying something like that when he brought her to the first crime scene. "I watched her profile my crime scene like it was a person."

Silas shook his head. "Yes. She can do all those things and more. She *feels* things, *sees* things the rest of us can't."

Barry thought back to that moment on Wendy Florren's porch. Olivia knew what was waiting for them on the other side of the door. She saw what came before.

"She can see to the other side," Silas added.

"The other side of…" Barry said but had to stop himself.

Silas said it for him instead. "The other side of here."

The night he pulled her out of Patricia Griffin's car. She was scared. She couldn't breathe. She was running from something. "That doesn't sound safe."

Silently Silas agreed. He thought back to the Nietzsche quote she used earlier in the day. "Spend too much time looking on the other side, and something on the other side is bound to see you. Kind of like a two-way mirror. She's had this kind of ability all her life. I think by now there are things that follow her around."

Barry didn't want to know the definition of *things*. "I heard some of the guys she puts away contact her later. Before they kill themselves."

Silas nodded. "Yes. They do."

"She said it was because she understood them and that they were abandoned. Abandon by who?" Barry asked.

"More like *what* than who. Olivia will tell you they were abandon by the force that used them to do the things that landed them in jail in the first place," Silas explained. "Once the killing is done and they're locked away, they're no longer useful. If they're not too far gone, they usually return to their previous state."

"So, you're going to have me believe they had no free will?" It sounded like a defense attorney's wet dream. A great case for insanity.

"Has she told you about the seven second theory?" Silas asked.

"She's mentioned it. I read some of what she's written, but I'm not well versed."

"Okay, this is the very watered-down version. There are multiple studies on human decision making. Some show that up to seven seconds before we make a decision there is brain activity—activity not initiated by the individual—at least not in the part of the brain responsible for conscious thought. It is Oliva's contention and others, that during that seven second window, there is the opportunity for something else to slip inside and take control."

Barry stood there, quietly taking in what Silas had just said. Silas could see him working it out in his head. "Mind control of some kind?"

Silas shook his head. "Olivia is an old school Catholic. She's more organic than that. She'll tell you it's a possession."

"She discovered this while working as a nurse? Are we talking about demons?"

"She worked geriatrics. The Alzheimer's units. If you read clinical assessments of some Alzheimer's patients as well as schizophrenics the symptoms, they display are eerily similar to demonic possession. It was the basis of her dissertation."

"So, the demon leaves the killer after it's done with them? You said the perps returned to their previous state. What does that mean?"

"For the most part these offenders were never the best society had to offer, but in some cases, they did undergo a significant role reversal. You've heard the news reports where the neighbors are interviewed, and say, 'Oh we just can't believe he did something like this. There were no signs. He's one of the nicest people you'd ever want to meet,' " Silas explained.

"And some demon selected them. Why? Because they were good?" Barry asked.

"Or because they were weak. Or, maybe, simply because they could. Who knows?"

"And this darkness follows Olivia? Why?"

"She'll tell you it's because they want attention. They want someone to notice them, and she can. She's a damn beacon in the night to them."

Barry didn't even know what to say. They heard Olivia leave her room. She headed for the bathroom, slamming the door behind her. The sound of running water came next.

"What does Mark's brother have to do with this?

Anything? Nothing at all?" Barry asked quickly. Jason's death had to be connected.

"Best I know, whatever happened when he was murdered validated her theory," Silas said. "My guess is she faced her first demon."

Olivia came in smelling like toothpaste. Her face was pale, but the color was beginning to creep back into her cheeks. "Don't ever let me drink tequila again," she said to Silas before sinking down on the couch. Alvin followed her, and she pulled him into her lap.

"We need to talk," Silas said before Barry could.

"Me, first," Olivia told him. "You both should sit down."

The two men looked at each other and each took the seat closest to them. Barry in the chair beside the couch and Silas next to Olivia.

"The message our UNSUB left on Tiffany Kelly's phone is something I've heard before. Ten years ago, Jason, Mark's brother, was killed by someone who had already ripped out the throats of four other people. I was at her bedside when she died. Her last words were 'Jason says hello from Hell'. I don't know about the two of you, but that sounds eerily similar to what we heard today."

Olivia watched them carefully for their reactions. Barry remained his stoic self. Silas reached over and squeezed her shoulder. Now at least he knew why she had been crying, and why she needed the tequila.

"I'm reworking the profile because I think our UNSUB stopped being on his own when he killed Patty Griffin. He won't stop until we stop him." Olivia got the look in her eye that was guaranteed to make Silas's skin crawl. "I think it's why I was confused in the beginning when I said he was older. It's the other influence that's older. And vengeful."

"By other influence, I'm assuming you don't mean a partner. At least not the conventional kind," Silas surmised.

Olivia just looked at him. "What do you think?"

"That you're right. As always about these things," Silas admitted.

"You're the one that said they follow me," Olivia acknowledged. She didn't look happy at the admission. "You told me not to discount it, and I did because I didn't want it to be so."

Despite what he and the agent had just discussed, Barry was still struggling to comprehend it all. Hearing it from Olivia made it real. He had to get up and move. Watching and listening to them wasn't helping.

"For once I'm truly sorry I was right," Silas told her with another squeeze to the shoulder. "Do what you've got to do, but you're going to do it from somewhere other than here."

"Why?" Olivia asked.

"What do you keep locked outside the house?" Silas asked.

"All three gates to the backyard and the little house," she answered automatically.

"The dog door is pretty big," Silas said looking at the greyhound who was on her bed surrounded by every stuffed toy she owned. "So, I'm guessing you left that open."

"The dog door doesn't work if it's not open," Olivia told him.

"When I got here today the gate by the kitchen and the door to the little house were unlocked. Our UNSUB is on the smaller side. He could have crawled through the dog door and unlocked the door to the little house. A ladder was conveniently left leaning against the house under the windows of your new upstairs addition. The bedroom window, just above where the ladder was stowed was conveniently left unlocked, but not open. The UNSUB has been here, and I think he was giving himself plenty of options for when he returned."

"How could he know where I live?" Olivia protested. She was so close to getting her house back that she didn't want to leave it.

"Unclear," Barry finally spoke, turning back around to rejoin them. "But I talked to a VIA bus driver this afternoon who confirms he dropped our UNSUB off in this neighborhood as recently as two nights ago."

"And someone wanted to get rid of the dogs. They were gone when I got here. I'm sure it was our guy," Silas added. "He's the only one with a reason."

Olivia gave Alvin a squeeze.

"The young kid out there, Officer Baby Face, found them and brought them back. None of this makes this place safe. You cannot stay here." Silas's tone told her it wasn't up for discussion.

"What am I supposed to do with the dogs?" Olivia asked. "I'm not leaving them here. It's not safe for them either."

Barry and Silas looked at each other. They knew she was right. Hurting one or both of the dogs would hurt her. "Mark," Barry suggested looking for an immediate solution. Olivia was becoming more distraught the longer she had to think about it. "He has a house and a yard." Barry pulled the phone out of his pocket and stepped away.

"If all this happened today with the dogs then…" Olivia stopped. "Martin."

"I have the kid outside checking him out," Silas assured her.

"He hired two new painters to finish today." She felt nauseated at the thought of this intrusion into her home. Her refuge.

"Go pack some things," Silas suggested quickly. He wanted to keep her moving. Keep her from thinking. "Jessica Tate is bringing her video from the other night to police headquarters. Maybe you can pick out the UNSUB from some of the footage. Right now, that is the only way I can think of how he would find out who you are. The girl has a big mouth, loves the sound of her own voice, and I'm sure loves looking at herself on tape."

Olivia looked at him. Silas was afraid she was going to tear up again. He placed his hands on both her shoulders and looked into her eyes. "It won't be for long. You and I both know he'll escalate quickly from this point."

"If he thinks I'm gone, he could lash out somewhere else, or at someone else. Keeping me here—"

"Is not going to happen," Silas said, his tone firm. "I won't risk you."

Olivia had to walk away from the confession. She carried Alvin with her to the bedroom.

Inside the downstairs bathroom, the water turned on by itself.

Chapter Twenty-One

Barry didn't have to wait long. Mark came running whenever Olivia needed him. Barry couldn't help but notice the disappointment on Mark's face when he realized she wasn't there.

"Thanks for taking them," Barry said as he clipped Daisy's leash to her collar.

"What's the little one's name again?" Mark asked, avoiding direct eye contact.

"Alvin," Barry said, and the little white schnauzer perked up his ears.

"Thanks for doing this," Barry said.

"Of course."

Barry followed his former partner outside as he loaded Daisy first and then Alvin in the car. Daisy was much more skeptical than Alvin. But she did have the whole backseat to herself. Alvin immediately jumped to the front.

"Why didn't you talk to me before asking to be reassigned?" Barry asked.

Mark shifted from one foot to the other. A sure sign he was nervous. "Barry, please, don't make this awkward," Mark asked. "It's nothing personal."

"It doesn't have to be awkward," Barry said. "We've known each other a long time. Been through a lot of shit. I just wish you had said something."

Mark nodded. "I know."

"You want to say it now?" Barry asked.

Mark looked at him.

"You want me to say it?" Barry waited for a response, but not for long. "You should have talked to me about her. About how you felt."

"What was there to say? It's me. It's always been me. Not her."

It was exactly what Olivia had said, but Barry would never tell Mark.

"It would have been selfish and stupid of me to say anything. It was a crush. Nothing more. I just need to not see it, at least not right now. I need some time."

Barry nodded understanding. "I get it. Let's do go have that beer. When you're ready."

"Yea. I'll let you know." Mark rounded the car to the driver's side. "Just don't hurt her. Don't be your usual asshole self." Mark smiled, an old familiar one.

Barry smiled back. "Good advice. I'll do my best." Barry thought it would probably be best if he didn't tell Mark that with Olivia his usual asshole self was the last thing he wanted to be.

****

Jessica Tate was setting up in the media room at police headquarters when Silas and Olivia arrived. At least the reporter didn't keep them waiting. But she did bring the news station's attorney back with her.

"There's close to five hours of film," Jessica said to Silas flashing one of her bright camera smiles.

"Agent Branch, I need to know that we are going to get the film back," the attorney said. "We complied with your immediate request, but because of your insistence we did not have an opportunity to copy it."

"You can copy it later," Silas said. "If we find

something of value, we will have to seize it for trial."

The attorney started to say something else, and Silas held up his hand. "Look, we'll work it out, but right now Dr. Osborne needs to review this tape, and the quicker we get started the better."

The attorney thought about speaking again but decided against it. He retreated to a table in the corner of the room. He had enough of the agent last night.

Olivia took a seat next to Jessica. "I'm mainly looking for crowd shots. I need to see who was there."

Jessica nodded and started forwarding the tape. "I just want to say, I'm a big fan."

"Of serial killers?" Silas asked, pulling up a chair next to Olivia, casually leaning one of his legs up next to hers. His encroachment on her personal space set off a perimeter alert heightening her senses. She felt boxed in between him and the reporter.

"Your books, Dr. Osborne," Jessica said, tugging Olivia back to the conversation. "I know where you got the name. Victoria Winters was my favorite character. I used to watch that show. I thought it was cool in black and white. That is where you got your pen name, isn't it?"

"What's she talking about," Silas whispered.

The question was innocent enough, Olivia just didn't know why Silas had to ask it while he leaned against her shoulder, another invasion of her personal space. He felt warm and brought with him soothing hints of woodsy spice wrapped in deeply masculine smells.

"Paranormal soap opera from the late 1960s," Olivia told him quickly. She focused on her surprise that Jessica Tate had even heard of the campy cult classic.

"You're not old enough to have watched that program" Olivia told the reporter.

"Neither are you," the reporter replied. "I'm from a really small west Texas town. The only way we could get cable is to have one of those huge satellite dishes. My older brother liked anything creepy, so we watched a lot of the *Sci-Fi* channel after school before our parents came home. The paranormal shows were my favorites."

"Who's Victoria Winters?" Silas asked, continuing to press against her shoulder.

"She was the poor nanny living in the creepy Collins estate surrounded by ghosts and a vampire. She was just trying to live her life," Olivia explained.

"I can see why you identify." Silas's phone rang, and he was gone as quickly as he came. He left her alone with an empty space and the reporter.

"So, what made you want to come back to San Antonio?" Jessica asked as she watched the agent walk away.

"Family."

"He doesn't live here, does he?"

Olivia followed the reporter's gaze over to Silas. He might have ditched the FBI suit for a button-down and khakis, but he was still impressive to look at. She had seen the look on other women before and realized she didn't like it.

"No," Olivia said firmly. Firmer than she had intended because Silas glanced her way. His eyebrows pinched together, wanting to know what was wrong, but she ignored him.

"That's too bad."

Olivia told herself to focus on the video feed and not the annoying woman next to her. The camera was currently perched on the edge of the news van bay and left to film on its own. Occasionally she caught a glimpse of Jessica's legs. When she did slow the film for a better look the audio kicked in and there was constant random chatter between the reporter and cameraman.

"Would you ever give me an interview?"

"Why would you want to interview me?"

"I think it would be interesting to know what it's like to be you."

"I'm not interesting," Olivia said. "Can you turn up the volume?" The UNSUB had to have heard the reporter talking. It's the only way he could have known who she was. On the screen in front of her, the crowd was just beginning to gather. As much as she didn't want to hear the reporter drone on, she might eventually say something useful.

"Uh, yes, you are. Your connection with, you know," Jessica waited, wanting Olivia to fill in the blanks.

"With what?" Olivia asked. She didn't want to talk to the reporter and certainly wasn't going to make things easy on her. Olivia was currently staring daggers into Silas's back, willing him silently to come back and save her.

"You know, your connection with the *other side*," Jessica said.

"I don't have a connection, Ms. Tate," Olivia said. Across the room, Silas was engrossed in whatever he was listening to on the other end of the phone jammed in his ear.

"That's not what I heard. And with everything going on in Atascosa County right now I thought it might be a great tie-in."

"Livie, can you please find out where Martin Mendoza is," Silas requested, looking back at her again. "I need to send the lieutenant his way."

Thankful for the reprieve, Olivia pulled out her phone and did as Silas asked. She looked at Jessica who was watching her and Silas. "When this is over, if you tell me about Atascosa County, I'm sure we can work something out," Olivia conceded.

****

Barry was about to get in his car and head back downtown when his cell phone rang. It was Agent Branch. Neither of them wasted time on a greeting.

"Go see the kid in the car. He's got Martin Mendoza's info. Livie just got off the phone with him. He's at a place called *Jaxx* off of Thousand Oaks. Do you know where it is?"

"Yea, I know it," Barry said. The place had a regular set of barflies. If memory served his first ex-wife had lived in some apartments near there. They played darts there a time or two. Ancient history. Nothing he would share with the agent.

"Good. He's expecting you."

Barry went to see 'the kid in the car' and tried to set aside his annoyance with Branch's flippancy toward Officer Brad Harris whose fine patrol work had been instrumental in finding Patty Griffin's car. "Officer Harris, Agent Branch said you had something for me."

"Yes, sir." He handed him Martin Mendoza's info, car details, date of birth, and home address. No record. Not even a traffic ticket.

"Did you see the painters today?"

"Yes, sir, but from the rearview only. I was instructed to stay out of sight."

"I get it. Just tell me what you did see."

"Four guys. Two older Hispanic men came in Mendoza's van. A pick-up showed up about the same time with two younger white guys. That's about it."

"Either one of them look like this?" Barry handed him both sketches and watched the young officer look over them.

Officer Harris shook his head. "I didn't see their faces really. One of them was taller and he had a ponytail. The other was shorter, probably fits the description of the guy in the drawing, five four or so. He could have been bald, but they were both wearing painter hats so it's hard to say. Sorry, sir."

"No, it's okay," Barry said. "You were doing what you were told."

****

"Is it true we have an excommunicated priest in our city? Do you know him?" Jessica continued.

"I thought we were talking about me," Olivia said carefully deflecting the question. She hated playing these games, and she so did not want to discuss excommunication again, but that was what she would do until Silas freed her from this woman. Olivia also decided for the first time in her career that she really needed a publicist. She did not want to be known as the forensic psychologist, horror writer who communed with 'the other side'. She desperately needed a new life.

"Stop the tape, stop the tape," Olivia said when she saw a familiar face.

Jessica jumped at her sudden outburst, and Silas

headed back their way.

"Oh, Lieutenant Bartholomew," Jessica said as she leaned forward to see what Olivia was seeing.

"No, actually that's Sergeant Austin," Olivia corrected her, watching the reporter and Mark speak for a moment.

"What is it?" Silas asked, leaning over her shoulder this time, not taking the time to sit.

"Right there," Olivia said, pointing at the screen. "Go back slowly. Turn up the sound," she instructed the reporter.

"We're not even filming," Jessica told her as she rewound the feed.

"No, but you're talking," Olivia said. More like babbling really. Silas was right. The girl talked a lot.

"Stop there," Olivia said.

"That's Olivia Osborne." It was no mistaking it was Jessica's voice. Her legs were just on the edge of the camera. "What's she doing here? Why would the FBI be here? Search Bexar County tax records again and find out who lives here."

On screen, Jessica's legs disappeared from view revealing two people standing behind her. One was Mike Stone, Wendy Florren's boyfriend, and the other was a much shorter man wearing a long sleeve t-shirt and cargo shorts, ones that fit this time. He had ditched the cap and wig but was still wearing the aviator glasses, despite the setting sun.

"That's him," Olivia said, pointing to the screen. He'd been standing there even before Mark arrived. He'd been waiting for the show to begin.

"Son of a bitch," Silas said as he stared at the back of Jessica Tate's head. She had led the UNSUB straight to Olivia simply because she couldn't keep her mouth shut.

"I think we're done here," he told the reporter.

****

Martin Mendoza's van was exactly where Silas said it would be. There were also quite a few motorcycles parked outside *Jaxx*. The weather today would have been perfect for a ride. Once upon a time, it was how he would have spent his afternoon. Barry's eyes took a minute to adjust once he stepped inside. The place was always dark, no matter what time of the day. The local basketball team was playing on the TV opposite the bar, volume down low. A few big guys in leather jackets were throwing darts. The only other patrons in the place, so far as Barry could tell, were two older Hispanic men sitting at a high-top table next to the empty pool table. They didn't seem interested in anything but the beers in front of them. Barry flashed his badge and Martin introduced himself. The man with him was Ramon. Barry knew from Olivia he was the tile guy. The handyman immediately asked if she was alright.

"She's fine. I'll tell her you asked. I'm just interested in the two new guys you hired to paint her house."

"Please don't tell me they took something. They seemed like good boys. I swung by there just as they were finishing up. Looked like they did a good job, too," Martin was clearly concerned.

"No, they didn't take anything," Barry was quick to reassure him. "Just some things going on in the neighborhood. Just wanted to have a quick chat. So, have you worked with these guys before?"

"No, sir," Martin said.

"How did you find them?" Barry asked.

"I do some work at the Y across the street. I put up flyers asking if anyone wanted to make some extra cash."

"You paid them in cash?"

"Yes, sir."

"Today?"

"Yes. They were done. Dr. Osborne should be happy."

"She is, very," Barry smiled. "Do you have their contact information?"

"Yes, sir, right here." Martin pulled out his phone.

Barry pushed one of his business cards toward him. "Go ahead and send their contact info to my cell phone. Does it happen to include an address?"

Martin nodded.

"Their names?" Barry asked while Martin scrolled.

"Tyler and Buzz."

"Is that a real name?" Barry frowned.

"Doubt it. The kid is bald, but he didn't correct Tyler."

"Did they ride together?" Barry's phone pinged as he received the first contact.

"Yes. Tyler drove. Buzz doesn't have a car. Rides the bus."

Barry nodded. "Do you happen to know if these two guys knew each other? Before the job, I mean."

"I think Tyler said they used to work together," Ramone said, while Martin scrolled for the next name. "At Rivercenter Rehab, over on Jones-Maltsberger. My mom stayed there after her knee surgery."

Barry nodded. A rehab facility would have

orderlies and nursing assistants. Olivia had pegged him in that role. It sounded like he was onto something, at least he hoped so. "They still work there? Do you know?"

"Tyler does, I think," Ramone said. "We spent a long time talking about my mom."

Barry's phone pinged again. He smiled. "Thank you, Mr. Mendoza. You've been very helpful. And the place does look great."

Back in his car, Barry pulled up the two contacts Martin just sent him. The first one, Tyler Ames lived in an apartment complex not two blocks away, just down Thousand Oaks. The next one was the same name as the bottle of wine used to kill Wendy Florren. Barry would have to check Meeks' report but was pretty sure the second name and the wine brand were the same.

He didn't blame Martin. Obviously, he didn't know the kid was lying. Martin didn't look like much of a wine drinker. He'd been drinking a beer straight from the bottle. Buzz listed his address as 3524 Blossom Pointe, same address as Wendy Florren. The cell phone number he gave was Patricia Griffin's. This Buzz was one sick fuck.

Barry sped down Thousand Oaks toward the apartments as he listened to Tyler's cell phone ringing in his ear before it rolled to voicemail.

Chapter Twenty-Two

"Well, at least we know how the UNSUB found out who you are," Silas said. Two days later than they should have. The captain told Silas the lieutenant had a bad feeling a couple of days ago and had requested an unmarked car to put outside Livie's place. But there were no grounds. The lieutenant had known something. Silas couldn't help but wonder if his own personal issues with the officer had hampered his ability to align himself with this man. And vice versa. If their working relationship had been more harmonious, maybe Barry would have come to him. Together maybe they could have found a way. The two days without the UNSUB getting to Livie was a gift. They had been lucky pure and simple. It wouldn't happen again. Silas needed to sort out what was going on in his own head sooner rather than later.

"Where are you taking me?" Olivia asked.

"I meant what I said earlier. You're not going back home. I'm going to hide you away until this thing is over," Silas told her as she followed him out to his car.

"I can't take my own car?"

"I think it will be just fine in the SAPD parking garage. Don't want you trying to sneak out at night." They got into the rented SUV, but Silas made no move to start the vehicle. He was staring straight ahead, his hand still on the key in the ignition.

"Are we going or what?" Olivia finally asked. She was tired. She just wanted to collapse somewhere. Even if it wasn't her house, she needed some downtime.

"If you were going to sneak out, would you go to him?" Silas finally asked.

"What?" Olivia asked.

"Don't make me spell it out," Silas told her.

It went quiet between them until Silas couldn't take it anymore. "I'm putting you in the room next to mine," he said.

"Is that a good idea?" The words were out of her mouth before she could stop them. Olivia wished she could take them back. That's why it was best for her to be alone when she was this tired. She was full of emotion, and she could be impulsive.

Her words prompted Silas to turn her way. He leaned in across the console, shrinking the space between them. "I need to say something," Silas said, his eyes focused on her this time.

"No, you don't," Olivia said. It was just like Silas to have a discussion she didn't want to have when she couldn't get away.

"Are you and the lieutenant…?"

"Silas, please," Olivia said.

"It's just that I need you to know something."

"I don't want to talk about it," Olivia turned toward the passenger side door and rested her head against the car window.

"Just like you don't want to talk about what happened in Tampa?"

Olivia took a deep breath. She had known this was coming. It was here now, and she couldn't run from it any longer. She turned back in Silas's direction, but she

didn't look at him. "Look, I know it was a rough case."
Two girls dead, ages twelve and thirteen. Silas called
her because there was no one else to help him make
sense of what had happened. And he was right to know
it was *other worldly.* "You don't have to apologize. I
get it. It was emotional."

"What? You honestly think what happened in
Tampa was what…about the case?"

They'd been the only two left in town. After the
arrest and confession, everyone else headed home. Silas
wasn't sure why they didn't. They were eating dinner
together. Sharing sushi, indulging in sake bombs.
Getting more friendly than professional.

Olivia was gone the next morning before he had a
chance to tell her it had nothing to do with the case or
the alcohol. It was all about her. He needed to make it
right if he ever hoped she would give him a chance.

What had happened in Tampa in those brief but
intense moments didn't mean anything, even if it felt
like it did. Olivia had been telling herself that ever
since.

"It's very important you hear what I'm saying."

Her eyes made their way to his face.

"You always discount yourself, Livie. I've watched
you do it for years despite the fact you have
extraordinary gifts. Don't discount yourself with me. I
see you for who *you* are. It might have taken awhile,
but I see."

Silas snuck another glance her way. He thought he
saw a hint of a smile. No matter how much they
bantered back and forth they always came together in
the end.

"The lieutenant and I are not that kind of friendly,"

Olivia finally admitted.

Silas nodded, feeling more satisfied than he should. "Not yet."

"No, not yet," Olivia confirmed. For once she was uncomfortable with the silence. Maybe she was afraid of what Silas might say or worse yet, do.

"Is it too much to ask you to hold off on that?"

"You've been promising me dinner. I'm going to have to insist on that before you take me back to your hotel."

Silas smiled. At least he had given her something to think about. "I would expect nothing less."

****

The complex was huge, and it took Barry a while to locate the right building. He could have stopped at the management office, but it was after six, and he assumed they would either be closed already, or it would simply take too long. Something told him time was of the essence. He hoped Tyler Ames was in the shower cleaning up from a day of painting, or maybe he was at work at his real job, but somehow Barry didn't think that was the case. He scanned the complex parking lot for pickup trucks while he roamed, chiding himself for not getting a description from Mendoza. There were too many to count. San Antonio might be a sprawling metropolis, but this was still Texas, and pickup trucks were everywhere. He radioed Officer Harris, who was still sitting in front of Olivia's empty house and asked him to get the description. He might need it for future reference, but really hoped he didn't.

Finally, Barry found building number fourteen. According to the number system, Tyler Ames lived on the ground floor. *Thank goodness for small favors.*

Barry wound his way to the end of the hall and around. This kid lived in the very back of this place. Maybe he liked the quiet. Barry found the door and started knocking. No sound came from the other side. No music, no TV. His best hope was the kid wasn't home.

Barry looked around for someone to ask. The breezeway was deserted. He tried calling the kid again. And heard the cell phone ringing on the other side of the door. No kid this age would go anywhere without their phone. The fact he wasn't answering it was a problem. Thoughts of Wendy Florren sprang immediately to mind. The kid was in danger.

Barry pounded on the door. "Police, open up."

Barry gave the kid to the count of five. He listened again. Nothing on the other side. Barry checked the walkway again for neighbors and still found none. No one was home on this beautiful Saturday night. He stepped back and kicked in the door.

"Tyler Ames, this is Lieutenant Barry Bartholomew with SAPD. I just want to talk."

No answer, just the sound of running water.

Gun drawn, Barry crossed the entryway in two strides and almost slipped from something wet on the floor. He looked down and saw water.

Focusing his attention ahead of him, he spotted the kid's cell phone and wallet on the dining table. It looked vaguely slim if Martin Mendoza had paid him three hundred dollars cash less than two hours ago. Barry would have expected to find keys to the unknown pickup truck with the wallet and phone, but there were none. The rest of the table was littered with fast-food take-out bags. Inside the small kitchenette drawers were partially open. A bag of trash bags sat out on the counter, yet the trash container in the corner was overflowing. It was a one-bedroom unit so continuing his search for Tyler Ames wasn't hard.

Barry followed the sound of water.

****

Olivia balked at the suggestion of Mexican food, even though she was pretty sure she hadn't had any for lunch. She flatly refused the mere suggestion of more tequila. She steered Silas to a cozy restaurant on the Riverwalk known for their old-world setting and premium cuts of meat. She felt like having something hearty to replenish her waning reserves, both mental and physical, and she knew the steak menu would appeal to Silas. He ordered a glass of wine while Olivia passed on that as well. She settled for sparkling water instead.

She looked around at the people occupying the tables near them. "What do you think they did today?"

Silas scanned the room and assessed their fellow diners. A fair number of diners were dressed for a night out. "Some of them are going somewhere special. Like that woman over there with the slinky black dress who keeps flipping her hair and trying too hard to impress the older gentleman sitting across from her. I saw an interesting historical theatre across the street. Must be something going on there. The rest of them are tourists. They probably spent their afternoon riding one of those boats. I wouldn't be opposed to taking a ride myself with you. Under all the lights in the trees, I'm sure it's nice, maybe even romantic. This Riverwalk of yours isn't so bad," Silas smiled.

Olivia took another glance around the room.

Silas reached over and took her hand. It forced her

to look at him. "What's up with you?"

"I'm just thinking that discussing serial killers and messages from the dead was not part of their day."

"It's not part of our day, every day," Silas tried to lighten her mood. "At least it doesn't have to be."

Olivia just looked at him and slowly withdrew her hand.

"So, if we're not doing it, do you trust any one of them to do it?"

Olivia didn't have to look anymore to know the answer.

"I know I don't," Silas said before she could. "A weekend strolling the river, taking in some play or a concert that's all well and good. But much more than a couple of days of that, and you would be bored silly. We both would. We would spend our time profiling the people around us for sport."

"Like the guy over there at the table near the window. He insisted his date sit on the same side of the table as him. First or second date, probably. Definitely a control freak," Olivia said. "His hand is already below the table. Trying to touch her inappropriately, I'm sure."

Silas smiled and snuck a glance across the way. "Should we warn her?"

"She'll figure it out," Olivia said. She reached for Silas's wine glass, and he called the waiter over.

"I think we're going to need another one," he said. Olivia passed the glass back and Silas finished it. "Besides, if you weren't doing this, what would you do?"

"Write." Although she hadn't done it or even thought about it all week. Not since Tuesday when

Mark called for help.

"Could you make a living from that?"

"Probably." She smiled, which he was glad to see. "If I fully devoted myself to it, got away from all the distractions."

"Maybe it's this place," Silas suggested. He had never seen her this way, and her return to San Antonio had not been under the best of circumstances. Losing her grandmother had been hard. She had been Livie's whole world. Despite its charm, maybe Texas wasn't the best place for her. With her grandmother gone, what did she really have here? "Honestly, I'm surprised you stayed. Do you know why?"

Olivia avoided looking at him. He was hitting close to home, but she couldn't leave yet. There were still ghosts here.

Silas took her hand again. "What you do, can be done in Virginia or DC. Wherever you want to be. And if writing is truly what makes you happy, then stay home and do it. Home doesn't have to be here."

****

The living room was across from Tyler's small kitchen. A couch and a recliner faced the wall where a big screen television hung. Boys and their priorities. The TV was on, but the volume was down. It was currently on some sport channel. Barry noted the basketball game had just ended. The win would push them closer to the playoffs. If Tyler Ames had wanted to keep up with the game, the TV volume should've been up. Except that would've gotten the neighbors' attention.

Ahead of him, Barry could see the bedroom. The corner of the bed told him it was unmade. A crumpled pair of jeans and a t-shirt littered what he could see of the floor. Looking at the carpet he spotted a trail of wet spots. They led from the bedroom and into the kitchen. Barry looked down at his own feet. Like any potential crime scene, he had to be careful where he stepped.

From across the room, he heard voices a little too clearly. A couple, walking a dog. He also felt a breeze. That's when he noticed the sliding glass door to the patio was open…just enough for someone to slip through.

****

Halfway through dinner, both their phones went off.

It was a text from Barry.

—*We have another one.*—

Chapter Twenty-Three

"You don't have to come inside," Silas said. If it had been up to him, he would have dropped her at the hotel, but knowing Olivia, she would have walked down to get her car and showed up at the crime scene anyway. At least this way he could keep an eye on her.

"You did not just say that," Olivia said, exiting the SUV before he could answer.

After more than half of her dinner, she was back to her old self.

They didn't need to know the apartment number. All they had to do was follow the lights. The same place Barry thought was deserted an hour ago was now attracting a throng of onlookers. Jessica Tate was already on scene.

"Fancy seeing you here, Agent Branch," the reporter said as she saw Silas and Olivia approach.

Olivia spotted Mark first. He was in the kitchen with one of the techs from the other night. "Thank you," she mouthed his way. It meant a lot that he'd rescued her fur babies.

Mark smiled. "No problem." He might have asked for reassignment, but he couldn't say no when Barry called and informed him, they had another victim.

Silas caught Meeks coming out of the bedroom. "What have we got? Is it our painter?"

"Looks like it," the medical examiner confirmed.

"So, do you work every day?" Olivia asked the older man. He was retirement age. Wasn't he sick of this already?

"Technically I'm off, but I was just down the street at the golf course. When the lieutenant told me what he had, I couldn't resist coming to take a look." He stepped closer to Olivia. "Our subject has gone off script."

"Gone off script, how?"

"Male victim. We can preliminarily state it's Tyler Ames, but he removed the penis. Post mortem. I think he might have been having a bit of fun."

It was for shock value, the thought crawled across Olivia's conscience. *Is everyone paying attention?*

"And he left another note. I'm guessing it's for you," Meeks told her. "I'll do the post in the morning. Eight sharp, Lieutenant," the medical examiner said on his way out the door.

Olivia spotted Barry standing in the doorway of the bedroom. "Son of a bitch left something for you."

Olivia brushed past Silas on her way toward him.

"You feeling better?" Barry asked quietly.

"Yes, thanks," Olivia whispered.

She felt a flash of heat as she crossed into the bathroom. The space was small, and it radiated energy, but only from the cross-over. Nothing else. A red haze punctured by swirls of gray and black. A fever had been building for years, and at last, he had the power to break it. He did this with purpose, a plan long in the making.

The message was written on the mirror like before. "It's blood. Used gloves again, I'm sure," one of the techs informed her. Again, the face looked familiar from the Florren place. *Kelly? Katie?* Olivia didn't know how the schedule worked, but she liked the fact it was the same techs working both crime scenes. Everyone was up to speed.

"Jesus," Silas said as he stepped into the bathroom just behind Olivia. They hadn't moved the body. Barry wanted her and Silas to see it first. It was getting crowded with all of them in there.

"Give us a minute," Barry said to the tech by the body and the one inspecting the bathroom counter. Barry shut the bedroom door behind them as they left leaving him alone with Olivia and Agent Branch.

There was a mixture of water and blood smeared all over the floor. The body remained in the tub, which helped on available space. Bright red arterial spray coated the room. A fight had ensued, but the victim had been at a disadvantage from the start. Naked, wet, and unsuspecting. The shower curtain was yanked down, and the rod pulled completely out of the wall leaving behind holes in the plaster.

"Meeks thinks the first blow was to the kidney. After that, it was pretty much a hatchet job," Barry explained.

" 'Psycho' come true," Olivia murmured.

"You could say that," Barry agreed.

"Blitzkrieg attack again," Silas said.

"At some point, Ames went down," Barry said, noting the large laceration near the victim's temple. "Probably struck it on the faucet. Meeks said the penis was removed postmortem. I guess there's something to be said for that," Barry said.

"Circumstances put him at a disadvantage. The victim looks like he could have been capable of overpowering his attacker if he hadn't been surprised. Again, our guy is working with what he has," Olivia commented.

All three of them looked at the body. Young healthy male. The puncture to the kidney might have been the first contact, but nowhere near the last. All wounds were at the waist and below.

There was dark energy swirling around the room looking for a place to go. It wouldn't stick around. It would burn itself out soon. The attack was brutal, but what it left behind was empty, almost hollow, without shape. After he unleashed the brutality and found his gratification, he took the real energy with him.

"This killing was different. It was personal," Olivia said.

Barry shifted uncomfortably at her statement. She hadn't heard the details of his conversation with Martin Mendoza. She and Silas had walked in blind; the only information they received was his text about the body.

"This encounter was not opportunistic. He chose this victim. He got a different kind of gratification from inflicting pain this time. He enjoyed it."

"Is that why he removed the penis?" Silas asked.

Olivia nodded. "I'm sure this guy was an asshole to him."

"We did find the penis in his mouth," Barry pointed out.

"Maybe that's how he did his talking," Olivia suggested.

"Martin and Ramone both said the kid didn't talk much. They knew Buzz wasn't his name, but they said the kid just went with it," Barry told them.

"I'm sure this kid has been bullied all his life. He's

learned how to get by."

"So, Dr. Osborne, is it safe to say you think this is about some personal revenge?" Silas asked.

"I think this is evidence of what he does to people he doesn't like. He has shown an interest in hurting Lieutenant Bartholomew," Olivia reminded them. She and Silas both looked to Barry.

"Please start at the beginning, lieutenant so we can get to know this other side of the man we're looking for," Silas requested.

While Barry talked, Olivia pulled out her phone and started a search of her own.

"Meet twenty-two-year-old Tyler Ames. He was one of the painters Martin Mendoza hired to finish your house. Mendoza found him at the Y down the street where he had put up flyers. Tyler and someone named Buzz took the job. According to Mendoza the two boys knew each other vaguely, so it's unclear if they both saw the advertisement at the Y or Tyler contacted his partner. According to Mendoza's man, Ramone, Tyler and Buzz worked together before."

"Where?" Olivia asked.

"Rivercenter Rehab, a few blocks away."

"There's our health care connection. How did you put together that this was done by this Buzz?" Silas wanted to know.

"From Martin Mendoza's description. The kid, Buzz, admitted he shaved his head, and he doesn't have a car. Tyler did all the driving. I felt like I was close, but I knew for sure when I checked my phone for the contact information Mendoza sent me. Buzz is obviously a nickname. The name he gave Mendoza was the name of the bottle of wine used to subdue Wendy

Florren. The address he gave was also Ms. Florren's. And he gave Mendoza Patricia Griffin's cell phone number as his preferred contact."

"This guy is twisted," Silas said, his eyes going back to the victim.

"He's a resourceful deceiver," Olivia said. "He's playing games." *The deceitful spirit will not outwit us, for we are aware of his schemes.*

"The water was still running when I got here," Barry continued. "It was cold of course. Keeping the water running would wash away anything he might have left behind. Looks like the UNSUB at least attempted to clean up—again. There was a box of trash bags sitting on the counter in the kitchen. I'm thinking that's what he ditched his clothes in. He would have been a bloody mess."

"I'm guessing we don't know if any of the victim's clothes are missing," Silas commented. "Are there surveillance cameras around?"

"Already requested. They mainly watch the parking lot, but we have no idea where Ames's pickup was parked, so maybe we'll get lucky. There were some wet prints in front of the closet. He probably left here in some of the victim's clothes. I have some of our guys checking all the trash bins across the complex parking lot for his kill clothes. The kid's keys to his pickup are missing. There's a BOLO out on it. Also, his wallet is empty. Mendoza said he paid him three hundred dollars in cash a few hours ago. Cell phone is still on the table."

"He won't keep the pickup long. He doesn't feel comfortable driving," Olivia told them. The more she thought about it, the more convinced she was he had some physical ailment that prevented him from obtaining a driver's license. Seizures maybe? The result of a head injury? He would also have to take medication. Again, it made him different than other kids.

"How did he gain entry?" Silas asked.

"Sliding glass door from the patio," Barry said. "The preferred method of entry for ground floor apartments."

"Again, the UNSUB took advantage of his surroundings," Olivia commented. She finally turned to face the mirror.

"And, then there's this," Barry said, referring to the message.

"Why don't we get the guys back in here to collect the body before we continue?" Silas suggested.

Barry called the ME guys back in while Silas went out the front of the apartment to have a look at the crowd. Barry and Olivia stepped across the bedroom out of the way.

"Any chance I can see you later?" Barry asked quietly.

"I'm at a hotel downtown next to the Alamo. I can add your name to my approved visitor list if you like," Olivia offered.

"I would," Barry assured her. He had seen her four nights in a row. It could become a habit if she would let it. "It sounds a little like prison."

"Could be. I haven't seen it yet. Haven't even checked in."

"He's keeping his eye on you." Barry said.

"He is."

Silas squeezed back in the room as soon as the

body was gone, and Barry stepped away. "I spoke to our favorite reporter. She will provide film again, even though I'm sure our guy didn't stick around for this one. And she agreed to hold off on connecting this to our serial."

"How did you manage that?" Olivia asked.

"I was noncommittal on whether or not they were connected."

"Room's clear," Barry called from across the way. There was definitely not enough space for all of them in here.

Silas shut the bedroom door.

"So, Dr. Osborne, what does this mean?" Silas asked Olivia as they all three looked at the mirror.

Behold, I am going to send my messenger, and he will clear the way before me. Who can endure the day of his coming? Who can stand when he appears?

"The verse is from Malachi 3:1 or some variation. *My, me, his* and *he* should all be capitalized. At least they are in scripture. Because they are not capitalized in this rendering, I suspect this message did not come from God, at least not tonight."

"Rather obscure scriptures, aren't they?" Silas asked. "Please tell me you had to look that up and you're not that well versed on the Bible."

"What do you think I've been doing on my phone? Updating my social media? They're definitely not verses I've seen before. I'd like to share them with Father Dominic tomorrow, if that's okay."

Silas nodded.

"Maybe our guy didn't capitalize them because he didn't know," Barry suggested.

"No. If they were his words, he would know

exactly what to do with them," Olivia said.

"So, what do they mean? If not from God, then who does this come from?" Silas had to ask.

Olivia sighed. She was glad she had a chance to eat and refuel before she came here. Her defenses were stronger than they had been all day. She was also glad she'd only had a half a glass of wine. The alcohol made her more vulnerable. Fortunately, at least for her, this scene wasn't the same as the others. Without the strong sense of malevolence, it was easier for her to process. The outside influence didn't drive this kill, it lurked in the background while the human hand wielded the blade.

"The message is not related to this killing. They are two separate things," Olivia clarified.

"And if it just happens to tie up some loose ends for this *outside influence*, all the better?" Silas theorized.

"The new sketches were released this afternoon. He knew it wouldn't be long before he was traced back to my house. Eliminating Tyler Ames gave him some breathing room."

"And the message?" Barry asked. She had not completely answered Silas's question.

Olivia shook her head slowly. "While this killing was about Buzz, the message is a reminder there is another. One that can take control of its human host whenever it wants. It is the source of these words, this manipulation of holy scripture." She wondered if the boy was even aware he left a message. He was more than a vessel. More like a revolving door.

Silas watched her drift just for a moment. "Talk to me. What are you thinking?"

Olivia shook her head, scattering the dark thoughts. "I'm thinking we're dealing with something very powerful."

"These words are from the Old Testament," Silas commented.

"Look at you, Agent Branch. You know more about scripture than you let on."

"Old Testament conjures up thoughts of fire and brimstone," he told her.

"For some," Olivia conceded. "The New Testament is more about light and salvation. I need to go back and work the profile. And find out when the UNSUB was no longer in control."

"Do we know at least who the message is for?" Barry asked. Right now, he wasn't sure who made him more uneasy—the UNSUB or Olivia.

"You. Me. Us. These things like attention."

"Do you have a clue what the message is?" Silas wanted to know. At least he thought he did.

"Seems pretty straightforward. 'I'm coming for you'."

The *you* part was what worried Silas. If there was a message from beyond this world, he knew it had to be for Olivia.

Chapter Twenty-Four

Silas did as he promised. He booked her a room next to his. She refused his offer of a nightcap in the bar, mainly because walking into the hotel, Olivia was hit with an *energy*. For a moment, she felt unsteady, as if she was standing on the edge of an abyss. Luckily, she reacted quickly and hopefully showed no outward signs of it. Silas's back was to her as he checked them in. They had relocated his room as well. Maybe she had never restored her electrolyte balance after her drinking binge. All she wanted to do at the moment was shut herself in her room.

"How did you score this place?" she asked Silas as they rode the elevator. The hotel must have been something else at one time. It didn't fit the cookie-cutter hotel their government travel per diem covered. Maybe that explained the weird energy she felt. She was picking up on something from the past. The building must have had a rich history because there were layers of something.

"I have a lot of unused travel points. I told my assistant I wanted something that reminded me I was in San Antonio."

Olivia knew what Silas meant. They traveled to so many places and did nothing but work. After a while everywhere started to look the same. Obviously, he had wanted here to be different.

"I think we're next door to the Alamo," Silas told her. Not that he had time to visit. Too busy doing what he had come here to do. He had already planned to add extra days to his visit when this case was over. Maybe he and Olivia could go together once this case was buttoned up.

Even for a local, Olivia wasn't sure how close they were to the historic fort. She might have been downtown once since she'd moved back. As a local, she didn't venture down here; the river was for tourists. The last time she saw the Alamo, all she could think was that it was too close to the chain stores associated with the mall next door. Olivia believed the stone ruins deserved a more picturesque setting, more like what could be found among the monuments in DC. No one could get lost there and stumble over a major department store. There was a beauty about the marble statues. They actually looked monumental.

Olivia was relieved when the elevator doors opened and deposited her on the twelfth floor. Her room was large even with the king-size bed. She was pleased to note the bathroom was also larger than what was found in a standard hotel. There was an odd familiarity about the place. Olivia locked herself in, ate the rest of her dinner, and indulged in a long hot bath. Her head was resting against the porcelain when the cool brush of wind against her cheek startled her. Again, she felt *off*. Maybe she drifted just below into a light sleep and didn't realize it. She reached for the towel and stepped out of the bath. The water no longer provided the refuge she sought.

Having traded the day's clothes for pajamas, Olivia padded down the hall barefoot until she found a soda machine. She indulged herself and went for the effects of a fully loaded soda. No diet drinks for her tonight. The caffeine combined with the sugar would definitely help adjust whatever was off with her. She reconciled the calories in her head as being for medicinal purposes.

Back in her room, her cell phone was ringing.

Silas.

"Did you just try and sneak out?"

Olivia shook her head even though he couldn't see her. "Absolutely not, Agent Branch. I just needed some caffeine. Now go to sleep."

"What if I'm not sleepy?"

"Then watch TV. I have work to do."

"Call me if you can't sleep." He hung up before Olivia could catch if there was some hidden meaning in his words. Better not to think about it. At least he was following her advice.

Olivia thought she heard the hum of the TV next door. Good. She needed to get to work. She went to her briefcase and pulled out the case file and photos surrounding herself with them on the bed. Not being brought into the investigation after three deaths left her feeling disadvantaged. The killer she met face to face didn't seem to be the one that had come before, so she needed to start at the beginning to understand his journey.

If the killer had come under the influence of a malevolent force, when and how had it occurred? And could she find it given the little information available? All she had were the actions of a killer. Where had he deviated? Where and when had he turned?

The first two kills, the EMT and the Kindergarten teacher were a month apart. Similar in method, strike to the face, stabs to the abdomen. No hesitation marks. Olivia stuck by her belief he had not killed before despite the blood lust he enjoyed while he stabbed them.

Of course, he enjoyed it. He had thought about this for a long time. Something in his life changed that gave him the power or permission to do it. Death of someone close perhaps?

He was methodical, but not overly intelligent. They were easy crimes of opportunity. He used his non-threatening demeanor to disable them and took advantage of their kindness. He could have gone on killing for a long time, especially if he stretched his distance with longer bike rides. San Antonio was a city full of parks, and trees were plentiful, so someone who used a bike as his means of transportation would certainly have had both the stamina and the geography to do that. At any one time, there were anywhere from twenty-five to fifty active serial killers across the United States, all unknown to law enforcement. Their killer had everything going for him. So, what changed?

Patty Griffin.

He was on his way to kill. The time was right, but then he fell. He was no longer in control. Everything changed. Including him. What prompted him to step out of his anonymous comfort zone? Was he pushed?

Olivia suspected it was at this moment, in these critical moments, that he caught the attention of something else. Killing Patty Griffin was the third of three blood sacrifices. Did that trinity summon something malevolent? Blood represented both life and death, it was binding. An offering.

He was an easy target. Despite not knowing who

he was, Olivia knew enough to know he was ripe for outside interference. He was weak, he was vulnerable, and he had already started down the path to destroy good by killing those who helped. Maybe that's what gained him the attention. He might as well have been waving a red flag. It was a perfect script.

Did this dark force have a purpose?

It must. It had a message. The first message was about the UNSUB. The one tonight was not. Olivia looked harder at the words from Malachi. In some translations, the message was about judgment to come.

—*Behold, I am going to send My messenger, and he will clear the way before Me. Who can endure the day of His coming? Who can stand when He appears?*—

If the capitalizations were removed, and they no longer signified the Lord, then did the messenger change the message? And was this a warning or a challenge?

Silas mentioned the Old Testament. The book of Malachi signified the end of it. It was the last book before the story of light began. It was a short book, and there were still theological debates regarding who actually wrote it. The Hebrew name for the book, *ykalm* meant "messenger". The aim of the book was to remind the people they were not giving God his due. But if the message wasn't from God, then did that mean that tonight's messenger wanted *its* due?

I hear you, is that what you want? Olivia thought.

The Catholic Church recognizes the existence of demons, sentient beings who possess their own will. As fallen angels, they are believed to be craftier than humans. They are ancient animations who retained their knowledge. This vast knowledge, this craftiness is how they sowed doubt and seeded confusion in the humans they chose to torment.

Olivia believed in the existence of demons as much as she believed in the sun, the moon, and the stars. She meant it when she told Silas that one cannot believe in the existence of evil without the existence of good. Their presence in her world was something she had been aware of since birth. Gran had schooled her about the energies, reminding her that they weren't all angels. There were two sides to every coin. To every story.

****

Years earlier—

"Happy Birthday, Livie." Gran slipped the slender chain around her neck.

Five-year-old Olivia traced the small silver cross with her finger. The chain was long on her.

"Don't worry, you'll grow into it," Gran said.

She did that sometimes. Answered questions Olivia didn't have to ask.

"I guess now is as good a time to tell you as any. After all, it is your birthday." Gran reached out and stroked her granddaughter's hair. "The women in our family have extraordinary gifts."

Olivia tried really hard to think about what that meant. All she could come up with was one question. "Did Momma have them?"

Gran hugged her close. She should have expected this and been prepared. "Yes, she did." She hesitated to say more. If she offered false promises Livie would know.

Olivia thought some more. "I don't think she liked them very much."

"You're not like your mother," Gran assured her.

"So, I have a gift? Are you sure?" Olivia asked.

Gran smiled. "Of course, you do, my dear. I'm very sure." She gathered Olivia into her lap and hugged her tight. Olivia had no idea how special she was. "You have the most profound gift of all. You're a reader. You see the end. It's why I gave you the cross. Let it be your guide. Always."

Olivia clutched the silver token. "My guide to where?" She didn't understand.

"Life. And death. You can walk in the twilight–that magical place where the dark and the light swim together. You are their equal."

****

Present day—

The buzz of her cell phone caused her to jump. Olivia didn't realize she was so submerged. It had been more than an hour since she started. She looked down to see Barry's name on the screen.

—*I'm outside your hotel if you're still up*—

—*Yes*—

—*Good. I brought dessert. It's a beautiful night. There's a rooftop patio. Want to meet me there*—

—*Excellent idea. I have nosey neighbors*—

—*Thought so. See you in two minutes*—

Olivia smiled, slipped on her shoes, and snuck out of her room like a teenager.

Barry was waiting for her by the pool. It was beautiful just as he said, and they had the whole rooftop to themselves.

She went to him and let him gather her in his arms.

"I'm glad you waited up," Barry whispered. His fingers trailed along her face as he bent down to touch his lips to hers. Not for the first time, he was reminded how he could get lost in her. "I think it was a good call not to go to your room," he admitted when Olivia broke their embrace.

She smiled. "Death gives you perspective, doesn't it?"

"It certainly does." He couldn't stop looking at her.

"So, you promised me dessert?"

"I did."

Barry led her over to the nearest table. "I don't know what else you like except coconut crème pie, but I swung by a little place I knew on my way here and got you a piece. I also, brought you sparkling water since I wasn't sure how you were feeling about the alcohol," Barry smiled. "I do have beer if you're up to it."

"No, water is good, and who would turn down coconut crème pie?"

Barry pulled out her chair, and she sat while he unwrapped the pie for her.

"You're not having any?" Olivia asked.

"I grabbed something there." He twisted off the cap to a beer instead.

"They should be closed by now," Olivia commented, spying the label on the bag. The restaurant had been a staple in San Antonio since the 1930s and was in their shared neighborhood.

"It is. Just have to know the right people." Barry leaned back in the chair and caught her watching him, expecting more. He would rather watch her, but this is where he was supposed to share. "My dad was a professor at UIW. He ate many meals there. I still know some of the old timers."

"Professor of what?" Olivia asked, genuinely

curious. Barry didn't talk about himself, and discussing his father obviously made him uncomfortable.

"Philosophy of all things." Barry said with a shake of his.

"The detective is the son of a philosopher? Interesting."

"One of the many points of departure for father and son," he said. Olivia knew there was more, but that was all she was going to get out of him tonight, so she didn't ask anything else.

Barry was content just to stare at her but decided he needed to say something rather than watch her lick her fork. She probably had no idea the effect it was having on him. This was the only time they would have together tonight. There would be no waking up next to her in the morning. "So, why are you still up? You've had quite the day."

"Homework."

"Reworking the profile?"

"Yes. It's as if we are dealing with two separate personalities."

"Could he have two personalities?" Barry asked.

"Not likely. Multiple personality disorder is incredibly disruptive, particularly when the slivers of self are so distinct from one another as we've seen in this individual. I'm not sure he could function in society if he suffered from MPD. And he obviously does function. He has a job, blends in fairly well. I should have said 'entity.' There is an outside influence at work here," Olivia admitted, watching Barry carefully for his reaction. It was one thing to discuss this type of phenomenon with Silas, but with the lieutenant, she was unsure. Olivia remembered how he had been the night he took her to the neighborhood after Patty Griffin's murder.

"Makes sense. It seems fixated on you."

Olivia put down her fork. *"Do you ever think these things follow you?"* She'd heard the question before.

"Did I say something wrong?"

She shook her head. "No."

"That is what's happening, isn't it? In the beginning, I was worried he was tracking you because you had seen him. Now I'm not so sure."

"What do you think?" Olivia asked. She had been too close to see it.

"I think it's more than that. Once he found out who you are and what you do…" Barry let his words hang there waiting for Olivia to pick them up, but she didn't. "If he had wanted to take you out, like Wendy, he could have done that already. He knew where you lived before we were onto him," Barry explained.

"You came to my house that night," Olivia said.

"I did, but it was late. From reviewing the bus routes, he would have already had to be back on the bus by the time I got there. Same thing with last night."

Had it really been only twenty-four hours? Olivia pondered.

"According to the bus driver, the UNSUB rode to your neighborhood on Thursday. He could have blindsided you if he wanted. We didn't even have his description at that point, remember?"

Olivia listened, but she didn't want to. So much had happened in such a short amount of time. It was hard to keep up, and she was either out of practice or fighting her natural instincts. She thought back to Patty's car. She had been too focused on finding the

UNSUB, she discounted herself. There had been another presence, from another place. The other side. That's where she had gone. She had caught glimpses of it when dealing with other entities, but never such a full emersion. Something from that place had crossed. Now they were both after her.

"The scripture tonight was about sending a message. You told Silas you didn't know who it was for. But you're the only one that's received one so far. 'Patty says hello from Hell.' There were no messages left at the first three crime scenes," Barry reminded her. "We both know some serial criminals leave notes behind because they want attention. But this guy isn't one of those. He killed because he wanted to, not because he wanted attention."

"He's spent his whole life trying not to call attention to himself," Olivia continued. "The messages started after the UNSUB was no longer in control."

She had just found the answer she was looking for.

"The first one was pretty straightforward. It told us why the UNSUB killed. But the second one, the message left on Tiffany Kelly's phone was a message you'd heard before."

Olivia pushed away from the table...her pie unfinished. She needed to walk around.

Barry followed her. "You're still alive for a reason. The message could only be for you. Maybe you should tell me what happened to Mark's brother since this thing is obviously trying to communicate with you."

Olivia went over to the edge of the roof and looked down. There was the Alamo as promised. It was as full of ghosts as her past.

Chapter Twenty-Five

Olivia had never told the whole story to anyone. She shared bits and pieces along the way when necessary, but she had never recounted what happened aloud. It played on a reel inside her head instead. To tell, gave it power. She parsed out scenes from the constant loop, but only to those on a need-to-know basis. One version for Mark and his parents, an edited version for the parents of a girl she didn't know, another version for Silas and the BAU, and a different version for Father Dominic. To share it all was too frightening. And yet she carried it around locked inside of her.

Why hadn't she told someone? Was it because she feared Nietzsche's abyss?

Olivia looked at Barry. Maybe the time had come. It had been on her mind since the case began, even before the messages. Barry was right, there must be a reason. She thought back to dinner with Silas. She had been whining about a life she wished she had. Silas encouraged her to embrace *this* life, the one staring her in the face. She couldn't run anywhere the monsters wouldn't follow.

"Jason was from San Antonio. That was the first thing we had in common. We were students at Marymount, and we were both looking into a series of murders in Old Town Alexandria in Virginia. Our mutual interest turned into a kind of obsession when we met. He was making a documentary about the investigation for his final master's project. I was hung up on the offender profile. I actually reshaped my entire PhD dissertation around it," Olivia began. She sounded wistful.

"You were with the FBI then?" Barry asked.

"No, not yet," she said. "All that started after."

"With your ability, I just thought…" Barry stopped himself from saying more. There was no denying it. Barry knew she was way out of his league, and he was in way over his head.

"There were four murders over a six-week period. All of the victims were connected to this little hole-in-the wall bar in Old Town. Jason had a contact in the police force. He got his hands on some profile information and a copy of the CCTV footage of the first victim."

"The murder was caught on tape?" Barry asked.

"Not exactly. It was parking lot footage. The actual attack took place just beyond camera range. She was alone in a parking lot at two-thirty in the morning, and she willingly approached her attacker."

Barry shook his head. "Why would she do that? Did she know him?"

"No. That was my first problem with the case. The BAU profile focused on a male offender. Statistically, it made sense, but after watching the video I knew it was wrong."

"The killer was female?" he asked. Not unheard of, but rare.

Olivia nodded. "That was my assertion. It wasn't a popular theory. There also seemed to be something strange with some of the evidence found at the crime scenes, but no one was saying. The original officers on the case had been removed and reassigned. It's like no one wanted to hear what they had to say. Jason wanted to talk to them, but their names were kept confidential.

"Jason and I knew we were out of the loop, but that's all we knew. Marymount's graduate school partners with the Alexandria PD. We had the opportunity to go on a ride-along with a couple of patrol officers. Jason talked them into checking out the bar. We spotted a guy walking a very drunk girl to his car. The officers ran the plates. The driver had priors, domestic violence, you know the drill."

"The officers followed the guy," Barry said.

Olivia nodded. "To a house. We were told to stay in the car, but Jason—"

"Shit. He didn't listen," Barry said.

"He never listened. Whatever was happening inside the house, he wanted it for the documentary."

"Did you follow Jason inside?" he asked.

She shook her head. "I stayed in the car, listened to it all happening on the radio."

Sort of. Some of it could not have been on the radio, but she decided to keep those details to herself. *So much for the whole story.*

"It was chaos. The girl was screaming, and I knew it was bad. They found her alive but covered in blood. They told Jason to stay with her while they searched for the guy. Jason was talking to her, trying to comfort her, but something was wrong, she was acting strange. I could feel it. She kept repeating the same word over and over. *Proximare. Proximare.* I'll never forget it."

Olivia saw Barry's brow wrinkle at the word. Even

saying it a decade later made Olivia shiver. She wrapped her arms around herself. Barry took off his jacket and draped it around her shoulders. "It's okay. It's just you and me here."

"Give me one of those," Olivia said, pointing to the beer. "Please."

Barry screwed off the top of one and handed it to her. She took a long drink. She needed it, even if it weakened her. It could dull the senses she didn't want to feel right now. It was a vice, and like everything else that was wrong with her, she owned it.

Barry placed his hands on her shoulders and squeezed. "Take your time," he coaxed as if talking to a witness. She guessed he was. Lieutenant Bartholomew was good at his job. She saw how the other officers acted around him. They trusted him, but more than that, they respected him. He cared about the people he tried to save every day. He did his job because it was the right thing to do, and he had his own wounds to heal. There was something dead inside of him.

"She kept leading Jason into the dark. I could hear him asking her to stop. Then the officers' voices, urgent. They found the guy. Dead. Just like all the others. And then I heard something else."

Olivia felt herself slip away. She couldn't stop it.

"Shots fired, shots fired. Officer needs assistance," I screamed into the radio. And then I ran for the house. I found them in the basement; Nash leaning over Jason, Jaworski on the other side. He had a two-handed grip on his gun, pointing at the girl across the room.

"I shoved Nash out of the way, but Jason was already gone. I knew it when I saw the blood. So much blood. And his lifeless eyes.

"I moved to the girl next. It was pure instinct. Nash reached out to stop me, I think, but didn't catch me in time. She was as pale as Jason, but her eyes were still alive. They were shiny, as black as night, and they watched everything I did. I pleaded for help, but neither officer moved.

"I stopped counting at three gunshot wounds, but there were actually four. When she stopped breathing, I started CPR. She shouldn't have made it out of the basement. Her name was Sophie. Her parents called me to the hospital the day they decided to withdraw her from life support. Once the ventilator was gone, she wanted to talk, but all that came out was a name. She repeated it over and over.

"Her mother was in tears. She asked me if I had any idea what it meant.

"I couldn't answer her. I had never seen anything like it. She should have been dead already. I stayed with them until the priest came. When he recited last rites in Latin, her body was wracked with seizures. When he finished, she opened her eyes for the first time in three days and spoke one last time. Her parents were huddled together crying softly. They didn't hear what she said. But I did. The priest did.

"I followed him into the hall, begging him to wait. He did. But he didn't want to. I knew it by the way he clutched his rosary. He hadn't stopped praying since leaving the room. He wouldn't even turn around and face me."

"Erase those words from your heart, my child. We might have heard her incorrectly."

I just shook my head. "Father, what does '*proximare*' mean? It's Latin, isn't it?"

"*Proximare*? Yes. It means 'come closer'."

"I almost let him get away, but I couldn't keep it to myself. I shouldn't have had to. 'You heard what she said. You know what she said."

" 'Jason says hello from Hell.' "

Olivia had become trance-like with the retelling, but she shook herself free. "There are signs to look for in a possession. One is speaking a language you don't know. More often than not, it's Latin. Another is speaking of faraway events. And knowing things you shouldn't know. This world is divided into two parts: good and evil. Those who say it's not, are only kidding themselves. Pure love and pure evil both exist. I know about the evil. I saved it in that basement."

Barry pulled her into him. He had no words. He silently stroked her hair until she regained her composure and broke the embrace. She looked up to the sky and took in a deep cleansing breath of fresh air. "Such a beautiful night for such a wicked tale."

"The officers? What happened to them?" Barry asked. He needed to pull her back from that faraway place.

Olivia shook her head. "Neither one of them went back to work."

"Did you find out why the other officers were reassigned?"

"I talked to Nash. Once. The other crime scenes had unidentified hairs, seemingly animal and some weird prints. It wasn't explainable."

"What kind of prints?"

"Suggestive of some kind of an animal. Hoof like. 'Cloven' is the word no one wanted to use. Nash said he saw her change. It was just a flash. Said he couldn't get it out of his head. She wasn't a girl. At least, not anymore. Jaworski kept firing until he emptied his gun because he saw the eyes of a serpent."

"Captain Zavalla said you were the only person left alive from that night," Barry said, wondering how much more there was. He hoped not much.

"Nash died a year later, heart attack. Just gave up on life. Smoked and drank himself to sleep every night. Jaworski only lasted six weeks after that night. He called Nash the afternoon before he did it. Said he couldn't get the image out of his head. He put the barrel of the gun he'd used to shoot Sophie, in his mouth, and pulled the trigger."

"You said she kept saying a name before she died."

Olivia could only nod. *Alleracsap.* She still heard it sometimes in her head. She finally mustered the courage to ask Father Dominic about it. He did the research and found it for her. It had been around the time they drifted apart.

"It was the name of the one who possessed her. I can't say it aloud. To speak it, gives it power," Olivia explained. Maybe it was one of the reasons she didn't talk about what happened.

"You were listening over the radio. You said you weren't sure what you heard. But that's not right, is it?"

Olivia looked away.

Barry went to her and pulled her back to him. "Remember, it's just you and me. What did you hear?"

"A growl. Jason didn't even have time to scream."

Chapter Twenty-Six

"How much does Mark know?" Barry asked.

"He knows it was bad. He knows they couldn't have an open casket. He knows I believed the girl, Sophie, was possessed. But he doesn't know what she said, and he never will."

Barry nodded.

Olivia didn't have anything left to say. She was emotionally spent. Barry led her back to the table. She hadn't finished her dessert, but she didn't want it anymore. She concentrated on drinking the remainder of her beer instead. Barry opened another one for himself.

"I swung back by the house on my way over. I didn't remember leaving the light on in the kitchen, but it was on when I drove by. I left it that way. Made the place look a little homier." He was searching for something to say.

Olivia nodded. She didn't have the heart to tell him that he was probably right. If he didn't remember turning the light on, then he probably didn't. More than likely the light turned itself on. Kind of like the water that turned on in the downstairs bath before she left. It was Alice, her forever roommate, keeping watch.

"I guess I should tell you, in case you don't already know, Mark has asked to be reassigned."

"What? Why?"

Barry just looked at her.

"Surely, not." Olivia shook her head. She should have known after their talk the other night. Mark had let her know he knew. She just thought they were going to be okay. She had taken it as a good sign that they were talking about it, even if not directly. "I saw him at the crime scene tonight."

Barry nodded. "He came because I called him. The captain plans to loan him out to Atascosa County."

Olivia nodded. At least she and Mark would continue to work together.

"He just needs some time," Barry assured her. "To get some perspective."

"I get it. I guess." She looked lost, defeated.

"There is something else I need to tell you," Barry said, reaching for her hand. "I'm falling hard here. Kind of like a free fall."

Olivia opened her mouth to say something, but Barry stopped her. "You don't have to say anything. Just listen. You have too much on you right now. I'm not going anywhere. But I do want you to do something for me." He reached for her other hand. "You're the only one who can do it."

"I'm listening," Olivia said.

"You have another life and given who you are and what you do, it's not going anywhere. Mark is easy. He'll come around. We'll work it out. The three of us. Together. But for the other part of your life, it has to be you and only you. You have to lead the way on that one."

Olivia looked away. *Silas.*

Barry reached over and stroked her face, bringing her eyes back to his. "Let's be honest here. Zavalla may have invited him, but Agent Branch came here because you're here. He came here for you, and it's clear you're struggling with it too. I don't know what happened between the two of you, and I don't want to know. It doesn't matter. You had a life before me. We both had lives before this, but going forward I need you to be absolutely sure about what you want because this, what's happening here, is different for me. *You're* different."

Olivia nodded. He was right, and she knew it. He was also telling her in no uncertain terms she needed to make a decision.

"Now I have to say goodnight, before I say to hell with everything I just said and beg you to come home with me."

Olivia smiled.

Barry reached over and kissed her forehead.

By a silent majority, they agreed he would not walk her back to her room.

****

Olivia just finished brushing her teeth when she heard a soft knock at her door. For a moment, her heart stopped. Was this some kind of a test? If it was, she wasn't sure she could tell him to go away.

"Livie."

"Silas. It's after midnight." She said through the door.

"You can trust me. I work for the government."

Olivia didn't answer.

"I'm aware of the time, but we're both still up."

"What if I'm not alone?" she finally asked.

"You might have been out gallivanting with the lieutenant, but you're alone now."

Olivia opened the door and then walked away, forcing Silas to catch the door with his foot. "I thought I said to call me if you couldn't sleep," he said letting himself in.

"I wasn't trying to sleep. And how do you know what I was doing?"

"I couldn't sleep. I was looking out the window and saw the lieutenant cross the street. Not long after that, I heard you leave. I was worried."

"You were not."

"Okay, not as worried as I would have been had I seen you leave with him, or if you'd invited him in here with you. I can assure you I'd have been here sooner if that was the case."

Olivia just looked at him, shaking her head. It didn't stop Silas.

"I was worried enough to check on you after he left."

"I really don't like you right now," Olivia told him.

"I get it." Silas watched her pace for a moment, her arms wrapped around herself. "It's not fair, is it? Me turning up like this?"

Again, Olivia looked at him. "The BAU was my idea."

"I saw he brought you food. Dessert, maybe? That was nice. Did it help? Is your metabolism off?"

"What?" She stopped pacing.

"I was flipping around the TV channels, and this refurbished, corporate conglomerate hotel was at one time named after a woman named Emily Morgan."

"I should know that name."

"You're the Texan. I'm just the military brat. But yes, you should know her. She was a woman of questionable employment who spent some time entertaining the notorious General Santa Ana during the battle of San Jacinto. Because of her help, he was captured. In exchange for his freedom, the general granted Texas her independence. The least they could do was name a hotel after her."

"Why are you in my room?"

"You let me in. I wanted to check on you. And to apologize. Before this was a hotel, it was also a hospital. The lobby downstairs, where I think you got a little woozy earlier and didn't want me to know, was formally the morgue. We're staying in what was once the psych unit. I'm sorry I brought you to the third most haunted hotel in the world."

Olivia sank down on the bed. "You really know how to show a girl a good time. I haven't felt right since I got here."

"I'm a little creeped out myself." Silas took the couch opposite the bed. "I could have sworn I heard someone whisper *'No!'* in my shower."

"This was the psych ward. You're probably lucky it wasn't something else," Olivia told him. "Just the same, no more TV for you."

"Probably should restrict my computer access as well. Considering what you said about Tyler Ames I did a little poking around in Tyler's background," Silas told her.

"And?"

"You were right. Again. Not a real nice guy. 'bully' was one of many words used to describe him. A few scrapes with the law and discharged from several nursing home jobs after questionable patient complaints. Inappropriate touching, fondling, what have you. Unsuccessful in gaining acceptance to nursing school. Seems he's employed now because his aunt's third husband is on Rivercenter Rehab board of something."

"And how does this impact our UNSUB?" Olivia was genuinely curious where Silas was going with this.

"I was just thinking back to what you said. He killed Tyler Ames out of revenge. Maybe for the first time, he had the courage or the support to do it. I was just wondering if maybe he made some kind of deal. Like maybe a *quid pro quo*."

Olivia considered it. "People make deals in this world all the time. Don't know why they wouldn't in the other."

"Considering that, maybe the UNSUB is trying to get to you not to hurt you, but because he wants you to help him."

It was certainly an interesting theory. Barry had thought something similar. Not that the UNSUB was coming to her for help, but at least he wasn't looking to harm her. *How could they see this, and she couldn't?*

"I know some previous offenders have contacted you after they were put away. After they knew what you could do. Maybe this UNSUB is one step ahead of the game and is trying to get you to help him before he gets put away."

"There's no going back from what he's done," Olivia reminded Silas. "At least not legally."

"Maybe he's looking to go to a better place when it's all over. Your recommendation on placement could go a long way towards how and where he spends the rest of his days. Or maybe he's simply looking to you for an escape."

Olivia shook her head. "I have no idea how I can help him."

Silas shrugged. "I'm just reaching for something. I've seen a lot. But I've never seen a serial offender go so off script. There has to be a reason. Some endgame."

"I'm not turning into some sort of demon dealer."

"Okay. Fair enough. Whatever that is."

"I'm not sure either, but I'm thinking you wouldn't want to owe them a debt. I think at this point our UNSUB does. Especially if the demon is the one who gave him the support he needed to kill Tyler Ames." Olivia was up and pacing now. She took a long look at Silas.

The look in her eye told him she was considering kicking him out. "If this place is freaking you out, I'm definitely not going back to my room."

Olivia sighed. "You're too long for the couch."

"The bed is yours."

"I'll get under the covers. You get on top."

Silas smiled. "How did you know…?"

"Stop right there," Olivia said, silencing him with a glare. "Just go get the blanket from the closet."

"Are you always this bossy in the bedroom?"

"My room. My rules. And we're sleeping with the light on in the bathroom."

"I'm good with that."

Silas did as he was told. He turned off the lamp on his side of the bed and unfolded the blanket. He turned on his side facing her but kept his distance.

"Can you turn over? Please." Olivia asked, hovering on the edge of the bed. He noticed, not for the first time the yoga pants were gone, replaced with what looked like boxer shorts with a touch of lace. And a whole lot of bare leg.

"No, I can't turn over. This is how I sleep. This is my side."

Olivia sighed and climbed in, pulling the covers up to her neck. She clutched the extra pillow she had in front of her and put her back to Silas. After a few minutes, she slowly worked her way over to him.

"Spooning. This is nice."

"Stop talking."

Silas draped his arm over her, very carefully. No sudden movements were probably best. She didn't stop him.

"You have my extra pillow," Olivia confessed. "I'm used to having one behind me."

"I see. Kind of like a nest. So, I'm guessing you want me to stay right here."

Olivia didn't comment.

"Remind me again why we haven't done this before."

"When I met you, you were too in love with yourself for anyone else."

"Yea, I guess there's that," Silas conceded. "If there's anything I could take back it would be that you didn't see me like that. And just so you know, if you're trying to make me jealous with the lieutenant it's working."

"I'm not trying to make you jealous," Olivia admitted.

"Then what are you doing? Do you even know?" Silas asked.

Olivia stirred, finding her place next to him.

"If you expect me to sleep, you're going to have to stop doing that."

Olivia stopped wiggling and went quiet again. She wasn't asleep. Her breathing was rapid, not rhythmic. Could be anger, attraction, or frustration. He wasn't sure. He was clueless when came to her—like this.

"If this hotel is haunted, how do you know my room is the safest place to be?" she finally asked.

"I never asked for safe. Maybe I was looking for some place better than my room...alone."

"You've stayed here the last two nights. What did you do then?" The words were out of her mouth before she could catch herself. "You really don't have to answer that."

Silas smiled to himself. She was just as nosey. "I have no problem admitting to you I was alone." Silas paused, hoping she heard him. Really heard him. "As for this, unsettled feeling I have, I didn't feel it like this when I stayed in the other room. What would you call it, some kind of energy?"

"These things are old. Hauntings probably. I'd call them echoes."

"Well, maybe bringing you into the mix caused a disturbance in the force. That whole looking back thing. Haven't you said that these things, spirits, or echoes, recognize when someone on the other side can see them? Don't they want acknowledgement?"

"Sometimes. A lot of the time," Olivia admitted.

"I still think I'm safer right here."

"How so?"

"The way I figure it, if demons won't face you without a human in the middle, what are some ghostly echoes going to do?"

****

Sunday...She sensed Silas was gone even before

she turned over to see the empty space. Olivia took a deep breath and closed her eyes. She thought she could still smell him. He was so loud in her mind. If she let him close enough was there an eye to the storm? A safe and quiet place behind all that noise? Is that where she went last night? The echoes hadn't whispered. She hadn't stirred.

She opened her eyes and saw the note.

—Woke up with a lot of unspent energy. Thought I would redirect with a run down the Riverwalk. Wait for me for breakfast.—

He'd even timed it. Such a Silas thing. Olivia checked the clock. He hadn't been gone long, yet it wasn't the sound of the door that woke her. It wasn't even him. It was the absence of him.

She heard her phone go off while she was in the shower. Once and then twice. She wrapped herself in a towel and went to check what was in store for the day. First was a text message from the captain. He wanted a briefing at ten.

The second text was Silas.

—I'm back and in the shower. Come get me when you're hungry. Or before. Your choice.—

Back in the bathroom, there was another message. Olivia blew it away as she dried her hair.

Silas was ready to go when she knocked. They decided to have breakfast at the hotel. Silas floated the idea that they might even have time to walk across to the Alamo before the briefing. "You're a good sleeper. You don't move. Couple of times I wondered if you were even still breathing."

"My grandmother used to say on good nights I slept the sleep of the dead."

"So, last night was a good night?" Silas smiled.

"Did you sleep?" Olivia asked instead. He didn't need her to tell him her answer.

"Really? What do you think?" Silas smiled. Olivia's eyes narrowed. She was on the verge of a smile. He liked seeing her this way. Timid, yet flirty. Interested. "Personally. I think we should change hotels."

"Actually, I think you could be right," Olivia conceded.

"This place getting to you? Wait, did I hear you correctly? I'm right about something?"

"We should leave. There was a message on my mirror this morning. It was four words. *Help me help you.* I would like very much to get out of here."

Chapter Twenty-Seven

Captain Zavalla was already on edge by the time they arrived. Barry, Meeks, and Frank from forensics were already there.

"Where are we at, everyone?" Silas asked.

"All our attempts to contact anyone related to Mr. Roche have come up empty," Dr. Meeks told them. "For all the fuss there was to try and steal his body, apparently no one wants to claim it."

Silas and Olivia exchanged glances. "His family likely wants no association with him or the actions that led to his death," Olivia suggested. "It would be a pretty safe stance on their part whether we're dealing with witchcraft or drugs."

"Thank you, Doctor. I'll have Sergeant Austin coordinate with the Atascosa County Sheriff. If the body's not gone in a week, let me know."

"Will do," Meeks said.

The captain took a sip of his coffee and seemed to be calm, at least for the moment. Olivia noted that while he might be explosive, it didn't take long for him to return to his usual self. "Frank, you're up. What did you get from the Ames murder last night?" Zavalla asked.

"Unfortunately, this will be brief. The UNSUB is consistent in his use of gloves. No prints on the sliding patio door. Nothing in the kitchen. He used gloves for the message he left on the mirror just as he did at the Florren house. We didn't find his bloody clothes in any of the dumpsters at the apartment complex. There is a church nearby and a strip mall just down the way. We're fanning out there today."

"Don't bother looking at the church. He won't set foot on the grounds," Olivia told him.

Frank nodded, ignoring his knee-jerk instinct to roll his eyes. By this time, he had looked her up online. He wasn't even going to ask; he was just going to do as she said.

"No discernable footprints in the apartment. He must not have been wearing the bike shoes. The water, running for who knows how long, washed away anything else he might've left," Frank reported. "If not for the dead bodies he leaves in his wake I would think this guy was a ghost."

"Of course, he wasn't wearing the shoes," Barry said. "He hitched a ride to Dr. Osborne's house and used the victim's pickup as his getaway."

"Keep in mind, he's not actually a cyclist. He's a wanna be," Olivia inserted. "He's pretending, imitating as best he knows how, but he's never going to actually pull off the masquerade. Frankly, he's probably more comfortable wearing work boots or whatever he had on when he was painting my house."

"Then how did he get there?" Silas asked.

"Since he didn't use the bike to leave, and he'd been painting at the doctor's house all day, he wouldn't need them. He had Tyler Ames for a driver. He probably never even left the area," Barry told him. "That assumption is based on the time you said you saw the painters leaving Dr. Osborne's house and the time of death. There would be no reason especially when he knew what he was coming back to do."

Silas nodded, obviously pleased with the lieutenant's assessment. A prosecutor would call that premeditation.

"Dr. Meeks, your turn," Zavalla said.

"As I initially theorized, it looks like he was struck in the kidney first. The wound would have disabled him and resulted in incredible blood loss. He used the knife on Ames just as he did on the first three victims."

"And the penis? Was it really removed?" Zavalla wanted to know.

"Postmortem, yes. And shoved in the victim's mouth," Meeks told him.

"The press gets none of that, people," the captain said. "Any theory on why?" the captain asked, looking specifically at Olivia.

"Since the killer and the victim knew one another, I'm assuming it was most likely a representation of their relationship. I'm pretty confident our victim bullied the UNSUB at one time or another."

"Do you think our victim sexually abused him?" Barry asked.

"We can't discount it," Olivia said. "We can theorize about him all day, but it's not going to get us very far. Even if the killer was abused by our latest victim, or someone else for that matter, I doubt it was ever reported."

"So why take a job with him?" the captain asked.

"To gain access to Dr. Osborne," Silas spoke. "Or he's coming into his own, and he decided to exact some personal revenge."

"I agree with Agent Branch's assessment," Olivia

confirmed.

"So, he's going down his personal list?" the captain asked.

"If he is convicted, it doesn't matter how many people he kills. He only has one life to give in return, if that is to be his punishment," Olivia said.

"Personally, I'd love to see a needle in his arm," Zavalla said.

"We reviewed some of the victim's personal information last night, and the term 'bully' is appropriate for him. I emailed you, Captain, and the lieutenant with the information I gathered. I didn't do a deep dive, but it does give us a few answers," Silas added.

"Then we really need to ID this guy. If he's been on the receiving end of bullying most of his life, as Dr. Osborne described, he could have a long list," the captain suggested. "Lieutenant, any leads on that front?"

"My feeling is this is his last personal kill. He'll be back on script soon enough," Olivia warned quietly. "He'll escalate sooner rather than later. This will all be over very soon."

They all looked at her, but no one spoke.

"I confirmed the victim was employed at Rivercenter Rehab on Jones-Maltsberger Road. I'm meeting with the interim director of nursing right after this to go over his employment file and see if we can find a work associate," Barry finally said in response to the captain's question.

"I'd like to be in on that, Lieutenant," Olivia offered. "Nurse to nurse might help, especially if she hasn't been in charge long. She might not have been there long enough to know staff relations. A lot of those places have a high turnover in upper management. I also have a contact who occasionally sees patients there. I'll follow up with him as well."

"Who?" Silas mouthed.

"Father Dominic," she said quietly as she reached for her phone to send a text. "We still haven't found the pick-up. I have some guys canvassing the Y today on Thousand Oaks trying to put our victim and the UNSUB together.

"Also, I heard back from the VIA bus driver working the route between Bitters and Alamo Heights on Friday night. He confirmed he picked up the UNSUB and dropped him off at Broadway and Sunset around eight p.m. and returned him on his last stop of the night at approximately ten forty-five. We now have confirmation he was in Dr. Osborne's neighborhood two nights in a row." Barry shifted in his chair with the statement. The killer had been outside watching her house. The officers hadn't gotten there until close to ten. He had been even later. *Too close. That cannot happen again.*

"We found no unknown prints on any of the gates to the doctor's backyard or the little house in the back. We even checked the dog door. There were some paint smudges on the back gate and the dog door, so I'm assuming he used a paint rag on whatever he touched. Also, none on the ladder. Only Mendoza and his crew," Frank reported.

"He's an opportunist," Olivia said. The thought ticked off some other subset of information stored in her head, but she couldn't place it.

"What were his pick-up and drop-off points?" Silas

asked. He had memorized the kill zone map in his head.

"Best the driver could give me was he's pretty sure both points were at the Bitters and Heimer stop. It's a pretty popular stop, with all the shopping and restaurants in the area."

"Isn't that right down the street from the Florren house? Damn it, he's got to live in that vicinity," Silas commented.

"There's a cluster of several apartment complexes within a couple of blocks," Barry told him.

"Then I suggest you find some officers and hit all the leasing offices of all those complexes. They're open today. Somebody has to know this guy. And given that we didn't get the sketch out until yesterday, and the fact no one watches the news anymore, we're going to have to use boots on the ground for this," Silas suggested.

The captain nodded Barry's way.

"Any word on Gail and Billy Wallace?" Olivia asked.

"Nothing. I'm hoping, considering today's Sunday, she'll come home. The kid needs to go back to school," Barry said.

"An occasional drive-by wouldn't hurt," Silas said.

"And we need to pull the guys from Dr. Osborne's house," the captain suggested. "Unless you have an objection, Agent Branch."

Silas seemed to consider it for a moment before deciding. "Pull them, since you need the manpower elsewhere. She's not going back to the house until this thing is over anyway. The house is alarmed, correct?"

"I armed it myself," Barry said. Olivia tried to look disinterested but saw the glance between Meeks and Frank.

Silas pulled Olivia aside. "I want to be there when you talk to Father Dominic."

Olivia shook her head. "No. My contact. My call. Besides, you're not one of his favorite people."

"I'm getting that a lot here. Maybe it's a Southern thing."

"Maybe it's a Silas thing," Olivia told him.

"But not a you thing?"

"Silas, now is not the time."

"I know. It just makes me crazy how close this bastard's come to you. I feel like we're running out of time. And there's still so much we don't know."

"We're close," she assured him. "I know canvassing the apartments covers a lot of ground in a short amount of time, but I really think this guy lives in a house. He was raised by a grandmother, aunt, something. They would have a house. I'm sure of it. Maybe he went home while he waited to kill Ames."

"Makes sense."

"You're good with scouting. You know how to hunt the hunter. Take Mark with you and go over the neighborhood again. Look for houses in need of repair or with overgrown yards. It should stick out like a sore thumb in the neighborhood. This guy's been on his own for a while now, and I'm sure he's let some things go."

"Wouldn't someone in the neighborhood have recognized him?"

Olivia shook her head. "Not necessarily. He blends in well. And no one watches TV. You said so yourself."

Chapter Twenty-Eight

Olivia had to argue with Silas, but she did get to leave in her own car. Alone. She was on her way to meet Barry at the rehab facility while he checked them out of the hotel. She thought she was going to have to argue with Barry about driving herself, but something made him drop the subject pretty fast. Maybe it was her tone. The one that said *back off, this is not up for discussion*. She had been surrounded by more than enough testosterone for the last day and night. She needed some alone time, even if it was only long enough to drive from downtown San Antonio to the northeast side. With one stop in between.

Olivia didn't tell Barry or Silas she was swinging by the house. It would have prompted another discussion. One that she would not have won with Silas. She might keep him in line at work, but she also had a way of acquiescing to him when she least expected it. She wondered if Barry could see it. She put it out of her mind. It was something she would have to think about later. There was a growing list. She usually didn't have to mull over personal relationships. Maybe because she avoided them, for the most part. Now, why now, of all times? Because those kinds of things came when you least expected them, or so Gran said.

Gran. She had always been there for her. Olivia still remembered the day her mother took her back.

Sarah had only been living on her own with her four-year-old daughter for a few months. Olivia missed her Gran and her little house even if she had to share a room with her mother. In the new place, she had her own room, but it was dark and loud at night. The night she crept down the hall to the bathroom she thought it was her mother who was crying. She did that sometimes after that week's boyfriend left. It hadn't been her mother crying at all that night, but it was the night her mother returned her to her Gran's house.

Olivia stood on the porch of the house she now owned. Her small hand in Gran's as they watched her mother pull away. Olivia knew she would never see her again. No matter what Sarah promised her. Olivia had learned not to believe her.

"What happened?" Gran had asked. Her only daughter just said her four-year-old scared her. "How?"

"I told her about the sad lady in the bathroom."

Gran nodded.

"Why did that scare her, do you think?"

Gran knew… "Because she could see her, too. She always sees them. It's why she takes the pills."

After Sarah left, Gran legally changed Olivia's last name to Osborne, her maiden name, instead of keeping Sarah's last name of Larsin. She at least wanted to give the appearance her daughter had been married when she had Olivia. Sarah never said who fathered her daughter. Gran suspected it was because her daughter truly didn't know. Olivia never asked. Just like Gran didn't ask things sometimes. She was never afraid of her granddaughter, even when Olivia knew things she shouldn't, and occasionally had playmates no one else could see. It wasn't long after she came back to live with Gran that Alice showed up. And to Olivia's delight, Gran didn't get scared, and she didn't make her go away.

It was Gran who told her about Alice. She had been Gran's friend when she was little, like Olivia. Except, Alice had been alive then. The two best friends were walking home from school one day when a truck took the curve by the house too fast. Gran got out of the way. Alice didn't.

Gran said Alice could stay, that she was a guardian angel. Gran believed angles were all around, and Olivia believed whatever Gran said. Gran knew things too sometimes, but she said she didn't know nearly as much as Olivia.

Olivia made the block and took the same turn before pulling into the driveway. No pickup trucks, no bicycles, and no cops. She was free to go into her own house. Silas had been in such a rush to get her out of there that Olivia had left her computer behind. She also decided she wanted something better to sleep in than yoga pants and a t-shirt. Before leaving, Olivia stopped by the kitchen. The light above the sink wasn't on anymore and she knew Barry hadn't had time to come by and turn it off. Alice was still watching out for her.

****

On her way to the rehab facility, Olivia stopped for her favorite soda at the only fast-food place left in the world where they still had carhops. She liked the place because of all the different flavors she could have added to her drink and because, during certain hours of the day, they sold a five-gallon vat of soda for roughly a dollar. She couldn't even remember what she had for breakfast. All she remembered was coffee and lots of it.

Olivia was waiting for her gigantic soda laced with vanilla and studying the sketch of the suspect when her drink arrived. Instead of handing her the drink, the cup slipped from the teenage girl's hand and slid down the side of Olivia's vehicle.

"Oh, ma'am, I'm so sorry." The girl standing next to the car window looked like she was going to cry.

"It's okay, it'll wash," Olivia told her, but the girl wasn't looking at her. She was looking at the paper in Olivia's lap. "Do you know him?" Olivia asked.

The girl nodded. "He comes here all the time. He was here yesterday afternoon."

"Was he on his bike?"

"Not yesterday, no. He was in a pickup truck with another guy, but he's usually on his bike."

Olivia remembered the fast-food bags scattered on the small two-seater dining table in Tyler Ames' apartment. They were from here. Did the UNSUB really eat after he killed the victim?

"Is he the one killing those ladies in the park?" the girl outside the car asked.

"We would like to talk to him," Olivia said carefully. "What do you know about the girls in the park?"

"I saw it on the news."

"You watch the news?" Olivia asked.

"On my phone. I have to. We have a pop quiz in government class every Monday. It's been on the news all weekend."

Olivia nodded. Thank goodness for public schools and pop quizzes. "Do you happen to know his name?"

"His friend calls him Buzz, but his real name is Jamie. He told me once. He seemed kind of nice."

Olivia wanted to open the door and hug the girl. Who knew one of their biggest breaks would come from one of the people Olivia had complained had no self-awareness and was always on their phone.

"Does he pay with a credit card?" Olivia asked.

The girl shook her head. "No. Cash. It's nice. That's when I get tips. Since they put in the card readers, fewer tips."

"I see," Olivia nodded. "Do you remember a last name? Do you know where he lives?"

The girl paused for a minute. "Not far. When he's not with his friend he's on his bike. I bet his friend Tyler knows," the girl offered.

Olivia nodded again. Tyler's name had yet to be released to the press.

"Should I tell somebody if I see him again?"

"Yes, you absolutely should." Olivia fished around in her purse and gave the girl one of Silas's cards.

"Wow, FBI, huh?"

"I'm sorry, I didn't get your name," Olivia said. The girl wasn't wearing a name tag. Maybe they didn't do that anymore. Maybe they shouldn't. You just never knew who you might run into.

"Brandi—with an *i*."

"Okay, Brandi with an *i*, what time do you get off?"

"Oh, not for another five hours. I just got here."

"Good. I'm also going to have some officers come by and talk to you, okay? And maybe some of the other people working. They might know Jamie as well."

"Sure," the girl's face lit up like a Christmas tree. "Let me go get you another drink."

Olivia nodded and pulled out her phone. She sent a

group text to Silas, Barry, and Mark telling them who and what she had found.

****

Armed with a new drink, Olivia arrived at Rivercenter Rehab just behind the harried interim director. She was fumbling with the keys to her office when Olivia caught up with her and Barry.

"I've got a unit on its way over there now," Barry said quietly.

"Hi, I'm Rebecca," the director said once she got the door open. She ushered them into an office not much bigger than a closet. The paper on her desk reminded Olivia of Barry's. "Sorry for the mess. I just took over this place a week ago."

Olivia nodded in sympathy.

"Thanks for coming in on a Sunday, Rebecca," Barry said.

"So, what's this about Tyler Ames? Why did you need to talk to me about him on a Sunday? Did we have another family complaint I don't know about?"

"Maybe we should shut the door," Barry suggested. He and Olivia found a place to sit, and he broke the news about Tyler.

"The employment files will be down the hall in my admin's office." Rebecca began fumbling with the keys again. She seemed genuinely disturbed by the news and overwhelmed by her job in general.

"How long have you been here, Rebecca?" Olivia asked.

"I was hired as assistant director two months ago and was not expecting the previous director to resign quite so soon. Baptism by fire, right?" she replied. Bewilderment filled her face as uniformed officers filed past her office window their chirping radios barely audible through the closed door.

"I see. Do you have another employee or have you heard about one that might have worked with Tyler? His name is Jamie? Or maybe Buzz?"

"Sorry, no. Not that I know of. I can't think right now."

After fumbling with multiple keys, Rebecca found the right one. "Employment files are here," she said directing them toward a file cabinet below the window.

"Do you know if there are separate files for former employees?" Olivia asked.

"I'm sure there are, but I have no idea where." Someone appeared in the doorway and right after her another.

"Becky, so glad you're here. We need to talk to you about Dr. Sadler. He's not happy," the second one said.

"It'll have to wait, Susan. I'll find you when I'm done here," the director told her before refocusing her attention on Barry and Olivia. "It never stops. No one is ever happy." She studied Barry, then Olivia.

Olivia sensed she was conflicted.

"Look, I'm not comfortable just letting the two of you go through all of our employee records. I don't think the Warm Springs board would appreciate that very much. I don't suppose you have a warrant?" she asked.

"I wish I did, but there's just no time," Barry said. "These are exigent circumstances here."

Rebecca sighed and crossed her arms.

"Look, I get where you're coming from. But I'm sure your board wouldn't appreciate the media discovering that Rivercenter Rehab protected a serial killer," Olivia added.

"Might make some folks hesitate to park Mom here for her twilight years," Barry said. "Not exactly a great way to start your tenure."

Rebecca held up a hand. "Fine, fine. You can review the records, but we're doing it together. At least I can say you were supervised, and the files never left my possession," she agreed.

"Lieutenant, why don't you and Rebecca get started on the files? Meanwhile, I would like to talk to the charge nurse. If I can get a last name, it will speed this up," Olivia said.

"Sure. The nurse's station is in the middle of the building. Take any hallway toward the center and you'll get there. Ask for Karon. She's familiar with all the staff."

Olivia looked back at Barry and the file cabinet. "I got this," he said. "Once I find Tyler's file, we can at least nail down a time frame for this Jamie. Go do your nurse thing."

****

The charge nurse was a steely grey-haired woman. As soon as she turned around and Olivia saw her badge, Karon Thornhill, she knew they had crossed paths before. Karon had been around for a long time. Forty years or more.

Nursing was an honorable profession, but it took its toll. If you stopped caring, you were jaded. If you cared too much, it ate you up inside. That was what it meant to be a nurse these days. With sicker and sicker patients and more and more regulations, it was no wonder in Olivia's mind why the numbers attending nursing school had dropped. The sad truth was that if the numbers ever did start to go up, there weren't going to be enough experienced nurses left to teach the new ones. Karon was an exception. She must have found a balance because she had managed to stick it out.

Olivia asked Karon about Jamie. She didn't know that name, but she did know Buzz. "Yep, I gave him that name. Can't believe he's still using it. But he hasn't worked here since I have."

Olivia resisted the urge to sigh heavily.

"Try one of the places down the street. I was at one of them briefly back when it was Habitat something. I think that's where I ran across him."

"Do you remember anything about him?" Olivia asked.

"Weird, twerky kid, but a reliable worker. Lived with his two old aunts. Rode a bike. I'm pretty sure it was because he had a seizure disorder or something," Karon said.

"Thank you," Olivia said.

"I know you too, don't I?" Karon asked.

"You might," Olivia hesitated. Even though she did remember her, Olivia would never have said anything. That was another time, another life.

"No, I did," Karon assured her. "I don't forget faces. You were a good nurse. No matter what anyone said." Karon leaned in closer across the counter between them. "Some of what you said, that stuff about there being a few seconds in the brains for something bad to get in?"

"Seven seconds, actually. A brief interval before the conscious mind engages in the decision-making process." Olivia felt herself opening up to Karon on her theory, and as she spoke, she realized how accurate her theory of demonic possession truly was. "There's a vulnerability in those seven seconds, a chance for an outside force to intercede. The potential is significantly more pronounced in Alzheimer's patients."

"Well, I'm a believer. Don't tell anyone I said this, but it is the only explanation for how some of those patients act in the end. The things they say and do." Karon shook her head as a chill scurried down her back. "It's why I stopped doing Alzheimer's and switched to rehab. At least here they are working towards getting better. For the other ones, there's no going back."

Chapter Twenty-Nine

Olivia went back to join Barry, who was scouring paperwork on the admin's desk.

"I found the application Tyler Ames filled out. His work history looks a little light. There are only two places listed on here even though we know from the background Silas sent there's quite a bit more."

"Given his personal history, it's not surprising he wasn't exactly forthcoming," Olivia said, peering over his shoulder.

"Stopping for a soda on your way was a lucky break," Barry said.

Olivia looked down at him. He was only inches away. "Vanilla soda has always been good to me," she smiled.

"The email was late last night. Guess you couldn't sleep either," Barry said.

"I knew that place made me feel off. Did you know it's haunted?"

"Yes, the city tried to pretty it up by calling it the Emily Morgan," Barry said. "I thought you knew." He had felt it, too. One of the many reasons he had suggested the rooftop. It helped alleviate some of the energy.

"No, I didn't. We're not staying there anymore."

"He wasn't kidding about lockdown." There were so many things Barry wanted to say, he just didn't know the right way to say them. That's why he told her she had to lead. He just hoped they both wanted to go to the same place.

"I'll let you know where we end up," she told him.

"I'd like that." He wanted to reach over and kiss her, but the vibration of his cell phone stopped him. It was Frank Tobias. "Please tell me you found something."

"Bloody clothes in a trash bin at the strip mall. Near them we found some small brown vials of something. We're going to head back over to the victim's apartment and see if we can find more. I'm having the liquid in the vials analyzed. It'll take a little time, but I should have an answer for you shortly."

"Dr. Osborne and I will meet you at the apartment. I want her medical opinion."

"Separate cars," Olivia told Barry. "After the apartment, we'll each take one of Tyler's previous employments. Neither one is far."

Barry didn't like the fact they were splitting up. No one should be on their own today, but her way made more sense. And he knew there was no use arguing with her. She might not be a federal agent anymore, but she still acted like it. It was coming through increasingly more. Maybe being around her own kind. He needed to trust her experience and training.

"You have a preference?"

Not a preference exactly, but Olivia knew where she needed to be. Where they all needed to be. "Wisteria Gardens. It's an Alzheimer's Unit. The nurse I spoke with used to work there with a Jamie. She claimed she was the one who started calling him Buzz. Father Dominic should be there all afternoon." Olivia just needed to text him and let him know she would be later than she expected.

By the time they made a copy of Tyler Ames' employment application and arrived at the apartment, Frank and his team had located more vials. These were clear this time, obviously the main source. There was also a handful of syringes.

"He had them stored in a shoe box in the closet. We hadn't gotten there, yet."

"Its street name is special K," Olivia said glancing at the vial. "Ames probably stole it from work. It can be used as an analgesic with less risk of respiratory distress issues which could be the reason, they have it at the rehab facility due to the geriatric population."

"What that blood-spatter guy uses," Frank said. "But doesn't it knock them out?"

"Yes, what the guy on TV uses," Olivia confirmed, frowning at the implications. "Depends on the dosage. It can also be used like ecstasy or as a date rape drug."

"What kind of a doctor are you again?" Frank asked.

"Not the kind with a prescription pad," Olivia said. "I've just spent too much time around some nasty perpetrators."

"He's not been using anything other than a blitzkrieg attack," Barry said.

"More changes ahead. None of them good," Olivia predicted.

Barry walked Olivia to her car and gathered her close to him before she could get inside. "Be careful."

"It's one stop," she told him. "I don't think he's going to accost me in the parking lot. Besides, I have the gun in my purse."

"You have a permit to carry, ma'am?" Barry asked with a smile.

"As a matter of fact, I do."

Barry bent down, and she met him halfway. She did like kissing him. It had been a long time. For kissing and everything else. Maybe that was part of the problem. Her hormones were clouding her brain.

"Father Dominic is going to be there," Olivia assured him when they found a stopping point. She looked around the parking lot. She had gotten distracted. Luckily the windows to Tyler's apartment faced the other way.

"You've worked with him before? I heard you tell Silas the Father didn't like him." The words slipped out before Barry could stop himself.

Something about the way he said it rubbed Olivia the wrong way. "There are a lot of places we're not welcome and it has nothing to do with the case. In Silas's defense, he has to commandeer a lot of situations that aren't pleasant. Do you think it's easy to come into someone else's backyard, take their toys and tell them we're playing a new game now? You have no idea what that's like. He has to come in hard and fast to get a handle on things. It's always easier to ease up once things smooth out than to seize control during a crisis. It's a tough gig."

She was defending him.

Barry nodded. He had never seen her so animated. He had hit a tender spot and unfortunately, the agent was in the middle of it. "I didn't mean it like it sounded. I apologize if it came across that way. I'm just trying to understand the dynamic and learn more about you and about what you do. That's all. You're right. None of us like outsiders coming into our jurisdiction and changing things up. We don't like to share."

Olivia's eyes narrowed. The word *share* caught her attention. Was there some other meaning in his words? She stopped herself. She didn't need to play psychologist in her own life. She also didn't need to go looking for a fight. She took a breath instead.

"We all met on a case in Virginia. Father Dominic was teaching at one of the seminaries in the District." It wasn't until she got back to Texas that Olivia was reminded of how old most priests were. There had been a constant supply of newbies in Alexandria. Priests were in as short supply as nurses. What were they going to do when they both ran out? "That was before Dominic…" she paused, pondering how to explain, and then decided straightforward was the best way, "before Dominic decided not to be a priest anymore."

Barry nodded. He hadn't known priests did that. He might have been raised Catholic, but he didn't practice. Not for a long time.

"When Dom left, he ended up in San Antonio. He's originally from the Dominican Republic, but he was assigned here in his early days. He felt he was being called back for some reason. Spending so much time away from here, I just gravitated to anyone with a San Antonio connection I guess."

Barry only nodded. He had no idea. He had never lived or worked anywhere outside San Antonio.

"We'll need to compare notes after our stops anyway," Olivia told him "You be careful too," she said.

****

Wisteria Gardens was serene. It offered retirement

living as well as onsite rehab and an Alzheimer's Unit. Olivia knew it once had another name. Maybe it was Habitat or something, as Karon had said. These types of facilities often changed ownership as frequently as they changed employees. Health care was tough these days whether you were a nurse or an owner and operator. So many regulations and so many changes with third-party payment and costs. It was a daily struggle to deliver quality care for the residents and ensure the reimbursement the owners needed to keep the doors open. Olivia personally had not worked at this location, but the struggle was the same everywhere.

Dominic's text directed her to the rehab portion of the facility. Since many of the residents were covered under the health plan, he worked for him and other case managers, and social workers were provided an office due to the amount of time they spent on-site. Even though today was his day off, Dominic was still here providing care. Today it was probably the soulful kind. Caring for elderly parents and family members, it was important the caregivers also take time for themselves. It was a daunting task for families and the former priest was quick to step in when for the caregivers when they needed time away. The truth was he missed his flock. And he enjoyed spending time with the residents. Every day was a new visit.

Olivia found the office easily. Dominic rose to greet her and gave her a warm hug.

"It's been too long, Olivia," he said.

His statement brought her immediate relief. Olivia had been troubled about how things ended the last time they spoke. She told herself they would not discuss the event today.

"Dom, you look good," she said and took the seat across from his desk.

"But you are hurried. How can I help?" he asked.

"I do want a proper visit, but today I need your immediate help. I'm looking for an employee named Jamie. I don't have a last name. He's probably an aide, or a personal care attendant. He worked with another aide named Tyler Ames. He also goes by the nickname of Buzz because of his shaved head. Rides a bike. Loner type."

By the end of her description, Dominic was nodding his head. "I know him. He hasn't been around much the last week, but as far as I know, he still works here."

****

Mark was driving while Silas briefed him on what Olivia had told him regarding what type of house they should be looking for. Before they started, however, they did a drive-by of the Wallace house, which still appeared empty, and then moved next door to Wendy Florren's.

No one had been there since Mark was there last. When the agent asked if they could scout the neighborhood together, Mark requested someone in evidence to give the house keys to Silas. Mark briefed Silas on the family situation. He had also kept in touch with the boyfriend, Mike Stone. Wendy's parents and her daughter were still in town since the funeral wouldn't be held until next week. The investigation prolonged the release of the body. Mark felt awful that the family had to wait so long for a proper goodbye. It made it hard on the ones left behind who needed to begin the closure process, something Mark knew all too well.

"Make sure we know when the funeral is. We need to attend," Silas said, and Mark agreed.

Mark unlocked the door and walked Silas through the crime scene.

"What a blood bath," Silas said, surveying the living room. The couch and sections of the flooring had been removed, but the grisly reminders of what was done to Wendy Florren would remain until someone ripped out all the carpet and washed the walls, or better yet, repainted.

Silas chided himself for not walking the scene sooner. Normally, he would have done it already, but time had just gotten away from him. Livie had been on site, and he trusted her instincts. What he saw prompted him to reach for his phone and call her.

"Where are you?"

"At Wisteria Gardens, an Alzheimer's unit. What's up?"

"I'm at Wendy Florren's. The sergeant is walking me through the scene now. Livie, this guy is—" Silas paused. This certainly was not the worst crime scene he had ever seen, but something about it got to him. Maybe because he knew Jamie, one way or another was coming for her.

"Silas. I found where he works."

"I'm coming to you." He turned to Mark, ready to tell him they needed to leave, but Livie was still talking.

"No," she rushed to stop him. "We don't even know if he's here today. What's wrong with you?"

"I'm worried about you," Silas said, aware Mark could hear everything he was saying. He didn't care. They were words that needed to be said.

"I'm here with Dom. He's getting someone to access Jamie's personnel file so we can get his address," Olivia assured him.

"SAPD can do that," Silas said.

"They can, but this is faster. We still don't even have a last name or date of birth. This kid keeps to himself. I'm in a building full of people. I'll stay in Dom's office if that makes you feel better. He'll never even see me."

"We've got to secure the place. I'm getting SAPD over there."

"Don't send the cavalry. Send a few units, in plain clothes. It doesn't take much to disrupt these patients' routine and make them confused and agitated. The facility will have lockdown protocols in place. Make sure SAPD works with the staff," she insisted.

Silas took a deep breath. Having her onsite, locked down or not, did not make him feel better.

"Alright. You're armed?"

"Of course, I am," she assured him. "Since I have you on the phone, I should tell you, in all likelihood our UNSUB has gotten his hands on some tranquilizing drugs."

"Jesus, Livie. How?"

Olivia briefly ran down what forensics found in the dumpster and what they ultimately discovered at Tyler Ames' apartment.

"He's changing again. He has a different objective," Silas said.

"He's either looking for a bigger target, or he wants more time with his next one," Olivia said.

"Or both."

Chapter Thirty

A few minutes after Silas and Olivia hung up, she texted him the reassurance she knew he needed.

—*Confirmed. He's not here today. Don't worry.*—

"Damnit, Livie," Silas said and slipped the phone back into his pocket. Just because he wasn't there now didn't mean he wouldn't be there later.

"How long have you known her?" Mark asked.

"Going on eight years now," Silas said. Had it really been that long? Maybe the days and weeks had slipped away from him because, for the last two years, Olivia had been in San Antonio. He needed things to slow down. Life was passing too fast. His job ate it away. Maybe because he measured his days in cases and number of kills. He was barreling down on forty-four and what did he have to show for it? A ruined football career, a law degree he earned but never used, and the FBI. It all looked good on paper, but what did he go home to at night when the chaos of the day grew quiet?

"She has a way of getting under your skin," Mark said, gauging the agent's reaction. He wondered if Barry knew. If things hadn't changed between them in the last week, Mark would know the answer. Barry needed to know if he didn't already. Mark just didn't want to be the one to tell him.

Silas looked at him. *Not him too.*

"She knew my brother," Mark said quickly. He could see the way the agent was looking at him.

Silas nodded. "Yes, his name was Jason. She told me about him. I'm sorry."

"It's been ten years now. He's what made me want to be a cop."

"My father lost his brother in Vietnam. I can still hear the loss in his voice when he talks about him. I don't think the number of years matters. He's still your big brother," Silas told him.

Mark felt his throat tighten at the thought. He hadn't thought about Jason like that in a long time. "I guess you're right." Mark cleared his throat and tried to clear his head. "Did Olivia ever tell you about it? I mean, what really happened?"

Silas shook his head. "Not all of it, I'm sure." He did know it was the case that got her noticed by the BAU. That and the gifts she brought with her.

"Yea. That's what I always thought. She kept the horror to herself. She shouldered it. She carries it with her to this day."

"That sounds like her."

****

"Brenda, she works in Admin, she's going to come in and get into the employment records," Dominic told Olivia. "They've gone electronic," he said.

"No one knows his last name?" Olivia asked. She was pacing, already tired of being in the little cramped room. All these offices with so much paper everywhere. Olivia wondered when modern technology was going to make it to this space.

"Let's take a walk."

The former father meant to the Alzheimer's Unit,

but Olivia asked to take the long route, so they could cover the parking lot. The fill-in charge nurse told Dom Jamie wasn't working today, but since they were out, Olivia wanted to have a look around. Maybe they would stumble across Tyler Ames' missing pickup. She had memorized the number in the plates 8675...it reminded her of some old song about a girl giving a guy her number. She couldn't recall the name of the song, but she couldn't get the lyrics out of her head.

"Do you still have the greyhound?" Dom asked.

"Yes, actually. And I've added another one. A little schnauzer." Olivia clearly wasn't paying attention. She was amazed at the number of black pickups there were. Of the three she had seen so far, none of them matched the one she was looking for.

"You should bring the dogs by for some time with the residents," Dom suggested. Animal therapy was good for patients in long-term care.

Olivia was in her own world. If the UNSUB wasn't here, then where would he be? He had a vehicle, so his range wasn't limited. Would he have it hidden away at his house? Was he out scouting her house? Or maybe someone else's? He had seen Barry's card. Could he be hunting him? Good thing Barry was far from the ground and the building had a doorman. It would be hard for the UNSUB to lie in wait. Why keep the pickup if he wasn't going to use it? Maybe they needed to call him into work just to see what he would say.

"I think the residents would love some dog time," Dominic said. "Olivia, are you with me?"

The sound of her own name caught her attention. "Yes, I'm sorry I just drifted for a minute," she apologized. "I should bring the dogs." Olivia followed

Dom into the unit. She needed to focus. This entire week had been surreal. She was right back in the game. Whether she wanted to be or not. "I'll bring the dogs," she promised him.

Olivia returned to San Antonio for Gran. First the forgetfulness and then a progressive downhill slide culminating in a cancer diagnosis. It was an intense six months. Then, when it was over, she made the decision to stay here and leave her old life behind because she wanted a new one. But what had her life become? Staying inside her four walls, creating a fictional world for others to live in. What had she found for herself? While Olivia wanted something else, this was all she knew. Maybe she should take Silas's advice and embrace it.

Maybe what she really needed, instead of running and juggling, was balance. The word was used a lot in the Behavioral Analysis Unit. She could still hunt the monsters, but on days she didn't she could spend her time bringing the dogs to a place like this. While she didn't regret leaving the nursing profession, she did miss the patients.

"How is Agent Branch?" Dominic asked as he held the door open for her.

"He's good. He's here in San Antonio for this," Olivia told him.

"Of course, he is," the former priest smiled.

****

Silas and Mark were exiting Wendy Florren's house when Silas's phone buzzed. He didn't even look at the screen, expecting it to be Olivia. He was disappointed when it was Captain Zavalla on the other end.

"Are you with Sergeant Austin?" Zavalla asked.

"Yes, sir."

"Put me on speaker."

Silas signaled for Mark.

"I just got a call from the morgue. Roche's body was released over an hour ago, but now the family is at the morgue, and they claim they never authorized a release."

"So, basically what you're saying is someone stole Roche's body?" Silas asked.

"Basically, yes."

Silas shook his head and wondered if this Roche guy was as much trouble in life as he was in death. He must have been, because someone was very intent on ending his life not only in this world but any other.

"Sergeant Austin, I know I've said I would loan you out to Atascosa County on this, but the Rangers are sending Sheriff Tennent in for a little sit down while they look for the body. I would like Agent Branch to assist me in speaking with him. I don't know why, but something about this guy just rubs me all kinds of wrong."

"I know what you mean. I got the same vibe," Silas agreed.

"No problem, Captain," Mark said.

"You alright on your own?" Silas asked Mark as they headed out.

"I'm just driving the neighborhood. I think I can handle it."

****

Barry didn't exactly strike out. Jamie and Tyler had both worked at Oak Hollow Nursing Home at one time. Tyler left first. Two people remembered Jamie but couldn't give a last name. There was one nurse who was willing to dig around some old call sheets looking for a name and contact number. She had a ready smile, and Barry kept one plastered on his face to ensure her continued cooperation. He got the impression he wouldn't have to try very hard.

"You know, I haven't been on day shift long, but I heard these guys were kind of creepy. Apparently, some of the residents complained," the nurse said as she rummaged through a drawer.

"Creepy, how?" Barry asked. He leaned slightly over the counter trying to get a look at the papers she was pawing through.

"A few of the female residents claimed one of them touched her." The nurse's face said what she couldn't put into words.

Barry nodded. At least he was on the right track. Definitely sounded like their latest victim.

"Oh, I remember hearing about that guy," one of the other nurses came over to join them. "But you're talking about his little buddy, right?"

"Yes, I'm looking for his buddy," Barry told her.

"His last name was Smith or something, but it wasn't spelled the usual way. I had more than one patient complain about him as well."

"What did he do? Or what did they say he did?" Barry said, correcting himself. He couldn't put words in her mouth.

The nurse shook her head, trying to remember.

"Remember my little lady down hall eight? How all she did was talk about the guy in her room with the fedora hat?" the first nurse interrupted. "She kept repeating the same story until her family finally got fed up and moved her down the street to Wisteria Gardens."

"I have a lady in hall two that told me that story this morning," the second nurse said.

"Ladies," Barry interrupted. "Back to the original complaint, please."

"You know it's so hard sometimes to know what's really going on with these residents. So much of the time they're confused."

Barry nodded, trying to hold onto his patience.

"Anyway, my patient said this Jamie kid would come up behind her and kiss her on the neck after she had a shower."

Bingo.

"Found it," the first nurse said. "Jamie S-M-Y-T-H-E."

"Told you it was spelled funny," the second one said.

****

Dominic led Olivia into the common room. It was full of light and filled with residents this Sunday afternoon. Some had family next to them, others were sitting all alone. At least on the outside. Who knew what went on inside their head or what scenes played before them that no one else could see?

Olivia imagined it as though every day of life was recorded on a slip of paper and put in a jar. Then one day, without warning, the recordings just stopped. No more new memories. All that was left were those slips of paper in the jar. From that day forward, every morning an unknown force shook the jar, opened the lid, and out floated one of those pieces of paper. That would be the memory of the day.

The odyssey could explain how Alzheimer's

patients sometimes knew their family and sometimes they didn't. How they seemed to shift between random events. They had good days, and they had bad ones. Olivia knew it was all a give and take, but what she couldn't shake was the knowledge that, among the birthdays and wedding days and the other joyous memories in a lifetime, there were horrors stored in those jars. She thought of her grandfather and the memories of a war that besieged him until his end. What if those were the only days that floated to the top? Some of those experiences should only have to be lived once.

"Dom, phone call," someone said from across the room. The care attendants blended in so well that it was hard to distinguish them from family. Olivia guessed that was a good thing.

"I'll be right back," Dom said. "Don't wander. I'm serious."

Olivia gazed across the room. At least the place was homey if you looked past the baby locks and alarms on the doors and windows and the fact every corner of the room sported a camera. Wandering patients were always a concern. Some of them were so unpredictable they had bed and chair alarms to alert the staff whenever they moved even in the confines of their own room. Those were the patients Olivia believed sometimes endured more than a day's worth of memories in a day. Or maybe they were the ones with the weakest synapses, frayed beyond repair.

"Young lady, young lady."

Olivia looked across the room to see a little white-haired lady beckoning her over with her hand. She looked back for Dom but didn't see him anywhere.

Olivia went to the lady. She was one of the ones sitting alone but she seemed to be enjoying the beautiful view outside.

"May I help you?" Olivia asked. "Can I do something for you?"

The little lady looked at her with gray eyes. Or maybe they were just milky from cataracts. *How did she see me across the room?*

"I just wanted some company." The lady laid an icy hand on top of Olivia's.

"I see," Olivia said, resisting the urge to take her hand back.

"I knew your grandmother."

"Really? How nice."

"Ginny Larsin," the little lady said.

Olivia was surprised. Maybe the lady's eyesight wasn't so bad after all. "What's your name?"

"Opal Collins."

The name meant nothing to her. She had been gone from San Antonio for years, but Gran did like to talk about her granddaughter. The lady appeared to be about the right age for one of Gran's contemporaries. Must be a not-too-distant memory Opal was reliving today.

"Well, Ms. Collins, how did you know my Gran?"

"We worked together at the school."

Olivia nodded. Her grandmother had been an elementary school teacher.

"She says to let you know she's doing fine. She's so glad you've come back home to stay. And she's very happy with what you've done to the house."

"What?" Olivia asked.

"Olivia, I told you not to wander." It was Dom. He was standing next to her, and his tone said he wasn't pleased.

"Oh, you're such a spoil sport," Opal snapped. She was looking at Dom, but her eyes weren't filmy anymore.

Dom slipped his hand into his pocket. Olivia knew it was the one where he kept his rosary. The air around them changed. Olivia felt a tickle on her scalp, like something crawling in her hair. She resisted the urge to scratch it. Her nostrils flared with the smell of something singed.

The thing next to her snorted at Dom.

"We have to go. Now," Dom told her.

Olivia got up without question, but Opal still held firm to her hand. The grip was strong enough to stop her. "Do you ever think about her?"

Olivia tugged at her hand, but Opal held fast. "Think of who?" Olivia couldn't help but ask. She struggled, but the old woman's grip was like a vice.

Something in Olivia's posture caused Dom to turn. He saw Opal reaching for Olivia's other hand, but he grabbed it first. The old woman released her.

"Sophie. She said to tell you she still feels bad about Jason."

Chapter Thirty-One

Barry thanked the nurses and went outside to call in the positive identification that would bring the entire SAPD to bear. Barry went back to the group message from Olivia and texted.

—*Jamie Smythe*—

At least they now had a name.

****

"I told you not to wander," Dom said as he led Olivia back to his office.

"She called me over," Olivia protested. "What just happened in there?"

Dom seemed reluctant to answer. He looked everywhere but at her until he couldn't anymore. "She's one of those we've met before," he said. "I would have told you not to engage her if you hadn't wandered off."

"She reached out to me," Olivia protested. She looked at him long and hard. "You know what she is, right? What's inside of her?"

"Like some of the others we've seen. Not herself," Dom admitted.

"I would say she's not herself. She's talked about a murder that happened a decade ago." Olivia struggled to keep her voice down.

"Most of them don't stay long. They just come and go. Some stay longer. Like with Opal."

"I haven't forgotten what you told me about the

name I gave you."

Dom was already shaking his head.

"I know, don't say the name."

Dom watched her, knowing there was more.

"*It* was there ten years ago. I think *It* is following me. *It* could be the one inside of her."

Dom turned his face away, but not fast enough to hide the worry that crept across it. "Or one of many," he suggested.

"Okay. *It, he, them*. We are talking about demons," Olivia reminded him.

"I know you don't want to hear this, but maybe we should be asking ourselves, why you."

"I would rather know why they're here," Olivia said.

"Maybe the answer is the same," Dom suggested. "I think you're a conduit."

"A what?"

"You're the flame. They are the moths."

Olivia considered his words. *Or they wanted something. What if what they wanted was her?*

"There seems to be more of them," Dom confessed. "Ana agrees with me."

"So, you've been communicating with Ana as well. Do you know she won't return my calls or texts? Where is she?"

Dom shook his head. "Don't know."

"Were you going tell me?" Olivia wanted to know.

He shook his head again. Clearly conflicted. "It's like a communicable disease. It started with just one infected. I'm pretty sure she was the host. She was a transplant, came in as a result of Hurricane Katrina. She was from deep in New Orleans. She held on to some pretty old traditions from her original country."

Olivia nodded, encouraging him to continue.

"Marceline Roche was her name."

Another Roche. No wonder Ana wanted to lie low. What was going on in Atascosa County?

****

"Hey, Officer Bartholomew," the first nurse who had been so eager to help came trotting across the parking lot, stopping him before he could reach his car.

Barry told himself to be polite but brief. He had decided he was heading down the street to Wisteria Gardens to check on Olivia.

"I know you're busy with something else, but there's a couple inside that needs some help. They're moving their mother in today and were parked in the back. The guy says that when he went to get the last load, he noticed his license plate was missing."

****

The man standing before Silas was of obvious Creole descent, with light skin turned the color of cinnamon from the manual labor he performed in the sun, combined with strong bone structure and piercing green eyes. Andre Roche's hair was thick and black, pulled back in a loose ponytail. No man bun for this guy. Although Silas had only ever seen Ferdinand Roche on an autopsy table, his much younger brother definitely got the looks in the family. Even though he was shorter by several inches, thanks to the European parts of his ancestry no doubt, Silas knew this man could give him one hell of a fight.

"So, you did not request Mission Park Memorial to come pick up your brother?" Silas asked. Sheriff Tennent was late, so the agent decided since he was there, he would take a run at the live Roche. The family had piqued Silas's interest.

"Would have no need," Andre said. He appeared disinterested in the whole thing. Not even annoyed that his brother's body was missing. Just bored.

"So, why today?" Silas asked.

"Today?" Andre Roche repeated.

"Why did you wait so long to claim your brother's body?"

"I didn't come to claim it. I came to identify it," Andre corrected the agent. "What you do with it after that I was going to leave up to you."

Silas nodded. He was telling the truth. He didn't call to have his brother buried. No brotherly love was lost there. Even though Silas didn't think he would let Andre know, they didn't need him to identify the deceased Ferdinand. His fingerprints took care of that. They were on file. Both in Texas and Louisiana.

****

Brenda from Admin called Dom as soon as she got in her office. Olivia followed him, unable to stay in the cramped little room.

"Jamie S-M-Y-T-H-E," she told Brenda as they waited for the computer to boot. "Thanks for coming in on your day off."

"Anything for the Padre, here," Brenda smiled.

Olivia gave Dom a curious glance. Normally he didn't advertise his former profession. He just shrugged her off.

"Current employee, correct?"

"Yes," Olivia said, clutching her phone like a lifeline. They had a name. All they needed now was an address and date of birth.

****

"It's the damnedest thing. Why would someone want to steal my license plates?" the man asked.

All Barry was interested in was where the truck was parked. He let the man prattle on while he followed him down the hallway. As described, he was parked in the far back.

"I wasn't even gone five minutes," the man continued.

If that were true, the UNSUB would have been in a hurry. Barry looked around the nearby bushes, and that's when he saw them. Tyler Ames' license plates bearing 8675. Olivia had reminded him of the song that neither one of them could remember the name of. The tune was implanted in his head now as well. The UNSUB must have been interrupted or he would have put these on the truck in front of him.

"To buy some more time," Barry muttered, scouring the parking lot even though he knew it wouldn't do any good. "What's your license plate number?"

The man rattled it off, and Barry was back on the phone updating the BOLO on Ames' pickup.

****

"Jamie Lynn Smythe. Hire date, December 12 of last year. He's a certified nurse assistant. Date of birth, April 10, 1992. Address is 4344 Blossom Circle. He has a cell phone and a home phone."

Olivia took a photo with her phone and sent the info in the group text.

"Where's the charge nurse?" Olivia asked Dom. "Take me to him or her."

"What, why?"

"Thank you very much for your help," Olivia said over her shoulder to Brenda. "I need whoever is in charge to make a phone call."

Dom didn't ask any more questions, just did as she asked.

Fortunately, the charge nurse was at the desk.

"Call Jamie Smythe and tell him you need him to work tonight," Olivia said to the woman Dom pointed to as the nurse in charge.

"Excuse me? Who are you?"

"I need you to call Jamie Smythe—the one Dom was asking you about earlier."

"Why would I call him? It's his day off."

"Tell him you need him to work," Olivia insisted. "Make up something. Just do it."

"I don't need him to work." The nurse looked to Dominic. "You want to tell me what's going on?" At that moment, four uniformed SAPD officers rounded the corner and headed toward the nurses' station.

"Just call him," Olivia ordered.

****

Olivia had been right about the house. She said it would stick out like a sore thumb. It was the only one that fit the description. He finally found it at the back of the neighborhood. The only thing he didn't know is if it belonged to their UNSUB or not. Right or not, it fit her profile. The lawn definitely needed mowing. The curtains were completely closed in the front despite the fact it had been a sun-filled afternoon. The shadows were starting to creep as the day surrendered to twilight. Mark stopped his car in front and got out. He took his gun and left his phone.

The gate to the backyard was unlocked. No sign of

pets. The lawn in the back was even worse—full jungle back there. No signs of life either. The garage was empty. Mark went back to the front and knocked on the door. When he got no answer, he retraced his steps to the back and tried there as well. Same results. The house was locked down tight. The whole area looked dead as far as he could see. The only thing that convinced him anyone even lived there was the garbage bin in front. It was pushed out to the street for pickup in the morning. Mark opened the lid out of curiosity. Not much in there. Just some fast-food take-out and what looked like a dog leash.

Mark went back to the car and got in. He looked out the window and considered the house. Maybe the owners weren't yard people. Maybe they worked on Sunday. It was obvious they didn't spend much time at home. What was he here for? He didn't have an answer. Maybe he should head down to the morgue and get caught up on the goings-on of Atascosa County. Besides, if the UNSUB had transportation, why would he be hanging around here?

****

Silas excused himself from the room after reading Olivia's last text. He asked Andre Roche to wait for him.

"Olivia, what are you doing?"

She had just ended a similar conversation with Barry. "I thought it was the best way to find out where he was," she said. "Besides, this whole area is crawling with cops. Barry sent over the foot patrol from the apartment complex. He is coordinating with them right now."

"Did he answer?" Silas asked.

"No, not yet. But if the phone is turned on, then it should ping off one of the towers and, now that we have an active warrant, we'll have the data sooner rather than later. At least that's what the tech guy said. A call from work shouldn't raise any suspicions with Jamie."

Silas mulled it over. It was an impulsive move, but it made sense logically.

"Where are you? Are you coming over here?" Olivia asked him.

"I'm at the morgue."

"I thought you were with Mark scouring the neighborhood," she said.

"I was, but something else came up. This Atascosa County thing just won't go away."

No kidding, but now was not the time to discuss it, but soon. "So, where's Mark?"

"If the lieutenant's coordinating, I'm sure by this time he's on his way to Wisteria Gardens. I want you out of there."

****

Mark made a slow cruise through the neighborhood. He would run home quickly and feed Daisy and Alvin. They were probably starved for attention by now, but he still had work to do. He'd feed them and then head to the morgue. He would be home late, but he would make it up to them.

Turning on the main street, Mark spotted a black pickup. It was parked in front of the greenbelt where they found Patricia Griffin. Weird coincidence. Even though he didn't believe there was such a thing as a coincidence in police work. Barry taught him that.

From where Mark was sitting, he could tell no one was inside. He didn't even have to pull out the BOLO sheet to know the plates didn't belong to the Ames kid's truck. Olivia had imprinted them all with some bad 80's song about some girl named Jenny and her number.

Mark pulled his car up to the front of the pickup. He got out and felt the hood. Still warm. So, where was the driver? Going with his gut instinct, he backed up and headed down Blossom Pointe.

That's when he saw a light on in Wendy Florren's house. Did he leave it on? It took him a second to remember the keys. Did Agent Branch give them back?

Mark checked the cup holder and saw they were there. Exchanging phone for keys, he decided he would just run in and turn off the light. It would take less than a minute. He shut the car door just as his phone buzzed.

Chapter Thirty-Two

The phone was ringing when the charge nurse approached her post. It was almost shift change. The dining hall was being cleared and the residents were shuffling back to their rooms to settle in for the night. It was the worst time for phone calls, but Julie was ready for this one.

"Wisteria Gardens, Nurses Station, how may I help you?"

"It's Jamie. Do they still need me tonight?"

Julie looked to Officer Stephens next to her and silently mouthed, "It's him."

Stephens, who had recently donned a pair of scrubs in an effort to fit into her surroundings for the sake of the patients, nodded back. Julie had been briefed on what to say and how to react.

"Hang on just a sec, Jamie. Let me confirm."

Julie put him on hold.

Officer Stephens had already written down the time and number of the incoming call and was twenty feet down the hallway headed for the vacant patient room that was serving as an impromptu command center.

****

The charge nurse found Olivia in the back walking the perimeter with the first officer on the scene. The officers in unmarked cars were instructed to park in the back and in front of the businesses located in the strip mall next door. The place needed to appear as normal as possible.

"He called. Said to give him an hour."

"Do you believe him?" the officer on scene asked Olivia as he watched the charge nurse go back inside to deal with what was ahead.

Olivia shook her head. She didn't know what to believe. Something was wrong. Maybe she had been too impulsive when she made the decision to call the UNSUB into work. But she had been doing what Silas loved to call *tightening the noose.*

"We can't afford not to," she told him. If their UNSUB was not coming into work tonight, then what was he doing while they were chasing their tails? Did he know they were here waiting for him? She had been trying to herd him, but what if instead, he was picking them off like strays? She still hadn't heard from either Mark or Barry. And she and Silas were halfway across town from each other.

The officer had plans to make and so did she. Olivia went back inside to the nurse's station. The charge nurse was nowhere in sight. She wasn't leaving here on time tonight. No one was. Julie was still on desk duty even though she was supposed to be stocking supplies, but in the chaos, she'd been told to stay at the desk and answer the phone.

Taking the call from Jamie had set things in motion. The staff was out on the floor, calmly asking family members to leave early tonight for a last-minute staff training session. The only training, they were receiving was what to do if the UNSUB actually showed up for a shift. The nurses and some of the aides were being replaced by SAPD officers. Any administrators on site were handling family issues.

Unable to stay out of the information hub, Olivia headed for the command center. The bed in the patient room had been replaced by a folding table where two SAPD techs, Diaz and Weiss, had set up workstations. She followed up with Weiss about the number from Jamie's file she had handed them as soon as they walked in. "Does our warrant give you access to live geo-position data on that number?"

"Technically yes, but don't hold your breath. We're not the CIA here. Real-time location is relative, but it looks like this general area," Weiss said, pointing to the green and black grid on his computer screen. "Within three to five miles," he translated. The graphics were confusing, and he didn't have time for a crash course.

"So, this phone is turned on?" Olivia asked.

"Yes. He's just not using it."

"Whose number is this?" Olivia pointed to the number Jamie used to call into work.

Multiple mouse clicks later, Diaz had the answer. "Patricia Griffin."

Damn him. Why? Maybe he didn't know they could track him even if he wasn't using the phone?

"Where was that phone last used?" Olivia asked, trying not to lean over Diaz's shoulder as he clicked more keys. This time it didn't take him as long. "Looks like both phones are in the same location."

****

Remember how when we were little you used to sneak into my room at night because you were scared?

Mark shook his head. But kept his eyes closed. Of course, he remembered.

319

I told you there were no monsters.

He bobbed his head up and down again in agreement.

I lied. I'm sorry.

Mark had the worst headache of his life. What had happened? He had taken a turn on his way to somewhere else. Somewhere he needed to be. They were waiting on him. He saw a light, went toward it, and now...there was a bright light hanging above him. Beneath him was a firm surface. Did he fall? Did he break something? He couldn't move.

"Oh, so glad you could join us." The voice came from above. He had just enough time to move the vehicles and grab the phone left in the cup holder. He was glad to see this one was still breathing, at least for now. "I'm not a doctor, so I was really unsure of the dosage. Tyler was the one into drugs, not me."

The eyes looking into his were blue, but blackness surrounded them.

"You know how this is going to end, right?"

Mark tried to shake his head, but his stomach revolted, and he knew if he threw up, he would choke on his own vomit. It might be a better option than the one ahead of him. Because it was coming. He knew it.

"Saint Bartholomew, you know how he died, right?"

He swallowed hard. He went to Catholic school. He knew.

"Skinning. He's the patron saint of Tanners. Ironic, isn't?"

Something silver appeared in his peripheral vision.

"You know, the Bowie knife has so many uses. The high carbon steel is more expensive, but it offers a better edge. It's great for times when you need a precise cut."

The face from above smiled and all he could smell was something old and acidic. He was rotting from the inside out.

"I saw you. On the TV next to the fat guy. And I saw you at her house. You sat on the porch, drinking and talking when all you wanted to do was fuck her. Tell me I'm wrong. That you didn't want to bend her over right there on the porch. I bet she'd like that. It's the uptight ones that surprise you." He sighed and brought the point of the blade directly in his line of sight. "But she doesn't want you, does she?"

Mark closed his eyes.

"I'll take that as a yes. Maybe it's the FBI agent she wants. I saw him too. Good looking guy. I'm sure he can fuck whoever he wants. I wonder if she'll let him use the handcuffs." Again, the smile, but this time the eyes changed. They were slits now, like a serpent.

He saw the pink of a tongue dart out to roll across the lips. It was forked.

I know who you really are.

The thought was in his head.

You ever wonder why people lie? Maybe because they've been doing it for eons? It is an original sin. I love you. You are the one I want. This won't hurt a bit. This won't take long. And my personal favorite — *monsters aren't real.*

Jamie blinked and his eyes changed back to blue. "You know I was having a good time until you came along. Just getting people to do what they do. It was a social experiment really. They wanted to help. A stupid choice on their part, but hey, still their choice." He gave a little shrug. "But then you showed up." The blue eyes peered down at him. Like looking at a bug under a microscope. Then the tongue darted in and out again.

"Why are you doing this?" Mark asked, his voice not even sounding like his own. It was dry and raspy. There was a great roar in his ears. It sounded like the ocean coming in waves. It must be his blood pressure combined with whatever drugs were coursing through his system. He vaguely remembered some kind of stinging sensation on his neck. Olivia had mentioned something about drugs.

"*This?* Why am I doing this?" Jamie asked, waving the knife around. "I've never had so much time before. Thought it might be fun. And because you spoiled my other fun, didn't you? You had to get involved and start poking around. Wendy's death is on you. You killed her you know. She opened the door because she thought I was you. Guess I showed her."

Mark felt the cold tip of the knife against his skin and heard the buttons of his shirt pop. One landed on the table next to him.

"I've never done this before, so please excuse me while I practice," the face above him said.

****

"Livie, I don't think you should be there."

Hadn't she heard this before? She spent her first eight months as a rookie agent in an office, rarely going into the field.

"Lieutenant Bartholomew can circle the wagons." Silas was still talking in her ear. "I'm going to spend a little time with the sheriff and then I'm heading over. I don't want to find you where you are now." It was the closest he could come to telling her to leave. "I mean it.

They don't need you there."

"I can't change what brought me here," Olivia told him.

Silas took a deep breath. He had heard this from her before. She felt left out. "I understand and hear what you're saying. But there are plenty of law enforcement officers who can do what you're doing right now. You, however, are the only one that can do what you do. Your safety is paramount to the BAU."

"What if there's a negotiation?" The defense sounded weak even to her ears.

"If he makes it off the premises, you can negotiate with him all you want when he's in custody and locked inside a little box. But I don't think that's how this is going to go down, and I don't think you do either." She heard him sigh. "Would it help if I told you *I* need you safe? Please, Livie."

Olivia didn't say anything for a long time. "I'll leave, but I'm not driving all the way downtown to police headquarters so someone can babysit me," she told him. "And I'm not going to the hotel to wait alone."

Silas sat in silence. Of course, she knew what he was going to ask next, but she had a point. Maybe he had better get used to the negotiation. She was a strong independent woman, and he very much liked that part of her. Silas also knew this was why the captain of the ship never got involved with his crew.

"I'm going home. I'll take Dom with me," Olivia consented.

Silas wasn't sure what the former priest could do, but he was better than nothing.

"We'll have some wine and I'll wait for you."

"I'll be there," Silas promised.

****

Olivia kept glancing at her phone.

—*I'm just making a quick stop*—.

It was his last text. He still hadn't arrived when she left.

Olivia watched her speed and kept checking to make sure Dom was in her rearview mirror. Jamie wasn't coming to work. She was sure of it. If she was the target, he would come to her.

****

Barry rolled into Wisteria Gardens with as much discretion as his unmarked cruiser could provide. The facility was in full lock-down mode, with a similar effort made toward discretion. Olivia was nowhere to be found.

—*Olivia, where are you?*—

Barry hated texting. As soon as he sent it, he wanted to take it back. He had mistakenly sent it in the group text when he meant to send it to just her.

Her reply rattled him.

—*Home.*—

****

Jamie heard the ping of Mark's phone. He saw multiple notifications on the screen. He hadn't heard any of the others. Too much screaming. At least that was the last of it. Good thing the neighbor lady and her kid were gone. He wondered if they were ever coming back.

He looked at what was left on the table. He was done. Shock was setting in. It wouldn't be long now.

****

They were all watching the time together.

"Can you get a GPS location on Sergeant Austin's vehicle for me please?" Barry asked.

"The Blossom neighborhood," Diaz said a moment later.

Barry thumbed through the series of texts to pass the time. He found one he had missed. There had been too much going on between them.

—*Nothing here. Going to feed the dogs.*—

"He's mobile now," Diaz said.

"What?" Barry was still looking at his phone. Trying to establish a timeline.

****

Jamie kept scrolling. *Reading. Learning. Realizing.* It was confusing at first until he realized which messages belonged to who.

He glanced at the man on the table. Heard his gasp. Death rattle. At least that's what they called it at work. His foot was still twitching. Not much longer.

Jamie went and stood over him one last time. "Oops, my bad," he apologized. He watched him for a minute longer. "Probably for the best, really. She wasn't going to pick you anyway."

Jamie grabbed the keys off the counter and headed for the car. He knew where he had to go.

Chapter Thirty-Three

"What do you think he's hiding?" Captain Zavalla asked the agent. They were viewing the sheriff through the two-way glass in the interview room. He wasn't a suspect, not yet anyway. They just told him the captain's office was unavailable. They were, after all, trying to take down a serial killer across town.

At least Silas had closed the distance between himself and Livie. The sheriff hadn't really been late. He had just gone to police headquarters instead of the morgue. Silas wondered if it was to avoid running into Andre Roche.

Silas shook his head. "Not sure, but it has more to do with than just drugs." If it was worse than the supply of the m and m—meth and marijuana—what the hell was it? The sheriff seemed like a man afraid of something more than just getting caught. Maybe legal repercussions were favorable over what else awaited him.

****

Weiss pointed to the screen. All police vehicles were equipped with GPS technology. Safety telematics worked like an airplane's black box, but right now what mattered most was location information. The blip on the screen was assigned to Sergeant Mark Austin. His car was heading south down 281.

Barry called his cell. No answer.

A quick text back.

—*On the other line.*—

Barry waited. But not for long. He didn't believe it. Based on what he could piece together from the time of the text Mark had more than enough time to feed Olivia's dogs. That would mean he should be heading back this direction, north on 281. Not south. Unless, of course, Silas had requested his presence elsewhere. But Barry didn't believe that either. The agent might not like him, but he would have followed protocol. He would have told him.

Barry had to know for sure. He made a call this time. No more texting. You never who was on the other end.

****

"I like what you've done to the place," Dom said after Olivia gave him the tour.

"Progress," she smiled. It was all she could do to wait and try and act normal.

She had suggested they sit on the porch, but Dom stopped in front of the downstairs bathroom first. The octagon tile caught his eye. "Is that onyx?"

"The black tiles?" Olivia asked as she went to the kitchen to grab the wine. "Yes. They were hard to find."

"They have certain properties," Dom told her. He wondered if she knew, but probably not. "Was it your Gran's idea?" From what Olivia said Gran had always been there for her.

"Gran's Gran actually. This house was a wedding present to Gran's mother. I think the family wanted her to stay nearby. The tile was original to the house, that's why I waited for it. It was important to me to keep with tradition," Olivia explained.

Dom nodded and wondered about the women in her family. "Is your family originally from Texas?"

"Best I know they came here as soon as Mexico won its independence from Spain in the 1820s."

"Before that?"

Olivia looked at him, rejoining him with wine glasses in her hand. "Why are you so interested in my lineage?"

Dom smiled. "You're troubled about what is happening. Agent Branch was worried about you. About your safety. It's why he sent you away. You're worried about him as well. I'm only trying to occupy your mind with other things."

Olivia finally handed over the glass. He hadn't asked, but she knew he wouldn't turn it down.

"And I'm just trying to reacquaint. We've let our friendship lapse. I don't want to do so again. The house is obviously important to you."

Olivia nodded. She would like him back in her life. He had a quiet and tranquil mind. "Massachusetts, I believe," she told him.

"Thank you," he said, taking the glass. "Did your Gran have your abilities?"

"Gran said I knew more than her."

"And your mother?"

Olivia took a sip of her wine. "My mother took a lot of drugs, hoping to drown out the voices."

"Did it work?"

Olivia shook her head. "Doubt it."

"You don't talk about her. What happened to her?" Dom asked gently.

"She went away. To Las Vegas she said. Because it

was full of lights."

Dom nodded. There was more.

"It doesn't matter really. I'm sure she still got lost in the dark." Olivia took another sip. "What kind of properties are in the tiles? You didn't say."

"Protection," he told her.

"From what?"

"Dark forces."

Up the stairs, Olivia saw the light come on in her new, empty bedroom. She was pretty sure that was where she left her purse but equally sure she had also turned off the light.

****

Silas's phone rang just before he was going to step into the interview room.

"Lieutenant?"

"Where's Sergeant Austin?"

Silas paused. "We parted ways in the neighborhood. I thought he was with you."

"No."

The one-word answer hung there, suspended while they both weighed the gravity of what it meant.

"Where are you?" Barry asked, praying he wasn't still at the morgue. It was a long way from Olivia.

"At headquarters." A sense of dread slipped over him.

"Get to Olivia. Mark's car will be there, but it won't be him."

Silas didn't wait for an explanation. He ran for the stairs leaving Captain Zavalla and Sheriff Tennent in his wake.

****

The car continued heading down 281.

Weiss and Diaz watched the dots on the screen. "The phone is moving with the car."

But Mark wasn't in the car, Barry was sure of it. Silas was the last one to see him. In the neighborhood. He went back to Mark's last text which had been sent over an hour ago.

—*Found something. Going to check it out.*—

Olivia was home. Jamie Smythe was heading her way. So was Silas. Until then, Olivia was on her own. Thankfully, she had the gun and the priest. Barry just wasn't sure which one she would need more. He dialed her number yet another fruitless time and envisioned the phone vibrating in her purse, forgotten on the kitchen counter. He knew she carried the gun in her purse. He found himself praying for Father Dominic to work a miracle.

****

Olivia climbed the stairs and witnessed the light switch itself back off. As soon as it was dark, she saw the splash of lights dance across the yard. She went to the window and saw Mark's car pull in the driveway.

She was half-way down the stairs when she heard the door open followed by shattering glass.

"Livie, come down here." The voice wasn't Mark's or Dom's.

The monster they had been hunting, the same one hunting her, was standing in the middle of her living room.

Olivia touched the silver cross at her neck as she went back upstairs. She wasn't convinced it was going to be enough.

****

"Come on, pick up!" Silas swore under his breath

with each passing ring.

Each failed call pushed him to drive faster.

The sirens behind him were gaining. Captain Zavalla had taken a cruiser.

****

Olivia entered the room, letting the gun lead the way. "You don't know me well enough to call me Livie."

"Don't, I?"

The former priest was in a heap on the floor at Jamie's feet. He went down with his hand in his pocket. He had been reaching for his cross.

"You were right about your mother you know. It's hard to find the light when all you seek is the dark. But she sure has been fun."

Olivia faced Jamie. The eyes were not his own. They were black slits.

Olivia had to blink away the image before her. It wasn't Jamie at all. It wasn't even human anymore.

****

Barry cruised the neighborhood. Jamie's house was dark. Mark wasn't there. Barry could feel it, but it had been the best place to start. He signaled for the cruiser behind him to take the house. He turned the car around and decided to go back to where it all started.

Rounding the block onto Blossom Pointe, Barry noticed two things. All the windows in Gail Wallace's house were lit up and a black pickup was parked in Wendy Florren's driveway.

****

"You're not welcome in this house," Olivia told the beast. Her eyes focused on the cross above the door, avoiding the black eyes. Father Dominic had blessed

331

the house when she moved in. It didn't matter he didn't wear the collar anymore. She had faith, and he still had his. It was all that mattered.

The cross shifted as if something was pushing it, but it remained in place, upright.

"I only want to talk to Jamie," she said.

The being's eyes blinked and turned to blue.

"How did you get here, Jamie?"

"I drove," he answered, but he sounded unsure as if he had just awoken from a dream. He looked around, and she watched as his vision cleared. "Do you like the paint?" he asked.

"Yes, Jamie, I do. You did a very good job," she told him. "Now tell me. Why didn't you let Mark drive you?"

"He's not here."

"You're not supposed to drive, are you?" Olivia continued. It wasn't the question she wanted to ask, but it was the only one he would answer. "That's why you don't have a car, isn't it? It's why you have the bike, am I right?"

"Yeah. The lights," Jamie sounded like he had something else to say, but the thought slipped away. He closed his eyes, and shook his head, as if in pain.

"The lights? They bother you, don't they?" Olivia continued. She had installed dimmers with the new fixtures. If she wasn't mistaken, the room was getting brighter.

"They cause seizures, don't they? If the lights are too bright or they move too fast. Isn't that right?"

"Enough talking to *him*!" The words came from Jamie, but it wasn't his voice. The windows shook with the force of it. He turned his head toward her again, the cords in his neck straining at the odd angle.

Dom stirred. It must have been the sound. His hand began to inch its way free from his pocket.

"You want my attention?" Olivia snapped. She wanted to touch the cross around her neck, but she held the gun instead because she needed both hands. It was aimed at the center of Jamie's chest. The demon was immortal. She couldn't kill it, but she could drive it out by destroying its host. It would seek a new vessel. She and Dom weren't viable options without an invitation.

"I have always been here," It hissed.

The cross above the door wavered again and began slowly rotating counterclockwise. Olivia fixed her eyes on it, and it remained in place. A lightning storm of pain flashed in her head as the stench of Sulphur rolled off Jamie and burned its way down her throat. She began to cough, her arms suddenly heavy with the weight of the gun in her hands. She retreated slowly, one foot behind the other, moving toward the bathroom, toward safety. She didn't have much time.

"And I already told you, you weren't welcome in my house," Olivia said raising her own voice despite the pain in her throat. The overhead light flickered, then brightened quickly, casting distorted shadows across the floor. The moment the intensity reached an impossible level, all the lights went out, pitching the house into blackness.

"Mark's dead. Just like his big brother." There was nothing of Jamie in the voice that seemed to come from everywhere in the dark.

The light in the hall behind her snapped on. A moment later, the one to her left in the dining room did, too.

When Jamie's eyes momentarily strayed to the light, Olivia sensed his surprise. Restoring the light had not been his doing.

'*Thank you, Alice.*'

"It was supposed to be Bartholomew, but Mark gave you the file at the crime scene. Bartholomew was with you on the front porch. Mark was the one on TV."

Olivia tried to put it out of her mind. Demons did that. They tricked, they taunted, and they twisted the truth to fit their needs.

"Of course, I knew the truth, but why spoil the fun?"

Olivia stopped listening and focused. "Jamie, why did you kill those women? What happened to you? Talk to me."

Jamie's head turned again, but he looked at her this time. The eyes transitioned back to blue, but she still saw darkness at the edge. "I told her not to stop. 'Mommy, I'm hungry,' I said. She promised me fries. But she stopped anyway. I told her he doesn't really need help. He just wants to hurt somebody, but she didn't listen."

"I'm sorry for what happened to you, Jamie," Olivia said, making sure to maintain eye contact. Dom's hand was free, and she could see the gleam of silver between his fingers.

"I watched him put his hands all over her. Over and over. No one came. No one helped." Jamie started to cry. "When he was done with her, he came for me. He threw me out of the car. They told me that's why I have the seizures, you know?"

Olivia nodded. She bit her lip against the pain in his voice. The lights began to flash off and on.

Jamie closed his eyes. "No one stopped for us. For her. Until it was too late." Olivia watched Jamie's face begin to change.

"Jamie, look at me!" she yelled as Dom drove the cross into his foot.

****

By the time Olivia and Dom made it to the bathroom Jamie was on the floor seizing. She gripped the gun firmly in both hands, keeping it aimed at Jamie. Dom held the cross. Horrified, Olivia watched Jamie Lynn Smythe's body levitate across the room and land upright on both feet just outside the bathroom.

His eyes snapped open, black and bottomless, and narrowed to slits. Lips peeled back in a grotesque smile. Olivia was mesmerized by the continuous shifting of the iris between black and... not blue... *green*. Emerald green. *Like mine.*

"*Alleracsap*, so pleased to make your acquaintance. Olivia Esme Osborne you owe me a debt."

****

Silas would've known he was at Olivia's house even if he hadn't been there before. The light show made it impossible to miss. He left the car running and bolted for the house, gun drawn. The first and only thing he saw was Jamie Smythe charging toward Olivia. Silas wasn't sure who fired first, but Jamie never made it inside the bathroom. He was clinging to life when the ambulance arrived.

****

Across town, Barry found Mark. He was on Wendy Florren's dinner table.

Despite there being a doctor just next door, there was nothing anyone could have done to save Sergeant

Mark Austin.

The first officers on the scene found Barry in the corner, his head in his hands, begging forgiveness.

Epilogue

Three funerals in three days. The last one was the hardest.

Wendy Florren was first. Her parents had planned to stay in San Antonio to go through the house to try and pack up to spare their granddaughter the task, but due to Mark's death, the house was once again an active crime scene. Olivia wondered what memories Wendy's daughter would carry with her. Would she ever go back to her childhood home?

Patricia Griffin was second. While Tiffany Kelly was in town Jessica Tate planned to speak to her about the friend she lost.

Mark's funeral was the last. The SAPD sent him out with full honors. The fact he died at the hands of a serial killer in the line of duty captured national attention. The captain, the mayor, the city council, State representatives as well as a Texas State Senator attended the services The BAU chief and the FBI Deputy Director joined Olivia and Silas as a sea of blue lined the streets outside the Cathedral of San Fernando. The most touching remarks during the memorial service were made by Lieutenant Barry Bartholomew.

Olivia didn't find out about Mark's death until hours after Barry found him. Silas insisted she go to the hospital as a precaution. After she was discharged, Silas drove her to SAPD headquarters to give her statement.

Once alone in an interview room, Silas told her about Mark. She begged to go with the officers to notify next of kin, but it had already been done. Alan and Belinda Austin had now lost both of their sons. They had one remaining child, a daughter, Madeline.

Olivia didn't see or hear from Barry other than at Mark's funeral when he eulogized his friend. Even from a distance, she felt his anger. She wondered who he blamed more, himself, Silas, or even her? Olivia knew she would carry her own burden of guilt. Mark had joined Silas at her suggestion. Silas had to remind her, as well as himself, that Mark had willingly accepted the assignment.

A brief inquiry ensued over Mark's failure to report his whereabouts prior to entering Wendy Florren's residence. The accepted explanation was that he entered the house simply to turn off the light he and Silas had left on earlier in the day. Where the black pickup was at the time of the sergeant's arrival was unknown. Since Mark didn't call in his location, there were many uncertainties. The inquiry concluded that based on the lack of communication, Sergeant Mark Austin was unaware of any possible threat to his safety when he entered Wendy Florren's house for the second time that day. The absence of defensive wounds indicated Jamie Smythe had immediately disabled him with a tranquilizing agent.

Having sustained critical gunshot injuries, Jamie was rushed from Olivia's house and straight into emergency surgery. He survived. Following his recovery, he would be remanded to the Bexar County jail where he would be held in solitary confinement for his own safety. He had no funds, yet multiple high-profile attorneys were lining up to visit him. A mental evaluation was pending. His childhood home, or at least the one he shared with two, now-deceased great-aunts, was still an active crime scene. Olivia doubted anyone would ever live in that house again. Jamie asked to see her. She'd known he would, but she had yet to decide if she was willing.

Dominic spent the night in the hospital and underwent nasal reconstruction surgery the next day. Before his discharge, he requested an audience with the Bishop of the Archdiocese of San Antonio at His Excellency's earliest convenience. Following that meeting, the Archdiocese sent a letter to Dr. Olivia Osborne. It sat unopened at her house for days.

With his request for extended leave approved, Silas remained in San Antonio longer than he originally intended. Just days before, he missed not being at home in Virginia, he now was reluctant to return. He wasn't ready to leave Olivia. They remained at a hotel downtown through the week before finally returning to her house.

In preparation for her return, and as soon as the house was released by SAPD, Silas arranged for Martin and his crew to come finish their work as well as do clean-up duty. He also requested they repair the floor where the former priest's cross made an indentation in the wood. Silas also hired two different electrical crews to inspect the house. All the wiring had been replaced when the renovations began, and all fixtures in the house were new. Neither company found anything wrong with either the wiring or the fixtures. Olivia assured him the light show he witnessed that night, the same one which caused Jamie's seizure, was a result of

Alice's intervention and left it at that.

Two days after Mark's death, sheriff's deputies discovered a burning body on a barren strip of land in Atascosa County. Following a dental comparison, the charred remains were determined to be those of Ferdinand Roche.

Silas had to get back to work. Olivia would not be far behind.

The monsters were waiting.

A word about the author...

I've been a registered nurse for more than thirty years, but my first passion has always been writing.

Growing up the youngest child of older parents I spent a lot of time entertaining myself. I discovered my love of writing through reading. I always wanted more. When I ran out of books I started writing my own. I have lived in San Antonio, Texas for almost twenty years and have adopted it as my own. I love the diversity of this city and its endless supply of ghosts which make it the perfect setting for the Olivia Osborne series. When I'm not writing I can be found with my family and any number of cats.

LisaComptonbooks.com